I AM KELLIE EARL

PEACE CARRIES A COST

Maggie Charters

BALBOA.PRESS

A DIVISION OF HAY HOUSE

I acknowledge the Traditional Custodians of the land and pay respect to their elders past and present.

Balboa Press books may be ordered through booksellers or by contacting:

Balboa Press
A Division of Hay House
1663 Liberty Drive
Bloomington, IN 47403
www.balboapress.com.au
AU TFN: 1 800 844 925 (Toll Free inside Australia)
AU Local: (02) 8310 7086 (+61 2 8310 7086 from outside Australia)

Print information available on the last page.

ISBN: 978-1-9822-9359-8 (sc)
ISBN: 978-1-9822-9358-1 (e)

Balboa Press rev. date: 07/06/2022

A big thank you to my accidental friends who ventured in-and-out of my journey and showed me the nuances of life. Also, I am grateful that my university friend, Olita Jepson, shared some of her history with me.

Sometimes, we have to accept our fate. In defiance, we might try to wriggle our way off destiny's winding path, defy moral fibres, and force open the slammed doors of disappointment. And then we envisage the light shining at the end of the tunnel and struggle to fortify, or justify, our very existence. We might compare ourselves to others, real or imagined, and embellish our lives with subjective ideals or precious jewels and riches. We might ask: 'Who are we? Why are we here? Is modern man any different to philosophers of old? Have we evolved?'

In reality, my readers have evolved. They no longer want to read about fairy floss romances in palaces. Instead, they want the proven and tried reality of flawed people who battle their innermost *dramas of conscience, justice and retribution*; people just like me. They want to get inside the minds of outsiders. And then they want to follow them on their tumultuous journey of recovery, as they find the true meaning of love and hate; even if it doesn't come till the last page of the book.

Yours truly,
B.M. Rising, aka Kellie Earl

CONTENTS

PART TWO

PART FOUR

PROLOGUE

1980

Exposed and naked, I stood in one of the prison's white-washed shower cubicles. There were full-height walls on both sides, and a waist-high swing door to preserve some modesty. The single head shower had a mind of its own, with both the temperature and water pressure fluctuating at will. Now warm water gently splashed onto my long, grey-flecked hair. I considered that, at forty five years of age, I was too young to start showing signs of ageing. But sometimes nature and attitude don't match. And besides, inside Fairlea Women's Prison I didn't have access to Andre, my private hairdresser of many years.

As I pushed any feelings of regret and self-pity to the back of my mind, the warm liquid washed away the dust I'd collected in my daily walk around the concrete yard. It snaked down my lithe frame. It cleansed my body, but not my mind.

The persistent dirt that caked my reasoning was untouched. Water has no impact on the grime that festers in your soul, and pusses your eyelids together till no one can look inside.

They say that your eyes are the windows of your soul. So maybe I don't have a soul. But that explanation is too simple. And my story is far from simple.

***

"Ouch," I mumbled, as I washed myself.

Cheap soap was in my eyes. Cursed reality! Wash, wash it out and away with the prison water. Wash everything out and away. If only I could. Some things stick, like mud hitting the fan.

In nearby showers, fellow prisoners splashed around, quickly sharing tales of their latest dramas; only interrupted by their bubbly laughter and quick grabs at love-in-the-suds.

"Five minutes left!" an impatient prison guard warns us, her shrill voice rises above the jailbird banter. "Hurry up!"

My prison life was under lock and key. I had order. Everything was predictable. Life's slippery slope was removed. When everything is taken from you, you no longer fear the night thief. You have nothing to lose, except yourself.

'Clunk, clunk', as awkward hands drop soap.

And then the water gurgles down the drain. All the prison showers synchronise; a symphony of archaic plumbing.

Water has a mindless direction, an indisputable path; an enigma birthed by the storm clouds. It's a soft texture that gives the 'kiss of life' to the beautiful flowers. Yet, with timeless precision it fiercely cuts away hard rocks as it purges across the thirsty land. Ultimately, someone controls its ebb and flow. They switch it on and off. They puff up the clouds with dew, and stir thunder into an angry rage of lightning sparks. They also decide the duration of our shower time.

Grizzle. Grumble. Not everyone wants to get out of the shower. They want to linger and lather in the mysterious flow of warm water. But they have no choice. They must do as they're told.

By opposing the rules of the society that birthed them, then being caught by the police, they lost control over their shower rights. Now they have no rights. They have no freedom except in their tainted imagination. Naked. Exposed. Just like me, they are prisoners of the State. Indefinite plodders of the prison yard dust.

But for fifteen minutes, the shower affords us pleasure. I appreciate its warmth. I feel like a smooth rock in a pristine stream, as I lather my tingling flesh with a slippery piece of prison soap. And in the final minutes in the shower cubicle, I close my eyes and tilt my face toward the shower head.

The water runs across my face and into the crease of my mouth. It tastes clean. Invigorating.

Enjoying my brave thoughts, I push aside the imminent danger of hostile prisoners. Some of them hate me. They call me a snotty-nosed toff.

Yet, in my shower cubicle, I breathe deeply, softly, biding my time. Then I notice my hairy legs.

"C'est la guerre. C'est la guerre," I whisper, remembering a catchphrase I once read in a magazine. "C'est la guerre." I must accept my fortune, without being too upset.

I remember the grand lady I had been, six months prior to incarceration: waxed legs and manicured nails; nothing but the best. After all, I had reached the pinnacle of my literary career as a popular author. Then midst the froth and bubble of popping champagne corks and salutations, I confessed to murder.

But why?

No one suspected me. I was too clever to leave a trail. Outside of my prison life, I was the master of deception. But like Tutankhamun, the real me had died behind a golden mask. People once envied my celebrity lifestyle. I was elegant and glamorous, to a fault. I mingled with the rich and famous. They relished my alluring smile. All the while I gleaned their banter for stories for my novels. No one knew that I battled the cruel voices in my head; the accusing tones of my alter ego reminding me of the abused child I had been. Kellie Earl the punching bag, the nothingness.

The cursed child.

Outsiders were dismayed when the police burst into my luxurious Sydney Harbour mansion and arrested me. My written confession had ended my life as a popular Australian author. Following that, my prestigious life-style gurgled down the plughole, like the shower puddles washing over my feet in the prison shower.

The world needed answers. I needed answers.

Truth known, when I lived in the bubble of the trendy nouveau riche, nothing made sense to me. My life was a charade. My sleep was racked with fear and flashbacks. My diamonds and party pearls were a sparkling juxtaposition on my dark soul. I could stand in the stream of a gold-plated shower with wall-to-wall gilt mirrors, and feel as putrid as a pig in mud. I felt violated. Tainted. The enemy within my soul constantly battled for supremacy. And no amount of washing or scrubbing could cleanse me.

I needed retribution.

Retribution.

PART ONE

1

Five names

1985

Today I am a popular fifty-year-old author with an exceedingly complex personality and heretical past. As such, I have the privilege of using five names. Of course, my choice depends on my mood and the activity I engage in. Now I will tell you the significance of each of my names.

Firstly, Akeila Zeneta Zirakov is the name written on my birth certificate. It is my least used name that I only attach to legal documents. Although I was born in Australia, I was conceived overseas somewhere; probably in Russia. Whilst pregnant with me, my Russian mother migrated to Australia with my older brother, Bolodenka Ziovy Zirakov, aka Billy.

Secondly, *Kellie Earl* is the familiar name my mother, Jana Sveta Zirakov, gave me to make me sound Australian. She desperately wanted our family of three to fit into her new home in Port Melbourne. She no longer wanted us to sound like Russian refugees. From that point on, we were known as the Earls. Ryan Earl was one of my mother's hangers-on who lived in our rented, single-fronted Bridge Street house in Port Melbourne. My mother briefly married him, in order to give us all the same surname. It seems that theirs was simply a short-lived marriage of convenience. For a while, my mother almost seemed proud of being called Mrs Earl. She felt that wearing a wedding ring gave her a position in the neighbourhood social order. She no longer typified a mail order bride. After all, she was a respected tax payer, wife and mother. Accordingly, she wanted her two handsome children to 'fit in' with the Australian way of life.

Sadly, Ryan was a dope-smoking musician who didn't do much for the environment or for our family. He was a true tyrant. One day, my mother caught him stealing her hard-earned waitressing money that she stashed under her bed. After that, I don't know what happened to him. My mother never spoke about him again. However, I remember that we ate a lot of minced meat after he went. Mother used to joke and call it Ryan's rissoles.

Thirdly, Mrs Kellie Bamcroft is the name I used in my fifteen year marriage to Carl Bamcroft. He was a highly-regarded bank manager who died too young. He liked to indulge in fine food and wine. Sadly, this lifestyle brought about his early demise. But the tragedy of his death was partially compensated by the millions of dollars I inherited from his estate.

Please don't prejudge me, for I truly loved Carl. I am eternally grateful for the precious time we shared. Obviously, becoming a wealthy widow enabled me to live the high-life whilst writing novels. Dear Reader, this is a creative activity that I thrive on, even more than my quest for life itself. And every writer understands my sentiments.

Fourthly, B. M. Rising is my pen name. This stands for *Bad Moon Rising,* which was the favourite song of my deceased brother, Billy Earl. Sadly, he died when he was only seventeen.

Writing my books under the pen name of B.M. Rising helps me to deal with the sudden death of my beautiful, teenage brother. His premature death is a pain that I carry to the grave. And I hope my use of the pseudonym brings credence to his memory.

My fifth name has an interesting story behind it. Years later when I was a prisoner at Fairlea Women's Prison, some fellow inmate called me Miss Zed or Zed. They considered my official name as being too much of a tongue twister. As mentioned, I ended up in Fairlea after I confessed to murder.

Overall, I enjoyed being called Miss Zed. This title seemed appropriate since 'Z' is the last letter of the alphabet. And I always get the last word in my books, as you will soon learn.

2

What is truth?

Dear Reader, I will take you on my twists-and-turns journey, as I sought truth and a sense of self- justification. As mentioned, I had multiple name changes along the way. These signified my transformation from being Kellie Earl the abused child, into Miss Zed, the cold-hearted murderess. And then I grew into a composed middle-aged woman who seemed to have redemption and a grip on life. Please be aware that this was not an easy task.

In this book I will share mine and other compelling stories; stories I heard whilst I was 'doing time' in Fairlea Women's Prison. Along the way, you will gain crucial insights into the mechanization of tangled minds. It's a place where lies become half- truths, and imagination protects one from life's harsh reality.

Although my story will place you *in situ* with the worst of the worst examples of humanity, rest assured it will help you to understand any biases a murderess harbours. Some are real whilst others are imagined.

C'est la vie.

"I am innocent," the prisoner always pleas. "I was set up."

But sometimes this is not far from the truth, as you will discover. Occasionally, the true villains appear as victims. And vice versa.

The jury can get it wrong. Witnesses can be fuddled or bought. And innocent prisoners become the walking dead.

As you follow my story, you will feel my universal pain and joy. You will realise that the shackles one throws over their mind, are more claustrophobic than any bricks and mortar prison cell. And the seismic issues that philosophers-of-old grappled with, are no different to modern-day conundrums.

We are no smarter than the ancient philosophers. And their truths become our truths. The innate desires and ambitions that drove the ancients in their quest for power and belonging, are still blatantly evident in our modern world.

As much as we like to think that society has evolved and we are more humane, we are still one rock away from stoning an innocent prisoner; or one vote away from reinstating a public hanging. But these are universal issues. For the time being, I will try to focus on my journey and my amazing discoveries, rather than veering into social tangents. After all, this book is about my journey and how I reached the light at the end of the dismal tunnel.

Undoubtedly, you will endeavour to find justification for my murderous act, as you seemingly place your troubled head on my lumpy prison pillow. You want to believe that I am innocent. You will find me 'too cute' to be anything short of charming. Perhaps you will label me as a victim.

No doubt, you will also side with the other incredible stories of my inmates. Your sympathies might favour the underdogs who fell foul of the law; the lost souls scurrying in the shadow of death in a place where morals are worthless. Overall, you will try to piece together our scattered mind-jigsaws as you lump us in the too-hard basket of prison misfits.

Notably, you might want to affix the blame on someone or something else; call it destiny or the wrath of the gods. But sometimes the blame is shifting and as slippery as my prison soap. People change their stories. They evolve. Their truth becomes a lie they don't want to face. And alibis become malleable clauses in the hands of clever lawyers.

C'est la vie.

Whilst many philosophers believe in the good of humanity, and strive for moral perfection, *Legalism* tells us that human nature is incorrigibly selfish. The only hope for humanity and social order, according to this school of thought, is to impose discipline from above. We need rules and boundaries. We see this happening in the prison system.

Further to this, it soon becomes apparent that 'truth' is also slippery. Even the wise philosophers have shifting definitions of its meaning. Nothing is fixed in concrete. Apart from authors who write the plot, no one can be omniscient and know everything. Instead, they each possess a piece of 'the truth'. Regardless, I eagerly searched for the truth, their truth, as I read tatty books in the prison library. Often, I was shocked by their hypocrisy and grand betrayal of their own values.

Yet, in a dank penal environment, reading about their flawed ideals opened a window of opportunity for me. Their timeless reasoning challenged my attitude. I took a different perspective on life. Things were no longer black or white. Human nature creates countless shades of grey. In the end, I wondered if humans are born inherently evil or good. And who's in control of our life? Is it fate, the gods or us?

I gleaned the sages every word. No knowledge is ever wasted. I soon realised that by understanding man's universal struggles, I could understand my own. I then became relevant. I was part of a broader system. Everyone is confused and unsure till they decide which school of thought they will follow.

As an inquisitive child, I struggled to find my true identity and a place in the world. I was lost in adult dramas. I desperately wanted my mother to talk about Russia and the life she left behind. I needed to know who my father was. But it was to no avail. Her pain was too deep to disclose.

And when I entered Fairlea Prison, I thought the truth would be hiding inside a bricks and mortar existence. I felt like a *tabula rasa;* a blank slate that is influenced by one's environment. I was a blank sheet waiting for society to write my destiny.

Indeed it did. But not in a kind way.

3

The novelist

Seneca was a Roman philosopher who shared his ideas on enriching people's lives. He said, "Power over a catastrophe can be achieved by overcoming one's attachment and aversion to external things."

(Seneca, 4BC – 56AD)

Whilst promoting detachment from external things such as wealth and sexual immorality, Seneca enjoyed all of the above. His contemporaries judged him harshly for his hypocrisy and his lavish lifestyle. Because of his blatant contradictions and *Pumpification* or satirisation of the gentry, they forced him to take his own life. If he didn't kill himself, he would have been murdered by the leaders of the day who demanded respect and god-like status.

Like Seneca, I also had this 'divided self' and seed of hypocrisy. Whilst I mingled with the rich and famous at lavish Toorak parties, I secretly laughed at them. Their lives were just as fanciful and empty as mine. We all had our demons to battle.

"More champagne, Mrs Bamcroft?" they politely asked me, when I escorted my wealthy banker husband, Carl, to their Melbourne mansions.

They knew that Carl had the means to give them bank loans for property development, or crucial advice to facilitate their investments. He was a financial genius who was much sought after. I could have ridden on his laurels. I didn't need to ever work again.

But Carl knew that I had a burning passion to write. It was innate. I loved immersing myself in my stories. Seated at a mahogany desk with a blank notebook before me, a pen in one hand and countless dreams in the other, I wrote many successful novels. Carl was my patron and best critic.

"Kellie, I really enjoyed your last book," he once said, when we shared a glass of wine in our spacious lounge room. The overhead fluorescent light shimmered on his soft, ginger hair as he smiled at me. "Parts of it were a bit sad though," he added. "I felt sorry for that young girl, Mixie, the drug addict. Do you know people like her?"

"Just made her up, dear," I lied, not daring to say that the frightened girl was a manifestation of me. I was the lost child clinging to the abandoned puppy.

"Mmm," he sighed, as he leaned back in his leather armchair and smoked his pipe. "You do a bloody good job, you know. You always suck me in when I read your novels. I started crying in the middle of your last book. That bit about the bird with the broken wing really got to me. It couldn't fly, and just got left behind by the flock. So cruel."

"Oh, Carl," I said, as I put my arms around him. "I am sorry if I made you cry."

"Come on," he teased, as he kissed me. "Isn't that the sign of a good author? They know how to stir our emotions."

For fifteen years, Carl was my soul mate. I still grieve for him. I lost my footing when he died.

And when I watched his large, wooden coffin being lowered into mother earth at The Melbourne Cemetery, the demons in me resurfaced. I felt angry and cheated by fate. My focus shifted from pining-away for my lost true love, to seeking revenge for the injustices that life dealt: the secrets about Russia that my mother kept; the untimely death of my brother; and the history behind my face that resembled no one I knew.

Who was I?

Although I looked the part of the grieving widow or the popular author with a flashy smile, I retained all my ugly childhood emotions. They were tucked away in my kaleidoscope of literary debauchery. So if I were an animal, I would be an arrogant grub turned into a flighty, beautiful butterfly. I could not forget my grisly childhood, despite turning into a minx who flew with a myriad of colour in her wings.

Fortunately, I could readily refer to my old diaries that I hid under my bed. On reading them, I could slip into the role of the child I left behind. I could bring her to life in the pages of my books. I was Mixie. I was the trembling, abandoned bird waiting for the cat to return, or the puppy no one wanted.

Mostly, I was yin and yang.

However, I find my personal contradictions and enigmas beneficial when writing a novel. An author must be able to embellish their fictional stories and characters with compelling storylines. Even painful childhood memories are useful. And I have many of these swirling in the chasms of my soul.

After all, how can one write a gripping story if they do not encounter real, interesting people and challenging situations? How can one gracefully fly through the treetops as a butterfly, if they've never crawled as a grub? How can you know how it feels to dangle on a cliff's edge, if your spirit has never been broken by despair?

Daily experiences feed the writer's imagination, as we watch and listen to people going about their daily lives. Mostly, we draft our stories from encounters with accidental friends and strangers who bump into us in cafes and bars. And then we find the words to fill the pages of our salacious novels. We bring their untold stories to life. If *Pumpification* occurs along the way, then so be it.

Touché, Seneca.

4

The Harvest Blonde

Although I often reflect on the child I used to be, please note that I don't want the focus of this book to be wholly on Port Melbourne. Nowadays, I separate myself from my childhood, as I engage in fresh story lines. Port Melbourne was merely the backstory to the unfolding dramas. Instead, I want to take you on my existential journey as I tried to find some meaning in life; as I sorted fiction from fact; and curiously noted how people push the limits in their universal struggles.

My quest all began when I entered the prison system at forty five years of age. As mentioned, I likened myself to a *tabula rasa* (a blank slate). And that is exactly how I felt. My life was going to be wholly influenced by the prison environment. It heralded a new beginning for me.

It seemed that by going to jail, I was given a second chance. As such, I had to learn new social skills and unlearn others. My mind was filled with fresh memories; some good and some horrid. I was given equal portions of respect and disrespect by the incarcerated women. Our lives became brutally entwined as we lived in close proximity. Some happenings were so bad, that previous horrors seemed almost insignificant. The contradictions of the human spirit still leave me flummoxed.

During my prison time, I shared my life with real people with real problems. Although mere numbers to the State, they became my true friends. I threw myself into their dramas. For a while, I forgot about my history: my past life in Port Melbourne and then in South Melbourne as a prestigious banker's wife.

Although it's called 'moving on', it's a bit like a mongrel dog dragging a broken leg. Your past never really lets go of you.

C'est la vie.

Therefore, by currently using the *nom de plume* of B.M. Rising, by donning sunglasses and dyeing my hair a shade of Harvest Blonde, I gained obscurity. Today I live in The Rocks in New South Wales, where no-one can connect me with the self-confessed murderess. I look like a beautiful, but ageing, James Bond spy. This is another thread in my ancestry. In reality, I am simply an ex-con trying to make my way in the world at large.

But there is still a huge story about the way I got from point A to point B; as I learned that the enemy of one's enemy may be ipso facto a friend. And as I planned this book and drew my timeline, I couldn't believe all the dramas that transpired along the way. I'm sure I filtered out some engaging stories in favour of others. But I had to compress several lifetimes into one novel, which is no easy task.

And when I looked at an overview of my life, it's as if the gods sat in their clouds and played marbles with my fate. One minute I was heading in one direction, and in the next breath I was rolling off on a different course. Sometimes, I rolled over the cliff edge. Looking back, the ground underfoot only seemed level when I was with Carl. And once he died, my whole world turned upside down in a huge landslide. All the marbles rolled helter-skelter.

Although I have a new identity, I am still the same person at heart. Changing names and dyeing my hair a pretty shade of Harvest

Blonde, doesn't change who I am. I'm sure you understand that living incognito is essential for my literary inspirations. I am not really eccentric, by donning a disguise. I am just covering my tracks. I am wily rather than wicked.

In effect, I want to separate the genius author from the killer I became. This is another theme in this loaded, loquacious novel. At the end of the day, keeping my true feelings and identity private is detrimental for my survival. What if people ever shouted, "There's the crazy killer!"?

But who's crazy, anyway? And what does being crazy mean? Different societies and cultures have different spins on this word. Later in this book, I will talk about the influence of war on our definition of 'crazy', and also how society has a shifting definition of' murder'. It's all about the time and place.

You might wonder why I still write, since I've got more money than I could ever spend. Why bother? Haven't the philosophers said it all? Why don't I just get on with my life? After all, I'm a free woman now. You might question why I am continuously compelled to scathe my surroundings for possible story lines.

Dear Reader, my quest to control my characters' destiny is a compulsion that spurs me on. It is innate; a universal drive amongst word smiths. For a certain time, each writer needs to withdraw into their secret world, where reality and fiction intertwine.

Sooner or later, writers must return to the real world. We must maintain a grip on reality, and know when it's time to put down our pen. And that, my friend, is the difference between insanity and sanity. Being lost in a fantasy world and being unable to return to normality, is similar to schizophrenia. The sufferers of this psychological condition are sometimes labelled as 'being crazy'.

It is evident that I relish playing God, as I insert and delete my imagined characters in my manuscripts. Some are stir crazy whilst others are not. I feel empowered as I write their destiny. It gives me a sense of control. I become the great creator who sets the moral boundaries. I determine the wavering path of destiny, as I close and open doors. I define the absolutes as I roll all the marbles across the floor.

C'est la vie!

5

1939

Now I return to my backstory. I will take you back to where it all began in the seaside town of Port Melbourne. To understand Miss Zed, you must understand Kellie Earl, the child she once was. A tree doesn't grow from nothing. First, a seed must be planted. And whilst I am in possession of my memories and marbles, I will throw all my seeds on the soil. The plot will take root and the seeds will flourish.

My story begins at the age of four when I knew I was different from the rest. My kindergarten teacher always found me challenging. Especially, during her story time when I used to act out what she was saying. The other children used to burst out laughing at me. Instead of encouraging me, the teacher exiled me to the sandpit. Sometimes, I had the company of another naughty child in the pit. But mostly, I sat alone to dig sand with a plastic spade.

The following year in primary school, I wasn't like the other school children either. They cried on their first day of school in Pickles Street, Port Melbourne. I never shed a tear when my mother kissed me "goodbye" at the school gate. Instead, I was swept by excitement. I raced toward my cluttered classroom in the B-wing of the school building. I couldn't embrace education fast enough.

Being a keen student, I was quickly socialised into the school routines. I conformed, rather than being chastised. I stuck to the predetermined pathway of education. I didn't want to have the life crushed out of me like an errant ant at the side of a road, or an unwanted rotten egg hurled against a wall during a protest march. And neither did I want to spend anymore story time in the sandpit.

By grade two, I realised that the compulsory 'John and Betty' classroom readers gave me a much needed class consciousness. *This is John. This is Betty.* Oh, how I remember those famous lines. Dear John and Betty familiarised me with an alien lifestyle. Theirs was totally different to the one I knew in the crowded, smog-filled town by the sea.

As I was growing up in the industrial town by Port Phillip Bay, I had vague inklings of the inevitable struggle I would face. I had a gut feeling that life wasn't always going to be kind to a Russian descendant who didn't know one iota about her heritage. Fortunately, I was a gifted child. And I had good teachers who worked with me. They saw me as a classroom blessing, rather than a curse. However, I soon realised that John and Betty were worlds away from my home in Port Melbourne. Instead of having a mum and dad, my mother's boyfriends came and went like flies on the kitchen wall.

When I was home alone, one of them fondled me. I was seven, at the time.

"I want to play 'doctors and nurses' with you, Kellie," he said as he lifted my dress. "If you say anything, I will cut off your fingers."

I believed his threat. And I remember the sickening smell of his tobacco breath, as he pulled me into him. Fear wreaked my small body. I clenched my fists. I was terrified. I truly believed he would cut off my fingers. His threats horrified me because I needed my fingers to hold my *John and Betty* books?

John and Betty's world was the family I yearned for. They gave me something to believe in. And I was glad when my mother's creepy boyfriend stopped coming to our house. For a while, things seemed safe. Maybe I could live a normal life like my book friends. I tried to push the sordid memories of him out of my mind.

But when I went to school, I wondered if any of the other children were fondled. I noted that they all had their little fingers. So maybe I was the only one. As always, I felt painfully different to them. I already knew that I was totally different to John and Betty. Unlike the fictional characters, I didn't have the happy, middle-class, meat-and-vegies existence they enjoyed. Neither did I have their stable home life with loving parents.

Instead, I had a tight-lipped migrant mother who looked like a beauty queen. Her silky, dark brown hair and soft, nut-brown eyes were striking. But she always seemed preoccupied. And I could feel the cold wall she placed around her heart. Maybe she didn't want to fall off the wall with Humpty Dumpty. Maybe she had her own sandpit memories.

By contrast, my older brother, Billy, was my best friend. Whereas I put my thoughts down on paper, he always spoke directly from his heart. We shared many happy moments; either watching the fishermen on Station Pier, or walking along the Port Melbourne beach. I simply idolised him and valued our time together.

We noted that we looked nothing alike. His complexion and hair were much fairer than mine. Also, he was much taller than me, and had a slight build. While I usually had my head buried in story books, Billy drew amazing pictures. I imagined his real father as being a famous Russian artist. Obviously, we had different fathers; fathers who remained anonymous.

Sadly, my mother kept her memories close to her chest and didn't divulge any secrets. She felt safer that way. I tried to do the same.

***

But all was not lost in those humble school years. And thank you John and Betty because reading and writing became my *raison d'etre;* my reason for being. By beginning with the simple reading of John and Betty's ventures, I soon advanced to reading more complex stories. I became enthralled by the world of literature. I realised that I could fantasise and lose myself as I turned the pages of a book. I could peer into the towering castles of kings and queens; in the land where everyone lives happily ever after; in that place where everyone went to the Mad Hatter's tea party, and there were no predators.

And then I started writing my own stories.

6

Grade Six

By grade six, I was blossoming into a beautiful girl, if I may say so myself. At least, that's what my mother's horrid men friends said. They liked the mystical beauty I possessed; inherited mostly from the father I never knew. When my long, shiny hair swept across my flawless face, it made me look like a high-end fashion model. Yes, I was pretty. And I knew it.

Thankfully, I excelled at school. I found much pleasure in receiving gold stars for my exemplary school work. The kindergarten sandpit became a distant memory. And I shuddered at the thought of being sent to the principal for *the cuts*, as the naughty boys and girls often were.

By contrast, Billy never got into trouble at school. He was always a model student. For two years he was the class captain. And because he was so handsome, he was always chased by girls. Sometimes, they befriended me, as a way to talk to him. But I sussed them out. I could be a right little bitch when the occasion arose.

"Sorry, Anna Ling, for not passing on your love letter to Billy," I said to one of the girls who chased him.

Hers was not the only relationship I sabotaged. I remember the day I came home early from school. Seeing the light on in Billy's room, I peered inside.

"Oops, sorry," I said, wishing I hadn't opened the door. Billy and Sandra Rogers were snuggled in his bed. They peered over the top of Billy's woollen blanket. "I didn't realise you had a visitor," I teased.

"Yes," Billy mumbled, almost dissolving into his mattress.

I instantly closed the squeaky door.

Within minutes, Sandra left his room. Looking embarrassed, she scurried out of the house. Thinking the coast was clear, I entered Billy's room.

"Well, well," I said to Billy. His blonde-tipped hair was dishevelled, and he had his t-shirt on inside out. He nervously sat on his hastily-made bed. "You told Mum you would be down the library doing school work."

"I got distracted," he said defensively. "I mean, she is pretty hot."

"You lied."

"Yea, well. Don't we all?"

He had me there.

"Don't say anything. Will ya?" he half-pleaded. "I really like Sandra."

"I thought Avril Young was your girlfriend."

"Not anymore." He smiled wryly, revealing his glossy-white teeth. "I don't like to commit."

"Commit?" I asked, as I sat down on his bed.

"You'll know all about it when you're older and start dating," he assured me. "It's all part of the game."

"Mmm," I said, as I noticed his splendid painting stuck on his wall. It was of a medieval knight fighting a blood-red and gold dragon.

"You can have my painting if you like, Kellie," he said, as he pointed to it. "It's just stuck up with sticky tape. If you like it, take it."

"Really?" I replied enthusiastically. I stood next to his brilliant picture to get a closer look. "This is lovely."

"Yeah, well, don't say anything to Mum. You can have that painting. It's our little secret."

Another secret.

"Oh, Billy. It's beautiful. Thank you so much. I will always love it."

"Yeah, well, go on. You can take it. Just rip it off the wall. It's all yours."

It was all mine. And that was the last thing Billy ever gave me.

7

Philosophy

By age thirteen, I was maturing both physically and mentally. Being tall, I looked much older than my age. In hindsight, I had an 'old head on young shoulders'. Such a cliché.

For a while I tried to believe in the good in people; even when their evil was blatantly obvious. I tried to enter that happy land that existed down the rabbit hole. I wanted to live with John and Betty.

When I tried to take my mind off the unpleasant men who visited our Bridge Street house, I created my own imagined haven on a mountain-top. It was a safe place where I could write my stories. By closing my bedroom door, I was able to build a protective wall around myself. For a while, I could shut the world out. I would not follow in Humpty Dumpty's tradition by sitting on a wall, waiting to be broken.

When people did harmful things to me, either physically or mentally, my mind wandered to a distant, pleasant place on my mountain-top. There I imagined stories about beautiful princesses and gallant princes. Instead of putting my trust in external things, be they people or possessions, I created a brave new world that I controlled.

Despite never hearing of the word 'nihilist', I had much of their logic ingrained in my psyche. I guess they were the times Billy called me a 'misery guts'. They were the times when I faced reality;

the times when everything seemed to be about doom and gloom, and hopelessness. Men were coming and going in our simple house. There were noises in the night; weird animal-like sounds coming from my mother's bedroom. During the day, my beautiful mother resembled a pallid ghost rather than a sprightly Cinderella.

I tried not to get involved in her world. I tried to ignore her friends when they visited our house. In order to escape my *black dog* depression, I walked to the local park in Esplanade East to get a bit of fresh air and sunshine. There I watched the kids playing on the swings or merry-go-round. They looked so refreshed and pure when they played with buckets and spades in the sandpits. For them, the sandpit represented playtime not punishment. We had the same truth, but a different perspective.

At the very least, my teenage logic would be a hornet's nest of skewered dreams that would impact on my actions and my writing. However, this time was vital in my formative years as a writer. It was the time my creative juices evolved. I often borrowed books from the local library. Through literature, I could escape into an imaginary world. It was a place where princesses were beautiful, and knights were noble. All stories had a happy end. And morals abounded.

But I could never entirely escape my childhood reality. At night when I lay in my bed, I could hear my mother walking along the hallway with her latest man. I heard their muffled laughter. Some stayed overnight. Others stayed for a couple of days.

During these tenuous times, Billy kept to himself. He stayed in his room listening to his radio, or drawing pictures in his art book. I avoided my mother's drop-kick men like 'the plague'. I felt their leering grins that accompanied their foul language. I saw their side-way glances that mentally undressed me. My skin crept.

But I always knew that they would go.

8

George Spiatis

Like my fountain pen, Billy and I became an extension of my mother's ego. She lived vicariously through us. She wanted us to have the education and riches that her displaced refugee status did not afford her. Her boyfriends were not a permanent fixture in our life. So there was always a glimmer of hope. But things changed for the worst when George Spiatis came on the scene. Mother simply moved him into our house without consulting Billy or me.

When George entered our humble house, a cold chill crossed my soul. Hell's fires hissed and spewed their venom. The 'fifth column' brought rape and paedophilia with him. George pretended to be part of our happy family. But all the time, he planned our demise.

George was a larger than life annoyance, being over six foot two inches by the old measure. Although he was always well-dressed in his tailored Fletcher Jones clothes, he reminded me of a paunchy, lazy wrestler. And I loathed the way he always blew cigar smoke around the house and in our faces. I hated his fat, greasy appearance. And I despised the way he laughed and touched my private places. He personified everything I hated in men. Everything I despised in life. Oh, God, I hated him enough to kill him.

In the afternoons when Billy and I weren't roller skating with the neighbourhood kids, we liked to watch cartoons on our television. It was our free time when we could relax. George was usually at the races. This enabled us to breathe easily for a while.

One afternoon George broke his usual routine, and stayed home. He sat in an armchair in our lounge room, like a fat bear sitting on the rocks beside a pond. He casually smoked a cigar whilst drinking a glass of whisky. Just watching him made me feel uneasy; like being in the eye of a storm.

At the time, Billy and I were seated on the nearby corduroy couch, watching cartoons on the television. We drank fresh milk while munching on cookies. We daren't talk to George, for fear of rousing his temper. Meanwhile, my mother was in the kitchen busily preparing Beef Stroganoff for the evening meal. The luscious smell wafted into the lounge room.

"You are a stupid boy, Billy!" George shouted at my bewildered brother. "You are nothing but a stick drawer. You think you will be an artist. Huh! What a joke. And you go out with your yobbo friends who are a pack of losers. You will never become anyone worth knowing."

As we sat on the couch, I felt Billy's feet shift beside mine. He clenched his slender, artistic hands in his lap. He bit his lip. I could almost taste his blood.

"That's a stupid show on TV," George hissed as he switched off the television. "Cartoons will never get you anywhere. Bloody idiots!"

Billy and I were dumbfounded. My stomach tightened. A cookie stuck in my throat. I started coughing. I took a gulp of milk. Billy looked down at his long, skinny knees that protruded beneath his cotton shorts. He lightly tapped his foot.

"And stop that stupid tapping!" George demanded. "You are getting on my nerves."

Billy and I glanced at each other. We picked up our almost-empty glasses. We headed for the kitchen, to see if Mother needed help.

"Get back here, you two!" George demanded. "I haven't finished."

Billy and I spun on our heels, and returned to our seats. We put our glasses on the tiled coffee table before us.

"When I say 'go', you go!" George commanded, spitting his words at us. "Not before that. I am the boss."

He chewed the end of his cigar. He gulped the last of his whisky. I thought, *perhaps he had a big loss on the races and was now in a bad mood. He was definitely intoxicated.*

I swallowed hard. I was shaking. Why had my mother brought such a horrible man into our house? Why?

"You need to learn manners," George roared. "Manners! You are grounded for a week."

Billy and I sat glum-faced. I almost cried.

With that, George burst out laughing.

"You two are robots," he spluttered. "You do what I say. This is so funny."

But I wasn't laughing. Part of me seemed to be dying a slow death. I think that's when I became a fully-fledged nihilist.

9

The Nihilist

At an early age, it seemed more logical to depend on myself rather than external forces. For a while, like the nihilists, I rejected all religions and believed that life is meaningless. I only found peace in my bedroom when I scribbled my thoughts into my diary.

My room was my little shelter that nestled at the front of our weatherboard house. There I found my ultimate power. With pen and paper, I captured the dreams and metaphors of youth. They were my thoughts that I alone controlled. No one could tamper with them. In the solitude of my bedroom, I began the drafts for my future best sellers.

I knew that I could not restrain my errant mother. I felt so weak and powerless. My home was not a safe haven. Yet, I could lord it over my fictional database. It was the only place where I felt empowered, one word at a time.

When I sat at my wooden desk in the corner of my room, I poured my heart and soul into my notebook characters. My words created real and meaningful people. They saw the rainbow colours of my bedroom window, when the morning sun broke through the blanket of night. They felt the crunch of scattered autumn leaves underfoot, as I walked to school. They smelt the salty sea breeze wafting across

Port Phillip Bay. They heard the squawking seagulls fighting over food scraps on the beach. They tasted the thick toast with its melting butter and smeared honey that was my breakfast. Mostly, they felt my universal pain; the *pain of antiquity* that permeated my novels.

***

In his free time, Billy was usually in his room creating amazing drawings. Mostly, he loved doing brilliant caricatures of his teachers, or elaborate paintings of monsters. He never disclosed what motivated his artwork. And I could only guess what was going on in his overactive mind. Did he also suppress his fears, and release them in his hideous beasts that breathed fire and destroyed life? In effect, did Billy create his own mountain-top experience in a place where his menacing minators ruled the world?

When I used words, Billy used ink. I turned pages. He turned heads. I infused my fictional characters with power and might. Billy did the same thing with his dinosaurs and ghouls. Both of us created strong, imagined creatures who wielded the mighty forces that we lacked. We told a story of a world far removed from the one we knew.

I used to wonder if Billy's father was a portrait artist for the aristocracy. Was Billy the result of a clandestine love affair my mother had with a Russian royal? Did an unknown Prince give her precious jewels in exchange for her affections, much in the same way George did? Did she live in a palace in Moscow or Venice? Was she envied by the peasants when she strolled their city streets in her diamonds and furs? While she flashed her glorious smile, did they cringe with hunger in the gulags?

Did she crave her homeland? Where did her heart truly belong? She was no longer a single, carefree girl. Is that why she secretly resented Billy and me? Did she feel obliged to take on a 'mother role', rather than relish it? Was her life an empty void where she missed the lifestyle of the rich and famous *vodka swillers*? Did she? Was she?

So many questions that she refused to answer. *Why not, Mummy?*

And more so, was my father a great philosopher or Russian revolutionary? Did he belong to the nihilists who were supporters of an extreme Russian revolutionary party? Like me, did he pore over his books as he scribbled his ideas into a notebook of some sort? Or perhaps I was wrong.

And what happened to my mother? Did something sinister stitch her lips with regret and trauma? Was she an orphan of the Gulags or the impoverished fishermen of the Volga River? Did her mother sell her to soldiers in exchange for vodka?

All these fanciful ideas consumed me when I imagined my heritage. At times, I almost begged and pleaded with my mother to tell me the whole truth. But she never budged. *Why not Mummy?*

But would I be able to cope with the absolute truth? Maybe ignorance is bliss after all.

So instead of persisting with her unremitting rebuffs, I conjured fantastic scenarios for my fictional beings. At least, I knew where they came from and where they were headed. Absurdity and extremity were the norm. My norm. In the same way that Billy dipped his brush in paint and ink, I dipped my pen into the chasm of my dictionary. I did my word-paintings whilst Billy produced his exquisite ink pictures.

Wisely, I hid my diaries and notes under the mattress on my bed. I didn't want anyone being privy to my secret thoughts. And I especially didn't want George Spiatis knowing that my writing had a consistent undercurrent of the toxic secret we shared.

Sometimes, in frustration, I ripped up my notes and threw them across my bedroom. An insurmountable anger surged within me.

My tears flowed. I hated myself. Nothing seemed fair. By night, my secretive mother was working somewhere in St Kilda. And George was taking advantage of his babysitting role in our home.

"I will stop giving your mother money," he warned me, one evening when he came into the sanctity of my bedroom. Like a haughty king facing a peasant, he sat on my bed-throne.

"If you say a word about our secret," he threatened, "there will be no nice clothes for all of you. And you won't be able to afford to live in this house. You will all be out on the street! Your mother will put you in a home for unwanted children. And they will rape and torture you."

This notion struck fear into my heart. I feared the devil I didn't know more than the devil I did. I remained silent. I wasn't prepared to take a gamble. There was too much to lose.

I know George paid our rent and bought expensive jewellery and clothes for my mother. He tried to buy favour with us by buying records for Billy, and popular books for me. Since he didn't have his own family, he tried to buy ours. Such a disgrace.

And my mother didn't really need to work. I think she only did it to get out of the house. Sometimes, I felt that she was trying to get away from me. Or maybe from the man I looked like; the father she refused to discuss. The man I secretly hoped would rescue me.

10

Hell's Babysitter

And neither did Billy or I need a babysitter; especially not George. George was the lowest of the scum. He made me want to strike out at society. I wanted to blame someone for the pain I felt. Mostly, I wanted to kill him.

"Look at me," he whispered, when we were home alone in the lounge room. "Oh, beautiful girl," he sighed, as he forced me to put my hands inside his pants.

I vomited.

And then I ran into my room. I needed to write. I needed to escape into my fantasy world on the mountain-top. Help me! Help me!

All my fictional characters were subservient to me. I chose who lived or died. Sometimes, I cast John and Betty into the sandpit where the naughty children belonged. I played God. I controlled their destiny.

I needed to write. Oh, God, I needed to write. Writing was the only voice I had. On a good day, I could titillate my readers with sheer delight; a delight that only I could imagine. By doing so, I gave joy to my readers, as well as to myself. I became the beautiful fairy who played in the rose garden; or the regal princess with the sparkling crown.

But my fantasy world was not always pleasant. From a safe distance, I could subject my readers to horrors that would shock or repulse them. It was nerve-racking. All the while I was totally detached from the dramas in my novels. My pen was merely the channel for a child's imagination. Whilst my fictional characters struggled against insurmountable odds in the valley below, I was untouched by the storm clouds that created their havoc. I distanced myself from the pain that was transferred from me to them. They floundered at the mountain base. They endured my pain and torment. They begged and pleaded, and scurried like blind mice escaping the lion's jaws of death.

Unlike the biblical Moses, I never met God on the mountain-top. But the mountain air in my mind was always fresh and untainted by George's cigars. There were no footsteps in the soft soil of my imagined haven. I was immortal. Soulless. Irascible.

The hot Australian summers and the chilly winters could not harm my soft flesh that was concealed in the pages of my creativity. I was omniscient, high above the storm clouds; out of reach of the common man. Far out of the reach of George Spiatis.

11

The Dead Lamb

In reality, George ruined my childhood. And no amount of writing books could erase him from my mind. He was the greedy wolf that raids the chook pen. He always lurked at the base of my imagined mountain. Sometimes, he invaded me. Then I hated him with an immeasurable passion; a loathing more intense than the raging bushfires that ravage Australia's forests. Because my mother naively invited him into our home, for a season, I also hated her.

After having a good day at school, I would come home to his ugly presence in our house. Although he had four houses of his own, valuable properties he inherited from his deceased mother's estate, he affixed himself to us; to our house. I loathed and hated him. And Billy felt the same way. George was like a limpet to our family.

George was the tyrant who destroyed our family. Each time he touched me, I vomited. The bile rose in my mouth, and stung my nostrils. I felt dizzy. My fragmented mind withdrew to my mountain-top. With Mother out of the house at night, George forced me into her bed.

"Akeila, Akeila," he whispered, as he invaded my sacred places. "You are so beautiful."

Oh, God. Why don't you hear me? Are you there? I silently pleaded.

Billy never knew about these assaults because he always had his headphones on. Out of earshot, he was nestled in the converted veranda that became his bedroom at the side of our house. Yes, that was his mountain-top. There he hummed along whilst listening to the radio that George gave him. *Bad Moon Rising* was probably playing.

But I was silently screaming for an escape. I was too afraid to scream out loud; too afraid that George might cut off my precious fingers. In my mother's bed, beneath the photo of the Bolshoi ballet that she proudly hung on the wall, George groped and molested me.

My skin felt putrid. I closed my eyes and pretended that I was somewhere else.

"Look at me, Akeila," he insisted, calling me by my Russian name.

I felt sick. I wished he would disappear.

"My Akeila," he purred, like a lion feasting on the carcass of a dead lamb as he kissed my face, and then my pert breasts.

Oh, please, cut me into a million pieces. Remove his acrid touch from my skin. I will kill you one day, George. I swear that I will! I screamed into my soul; into that inaudible place where no one hears.

Afterwards I scrubbed and scrubbed my flesh until it bled. But tangible soap could not clean away the sense of impurity that tarnished me. It could never erase the intangible fears that festered in my spirit.

If God existed, I didn't know him. Winged angels never scooped me out of my miry pit in the shadow of death, to place me in the green pastures with a watchful shepherd. Perhaps that was merely a story that someone wrote in their story book.

At an early age, I lost my soul.

12

Teen Years

George paid for Billy and me to attend the best private schools in Melbourne. As such, I gained excellent tuition in writing. I also gained exposure to the classics such as: Shakespeare, the Brontë sisters, Thomas Hardy and Lord Byron; an improvement on *John and Betty*. I gained academic recognition when I won several scholarships. This money paid for my school excursions. I was proud of myself.

But George liked to splash his money around. He liked to remind us that we were indebted to him. Did he expect me to be a grateful fifteen-year-old plaything? Did his expect his chattel to worship him?

As a sensitive teenager, I often withdrew into my secret world. Like a sword in a sheath, I always had a pen to scribble my thoughts down in an exercise book or diary. In the solitude of my bedroom, my imagination flourished. There I could stretch-out on the frilly, pink quilt that covered my single bed, and think about what I would write. My mind always took me to another place.

I imagined all sorts of villains and heroes that I inserted into my award-winning short stories. Yes, I won an inter-school writing competition with my story about a bold queen who conquered an empire.

Meanwhile at school, things seemed to go relatively smoothly for me; if one considers living with a paedophile as being the norm. All the while I tried to avoid George. In the evenings, I stayed close to Billy for as long as possible. And when I went to bed, I anxiously waited till I heard the click of the front door, indicating that my mother was home again.

One day, Ian Hoffmann, one of the Aboriginal boys from the local YMCA, approached me outside the YMCA's two-storey brick building. I had just completed my weekly gymnastic class.

"Hi, Kellie. Are you free this Saturday?" he asked, with a broad smile on his handsome face.

"Yes, why?" I asked, self-consciously.

"Would you like to watch a movie with me. We could go to the Bourke Street cinema and see Marlin Brando's latest film. I hear it's good there."

I was taken aback. What a surprise to be asked out by someone whom I considered as being the *biggest spunk in town.*

"Yes. Sounds good," I said, feeling flattered. "I'd love to go."

"Great. 'A Street Car Named Desire' is showing. And we'll go to the matinee," he enthused. "I'll pick you up at noon."

"Might be better if I just meet you under the clocks at Flinders Street Station," I replied. "It's less complicated. I'll catch the bus in."

"Ok. At noon?" he quizzed, tilting his head slightly. The sunlight glistened in his soft, black hair.

"Yes, that's fine," I replied. "Noon it is."

I felt extremely lucky. Ian was one of the nicest boys I knew. He lived somewhere in Garden City, which wasn't too far away. His younger sister, Georgia, was around the same age as me. I knew her from the YMCA. Although Ian's skin was dark, hers was as white as mine. She said that she was doing Secretarial Studies at J.H. Boyd

Domestic College in nearby City Road, and planned to leave school at the end of the year.

Ian said that he was an apprentice plumber. I wasn't sure of his exact age. But it didn't really matter because conversation came easily between us. He had the broadest smile with the whitest teeth. His mother was an Aboriginal from Darwin, and his father a German settler from Adelaide. Ian was much taller than me. I found this attractive because I was taller than most boys in my neighbourhood.

Mostly, I liked the idea of getting to know him a bit more; a lot more to be honest.

13

Ian Hoffmann

Ian and I met under the iconic Flinders Street clocks. It was a popular meeting place for young Melburnians. He looked handsome in his jeans and black leather jacket. His curly, black hair was cut short. It looked very stylish. I proudly wore a neat pleated skirt and pink cardigan sweater. I bought them from the new store on Bay Street.

"Hi Kellie," Ian said, with a broad grin on his handsome face. The crowds rushed past us as he lightly kissed my cheek. "The movie starts in an hour," he said. "We've got time to grab a drink and some popcorn, if you like."

"Sounds great, Ian."

Butterflies filled my stomach when we sat in the cinema, *cosying* up to each other and holding hands. His hands were a bit rough. But I figured that was from his manual labour. After the entertaining movie, we caught a tram along St Kilda Road. We headed toward the Queen Victoria Gardens.

"You're a great chick," he said, when we found a quiet spot in the park.

The green grass was soft to sit on. The surrounding trees were a mixture of autumn shades. A slight breeze was blowing. I was glad I wore my cardigan.

"I've got so much that I want to tell you, Kellie. So many things I want to share with you. You are such a special girl."

He wrapped his strong arms around me and drew me into his body. He lightly kissed my lips. His lips were so soft. I didn't want him to stop.

"Is that ok?" he asked, as he pulled away.

"Yes," I said, almost out of breath.

My face was hot and flushed. Everything was just perfect.

"I didn't know you felt that way," I said nervously. "We were always 'just friends' at the YMCA. And I bet Georgia has something to say," I teased.

"She's cool, Kellie. She encouraged me to ask you out."

"I am so glad you did."

I leaned over and kissed him, pushing my lips hard against his. My body tingled with delight. I didn't want to let him go. It felt wonderful.

We didn't need an orchestra playing music or a lovers' serenade. We didn't need fireworks exploding in the sky, or gondoliers sailing us into the sunset. All we needed was each other and the puppy love we shared.

14

Toy-Girl

Later that night, all hell broke loose at home in our lounge room. I stood in the hallway, dumbfounded. George's shouts and mean words bounced off the thin walls in our house.

"There is no way Kellie is having a boyfriend!" he yelled at my mother. "She is too young. And I am paying to put her through a private education. Doesn't that count for something?"

No response. I imagined my befuddled mother sitting in an armchair. Her long legs would be crossed in her blue Capri pants and ballet flats. Her full breasts would be partly revealed beneath her usually low-buttoned, check shirt. She was ready to work in the St Kilda cafe.

"You can't let her go about town with that Aborigine," George insisted, as he sat on the couch, like the king of his domain. "What will the neighbours think? We can't let her do it to us. And I don't want him calling her on my telephone and sneaking off with her again."

"Your telephone?" Mother asked with a quivering voice.

"Yes, I pay the bloody bills. It is mine. And this house is mine."

"George, it's rented," she protested.

"That shows how little you know, Jana. I bought it two months ago. I got sick of paying the rent. And I am here all the time. So I might as well own this bloody place."

"Oh," she half gasped.

"And when we are married, it will be your house. And all the other houses. So what I say should count. Right?"

"George, is that a proposal?"

"Yes," he grunted. "You will soon be my lovely wife."

All went quiet. I was shocked. George owned our house, and we could never throw him out.

"But Ian seems like such a nice boy," Mother insisted, after a while.

"No boy is nice. They all want one thing. One thing. And then they just toss the girl aside. Do you want that? Do you want her tossed aside? I don't. She is doing well at school. And she will be a lawyer one day. So you must focus on her future. I do not want her running around with an Aborigine! And that is the end of it."

15

Rape

That night, Mum went to work earlier than usual. She said that the cafe was going to be busy, and they needed an extra hand. But I felt that she just wanted to get away from George and me, and the impending drama over Ian. Billy also went out for the night, saying that he was having a sleep-over at his friend's house in Albert Park.

Around eight p.m., I put on my purple flannelette pyjamas. I wanted an early night. I couldn't believe that George owned our house. All the while I worried about what he said about Ian. He'd said some really nasty things. Did he really mean it? Oh God, George sounded so selfish and mean.

But would he abuse Ian and disgrace me in front of my friends? Or would he take it out on Billy and my mother? Would he harm them? George was capable of anything.

He owned our house and had unprecedented power over us. This thought terrified me.

And just as I was standing in front of the dressing table mirror, brushing my long hair, George stealthily came into my room. He reminded me of a lion entering its den. My heart pounded with fear. I felt my legs tremble.

"It's for your best, to end it with that boy," he said with a matter-of-fact tone, as he sat on the end of my bed. He seemed to believe his lie. "I am right on this. I am always right. You do not want to get involved with an Aborigine," he continued. "It will cause nothing but trouble for you. For us! People will talk. Now sit down on your bed, and we will talk about this."

Against my better judgement, I sat at the top end of the bed. I wished Billy hadn't gone out. I hoped my mother would return soon. *Please. Please.*

"I like Ian," I protested, as George moved closer. "I like Aboriginals."

"You just like sex," he whispered, and smiled like an assassin. "I will give you all the sex you will ever need."

And then he pushed me onto the bed with such force, that I was winded. Like a wild animal, he ripped my pyjama pants off me. Sheer terror filled me.

He was too heavy to push away. He pushed his mouth against mine. The smell of his breath was sickening. I punched him in the shoulder as I jumped off the bed. But he grabbed my hair. Like a primal caveman, he pulled me back onto the bed.

"Stop fighting!" he said. "Stop it. Just relax and you will come to no harm."

The pupils in his shit-brown eyes were dilated. He breathed rapidly. Beads of sweat formed on his brow. He was insatiable; in a trance. Bile rose from my stomach. I tried to kick him away. But the more I resisted, the more his grip tightened. I couldn't shake him off. I couldn't free myself.

He kissed me again. His rough whiskers scratched my face. I bit his lip. He slapped me. It stung like crazy. I spat into his jelly-like eyes.

He laughed. He laughed again. Louder. Louder.

Fight! Fight for your life. Silent echoes screamed in my soul.

I fought hard. I tried to push him away. My face burned with fury. Contempt. Hatred.

Mummy, Mummy where are you?

Nobody came. Nobody cared. My racing heart pounded out the seconds. My youth was stolen as rape killed my soul.

And then he rolled away.

16

The Investment

I missed my next gym class at the YMCA. I wanted to avoid Ian. How could I tell him that George was a mean racist and rapist? How could I? So I figured it was best to let go of my friendship with Ian. Better to keep quiet and hold it all in. Things would work out in the end. One day I would tell him the truth. I could always write a story about it, and hand it to him.

However, when I was walking home from school, carrying my heavy school bag, Ian crossed the road to speak with me.

"Hi, Kellie," he smiled pleasantly.

My heart immediately sank with guilt. "Hi, Ian."

"You weren't at the Y," he said. "I haven't seen you since we saw the movie. You don't take my phone calls. I thought we had something. So what's going on?"

"Nothing," I lied, walking faster.

"I'll carry that for you," he insisted, as he took my green, vinyl school bag. He walked beside me. "I thought you liked me."

"I do," I said, as I stopped to lean against a neighbour's fence. "It's just too complicated, right now."

"Complicated?" he asked, as he placed my bag at his feet. "Was I too pushy or something?"

"No." I felt my cheeks blush.

"What then? You didn't give me a chance." I avoided his eyes, and looked at the ground. "Kellie?" he asked with a breaking voice.

I bent over and picked up my bag. "I just have too much school work. It's a full-on year for me. You're not at school anymore. It's different for you. You don't get lumped with a shit-load of homework. I just don't have time for a boyfriend."

I turned away from him; from his misty gaze; from his indignity. With a heavy heart, I headed toward home. *One step. Two steps.* I resisted the urge to run to his arms. I pushed back my tears. I just had to tread water for a while; until someone threw me a life rope. *Three steps. Four steps.* Till then everything was on hold. I promised myself that everything would sort out in the end. One day Ian would know everything; when the time was right.

Later that night, Billy knocked on my bedroom door.

"Kellie," he called, "there's a note for you from Ian. It was in the letterbox."

I slowly opened my door.

"I was just doing a bit of homework," I said. "I am always so busy."

"Yeah, well, here's his note," he said, as he passed it to me. "It's got his initials on the back of it. So I assume it's from him. How many I.H.s do you know?"

"Thanks Billy. It's from Ian. But I don't want to read it now. I'm busy."

"He seems like a good guy. He hangs out at the Y."

"You boys always stick together," I joked, though I really wanted to cry. "Thanks for the note anyway."

I quietly closed the door, and lay on my bed. I opened the note. It read:

'That's your decision. Make sure you stick to it. No need to communicate again. Ian.'

I folded the note, and put it under my pillow. This was all George's fault. I hated him more and more each day. I wished I could just tell my mother the whole story. I rolled over in my bed. I breathed deeply, as I was instructed to do in gym classes whenever I felt exhausted and out of puff.

"Stick to the plan," I reminded myself. "Stick to the plan."

I hugged my pillow. My tears shimmered on its soft cotton. I hated hurting Ian. I felt like such a heel. He was such a great guy. But I had no choice. George would terrify my family if I went out with an Aboriginal. George was such a bigot; a hypocrite. Why did my mother ever bring him home? I wondered when he would die, and she would become a wealthy widow. He had a lot of houses. More than he deserved. But she could own all of them one day. Was that her plan all along?

"Stick to the plan, stick to the plan," I told myself. One day, my trap will snap shut on him.

Meanwhile, I hugged my tear stained pillow. I felt like a deflated balloon, or a broken light globe. Simply useless. Wasted. I inhaled. *One, two, three.* I thought I was drowning in regret. Exhale. *One, two, three.* I felt like a swimmer out of her depth. I tried to stay afloat in a sea of regret.

I closed my reddened eyes. I wanted to believe that good overcomes evil, and the princess is rescued by her prince. I dreamed of reaching the pot of gold at the end of the rainbow, in that place where our family would be free of George; in that happy place where John and Betty lived.

But George was always there like an evil force.

"Breathe, breathe," I told myself. "One, two, three."

17

The Party

Next week, Billy told me that Ian had a new girlfriend. I felt jealous. I hated her. I was 'sick to the stomach'.

"I thought you liked Ian," Billy said.

"Na. Well, not really," I lied. "We just went to the movies once. You know."

"Oh, ok," Billy said, with a little smirk on his face.

After that, I stayed away from the YMCA. I just didn't want to see Ian again. Neither did I want to run into his new girlfriend. Too many complications.

Fortunately, George offered no resistance when my school friend, Vicky Anders, invited me to her sixteenth birthday party. Feeling positive, I bought a quaint silver bracelet for her; something I would appreciate. It was gift wrapped in pink paper with a petite, silver bow on top. I knew she would love it.

My mother took me shopping for trendy clothes to wear. We settled on a slick, black t-shirt worn under a black, knee-length poodle skirt. It had a gathered black net petticoat. The swing skirt had a pink poodle applique on the fabric. This is how it derived its name. My mother loaned me a pair of her black stiletto heels for the occasion. My freshly-washed hair hung loosely about my shoulders. I felt all grown up. George wasn't there to comment.

In her new red Muntz Jet convertible, my mother drove me to the East Malvern party. The car was the envy of all. She said that she bought the flashy car with the money she earned from working in the evenings. And as I sat in its black, leather interior, I couldn't help feeling that she was slightly apprehensive about my going out for the first time; though she assured me that I had her full blessing and much more.

"Mum, are you ok with it?" I again asked, as her car pulled into the kerb outside Vicky's two-story brick house. Unlike our poky front yard, most of the houses in Vicky's neighbourhood had huge landscaped gardens.

"Yes, Kellie," she sighed. "Of course. Just a bit tired. Nothing to worry about."

Her beautiful, new diamond ring caught my eye. "Nice ring," I said.

"George gave it to me."

"Today?"

"Yes, before he went to the races. He'll stay there till late tonight. He wants to watch the trots. I will pick you up from the party at midnight."

Mum looked so beautiful behind the wheel of the car. Her black cocktail dress highlighted her slender body. Her long, red fingernails accentuated her shiny ring.

"Not working tonight?" I asked.

"No. I took the evening off. I'm meeting up with George, and then I'll meet you out the front at midnight. Ok, honey?"

"See ya then," I said, as I clutched Vicky's present.

I blew her a kiss as she drove away. I eagerly walked along Vicky's stone path that was lined with English Box hedges. As I approached her house, the sound of music coming from inside could be heard. I felt like Alice in Wonderland. I eagerly stepped onto the front veranda that was covered with climbing pink roses.

18

The Dance Floor

Apart from the noise of Vicky's party, it was a quiet middle-class suburb. Vicky said that her parents were at a party in Toorak, and would be home around two a.m. That gave her a free run of the house till then.

On the front veranda, two teenage girls were cosily sitting with two boys in a 3-seater wicker lounge. Their bodies were firmly intertwined. Out of their school uniforms, I hardly recognised my friends, Valda and Pam. They chatted amicably as they sipped drinks from their tall glasses.

"Hi, guys," I said, as I approached them.

Valda looked beautiful in her slim cropped pants and ankle boots. By contrast, Pam looked more stylish in her pencil skirt, scoop neck blouse and modest low heels. The boys wore jeans and striped shirts; straight out of a James Dean movie.

"Wow, Kellie," Pam said as she glanced at me. "You look great. Nice skirt."

"Thanks. You look good too. Is it a fun party?"

"Yeah," Valda said. "We're just hanging out here for a while. We'll catch ya later."

I quickly forgot about their canoodling as I entered the house. I had a quick look at myself in the hall mirror, to check that I looked all right. I took a deep breath. This was my night of nights. The first time that I was going to a party by myself.

Time for a drink, I thought.

I entered the lounge room where hoards of teenagers were gyrating in time to a Frankie Laine song. Disco lights flashed, sending rainbow colours around the room. The party atmosphere was electric.

I looked at the American-inspired fashions of the party goers. Although the oldest girl was probably only seventeen, they looked years older. Most of them were decked-out in the latest fifties gear, including Audrey Hepburn dresses, brooches and pearls, French plaits and beehives. Some wore mid-calf skirts and oversized sweaters, or sunray pleated skirts. Others wore a man's shirt over jeans. The boys fashions were influenced by Marlon Brando, complete with jeans, leather jackets and striped shirts.

Indeed, it was an eclectic Saturday night full of promise.

I boldly merged into the party scene.

"Hi Kellie," Vicky called. "I'm over here."

I immediately stepped through the throng of teenagers, and made my way toward the birthday girl. She looked stunning with her blonde, earth-goddess hair hanging loosely about the shoulders of her slim, black sheath dress. Her black back seam stockings were accentuated by her black stiletto heels.

"Happy birthday, Vicky," I said. I gave her the brightly-wrapped present. I kissed her cheek.

"Thanks, Kellie. I'm sure I'll love this," she bubbled, as she quickly opened her gift. "Oh-so beautiful, Kellie. I gotta wear it now," she squealed with delight, as she admired her gift.

I helped her put on her new bracelet. It looked perfect.

"Drinks are in the kitchen over there," she said, as she pointed toward a door in the corner of the buzzing room. "Just help yourself. There's vodka, wine, rum, coke and whatever."

"No worries. Will do," I replied.

I looked around the room at all the glitz and glamour of a group of teenagers. Just two weeks ago they'd been swatting for their mid-term exams. But tonight was about freedom and forgetting the stress of remembering textbook lessons, or the stress of finding a suitable job the following year. Tonight was about being a teenager and enjoying the magic of the moment, and having fun.

Everyone looked so happy and carefree. Tonight was party time with music by Patti Page, Tony Bennett, Perry Como and other legends.

C'est la vie.

19

Dutch Courage

I was determined to drink a glass of sparkling wine in the kitchen. I needed a bit of Dutch courage. A couple of girls wearing Peter Pan blouses and circle skirts had the same idea. We stood in a huddle around the food platter that was on the large kitchen table.

"Hi there," a handsome young man said to me. He seemed to appear from nowhere. His short, blonde hair was slicked back with hair oil. He looked very confident in his straight-leg pants and black turtleneck sweater. I soon forgot about Ian.

"Hi," I said, halfway through my second drink.

He touched my hand and smiled. "Can I join your little group?" he teased, as he put his arm around my shoulders.

I felt awkward, nervous and slightly drunk. "Sure," I replied.

"I'm Craig," he said. "Vicky's cousin."

"I'm Kellie, her school friend."

"Now that's out of the way, would you like to dance, Kellie?"

"Sounds good," I replied, and quickly finished my drink.

He took my hand and led me into the crowded lounge room. There were at least twenty youths cuddling and dancing there. A Perry Como song was playing, as Craig pulled me against his taut body.

We danced to a couple more songs before he said, "Would you like to sit on the couch?"

He pointed to one of the maroon, velvet couches in the corner of the spacious room. Another couple were already seated there, at the far end. They were in the throes of deep passion.

"Ok," I said, excited by the idea.

We sat on the vacant part of the couch. Craig instantly put his arm around my shoulders, and hugged me. It felt natural to be with him.

"Would you like a joint?" he whispered in my ear.

Without a thought, I nodded my head.

He pulled out a rollie and cigarette lighter from his pants pocket. He casually lit the joint and did the drawback. He passed the cigarette to me. I felt awkward as I took a long drag off it. I coughed and passed it back to him. Craig smiled. I felt amazingly calm. I closed my eyes.

"You ok?" he asked, as he kissed my cheek.

"Yes. I feel very relaxed."

"That's good," he smiled, and took another drag on his joint.

We sat together in the smoky room, sharing the joint. He kissed me passionately. I didn't feel self-conscious at all. The music was loud as party-goers smoked, swooned and swayed on the dance floor.

Craig and I shared another joint. By this time, I was feeling dizzy.

"Would you like to go somewhere private?" he asked. "There's an empty room just off the hallway. I know my way around here. I've been here heaps of times with my family."

Family. The word 'family' sounded warm and inviting.

Before long, I was lying on a single bed with Craig in one of the back bedrooms. I couldn't remember exactly how I got there. Maybe I walked. Or maybe I flew. But who cares? I didn't care about anything.

As Craig undressed me, he had a sense of urgency. Soon we would have to vacate the room for the next couple. But I didn't care. I was in the moment. Stark naked under the blanket, I imagined myself being in a large swimming pool. The warm water was splashing over me as Craig's hands sensually wandered across my body; soft and gentle. Wave after wave. His mouth was moist as it touched my lips. His tongue toyed with mine. Nothing was forced. We made love in the deep-blue sea bed.

Yes, it was love. Not rape. I wanted him. I needed him. I imagined our love boat gently sailing on top of the waves; gliding up and down with the currents.

After a while, I heard the bedroom door click shut as Craig left the room. Or maybe he was still there. I hugged my soft pillow. My drugged mind drifted in and out of reality, as I fell into a deep sleep.

***

"Kellie, good morning," Vicky said, as she gently shook me. "I phoned your mum, and she said that you could stay over last night."

"Oh, great," I said. My head felt like a ton of bricks.

"Are you ok?"

"Yes," I said, as I sat up in the bed.

"Here's your clothes," she said, as she passed them to me. "You had a fun time. Craig told me about it before he left."

"Craig? Oh yes, Craig," I mumbled, as I climbed out of the bed.

"Didn't catch his surname," I said, as I awkwardly dressed myself. "It's all a bit hazy. I really don't remember a lot."

"You drank too much. And it went straight to your head."

"Yes, straight to my head."

"And his surname's Anders. Same as mine."

20

The Outsider

At school on Monday morning, the girls talked about Vicky's party. Mostly, they said how great the disco lights and music were. I thought that having sex with Craig would enable me to get closer to Vicky and her friends. Maybe I would get to know her family a bit more, when Craig and I started dating. At least, that's what I assumed.

But I never saw Craig again. And Vicky avoided me. Her comments toward me were frosty. She made me feel as if I were a smelly piece of meat that offended her. Instead of being welcomed into her friendship circle, I was ostracised. I became the outsider.

It made me think of karma. Just as I had dumped Ian, Craig dumped me. It didn't matter that Craig initiated contact with me, and that he was the one with dope in his pocket. I became the slut.

And just when I didn't think things could get any worse, I missed my period. When I stopped menstruating, I put it down to stress. It was all the dramas in my life. But if that were so, why didn't it happen before; and why did I feel so sick?

Racked by uncertainty, I saw a local doctor. My worst fears were confirmed. I was pregnant. Tongues would be wagging. People would say that the apple doesn't fall far from the tree.

My mind went into a spin. How could I get pregnant so easily? None of the other girls at school ever fell pregnant. I just couldn't believe how quickly it occurred. And I was not ready to be a mother.

Who was the father of my baby anyway? Craig was too young to be a father. He had his life ahead of him, with plans of going to university. And he didn't even want to see me again. So how could he possibly want to raise a child with me? And I could never prove that Craig was the father. Therefore, he could simply deny things and say that I slept around; which wasn't true. And Vicky, being his cousin, would surely support him. Not me.

Then again, if George were the father, he would have serious explaining to do to the police. He would end up in jail, and my mother would never marry him or get his houses. There were many issues to consider.

Once I thought things through, I devised a clever plan; an ingenious plan that changed my life.

21

The Deal

"You want this house?" George asked, when I confronted him in our lounge room. His voice was devoid of its usual arrogance and bully rhetoric. "This Bridge Street house?"

"Yes, George. That's the deal. Put it in my name, or I will go to the police. I will tell them what you did. You will go to jail."

For the first time, I saw him cry like a child. I wielded all the power. He stood like a pathetic figure in our lounge room. His flabby body shook. His reddened eyes rolled. He reminded me of a prisoner facing the hangman. I almost laughed at him.

"Please don't tell the police. Please don't tell them. I will do anything, anything. Oh, please..."

"I am pregnant with your baby, George," I interjected. "Your baby!"

My words were like acid pouring over him. His face contorted. He ran his fingers through his thick, black hair. Sweat poured from his brow. Like sewerage flushing down a drain, his brown eyes flooded with pity tears.

"I now have evidence to prove that you raped me," I threatened. "They will lock you up."

He thrust a fistful of bank notes on the coffee table.

"There's a thousand pounds. I won it today on the horses. Take it all. Please. It's yours. You will need it for an abortion. I know a doctor who will do it. She will. Please do this."

"I want this house too!" I demanded. "Put it in my name, and I will not tell my mother or the police."

"I will pray to Saint Brigid every night," he blathered. "I will pray for forgiveness." He was a pathetic sight. His bloodshot eyes resembled road maps as they flickered in his head. "Please don't tell anyone."

"Just do it! Put this house in my name!" I ordered.

A couple of days later, I went to George's doctor. Within weeks, the Bridge Street house was put in my name. His hold over our family was finally broken. The irony was that my mother planned to marry George in the Bay Street church, not far from the house where I had the abortion. *C'est la vie.*

22

My Story Continues

Like me, you have probably realised that George sought revenge against a cruel world that made him feel inferior. As a child, George hated the way the school kids bedevilled him and called him a fat wog. He hated the way his priest singled him out for 'special favours'. Mostly, he hated his mother for sending him to a church camp where he was abused and humiliated by older boys. Now he felt justified in taking revenge. It seemed the right thing to do.

He used emotional abuse against poor Billy. No physical scars; just a lifetime of ridicule and put downs. After all, George's head was full of the condemnation he'd received as a child. I remember him calling Billy a weakling. Is that what the older boys did to George?

George was the eternal weakling. He picked on women and children. He tried to control my mother. He didn't want her going to university to become more educated than him. Mother's innate dream, apart from dancing in the Bolshoi Ballet, was to go to university.

"You're not going to university!" George exploded, when he found some pamphlets on university courses on the coffee table in our lounge room. "You have ample money. And you don't need to be working in the evenings either," he hissed. "When we are married, you will have to stop all this St Kilda business. You'll stay home."

"But I want something more," mother self-justified, as they sat in the lounge room. "The university course looks very interesting. I could graduate in a couple of years."

"No! You are not trotting off to university with all those studs prowling around."

"Studs?" she asked, tearfully.

"Those young men! They would love to screw a mature woman, like you."

"Oh, George," she pleaded, "it's not true. I've got brains, and I want to use them."

"Go and make dinner. That's the best way to use your brains," he taunted. "No better still, you're sitting on your best asset."

Mother's face revealed her humiliation. George wanted to make her housebound; to run to his beck and call. No more cafe working. Like my gold pen, she would be his and his alone.

I am not belittling mothers and housework, two things I never engage in for I have a paid housekeeper. It's just that being a housewife should be a woman's choice. If she wants an education, that should also be her choice. We need options far greater than just burning our bras.

However, I didn't forget my time in Port Melbourne. George didn't just quash my mother's dreams. He also bulldozed Billy's. He didn't want Billy growing into the world-renowned artist that he was destined to become. He planned the car crash that stole three young lives, including Billy's. Over and over, I considered the facts; trying to piece the bloody jigsaw together.

"Go home, mate," George would have said to the regular mechanic in his garage. "I'll take over the work today. You go home. Ok?"

Then I envisaged George carrying a spanner as he casually walked over to Billy's friend's car. Next he tampered with the latch on the hood. No witnesses. No fear of being blackmailed. In fact, George would have given Billy's friend a discount on the service. After all, he was the boss. He owned the garage.

"All good, mate," he would have said with his Greek accent, when the boys came to collect their precious car. "She's ready to go."

Billy and his friends anticipated a fun weekend of cards and booze in their friend's mud brick house in The Dandenongs. They had everything to live for, and no reason to die.

And then I imagined Billy's final moments. Their car spun out of control when the bonnet latch snapped and smashed back into the windscreen. Driving blindly, the driver crashed the car into a tree. All the occupants died.

Oh, how that sickened me. Knowing that George killed my brother caused untold misery. He fooled everyone with his false smile. He had everything planned to perfection. I just needed proof to have him convicted. I believed that he sent his mechanic home before tampering with the car that crashed. And no one wanted to talk about these issues with me. The police never investigated this line of enquiry. And why should they, since George had a squeaky clean reputation? He donated money to their charities and was a pillar of the community. Mostly, he supposedly loved Billy and me. He gave us a home and a private education. But it was the perfect cover for his debauchery. He'd committed the perfect crime.

23

A woman of substance

In my early twenties, I had a fairy-tail wedding to Carl Bamcroft. We promptly bought a modern 100 square home in Doncaster, an outer suburb of Melbourne. It had five bedrooms and four bathrooms. No expenses were spared. When George and my mother moved into their Albert Park terrace house, I decided against selling my Bridge Street house. I rented it out for a tidy sum. Despite the story behind its acquisition, it proved a good investment.

After fifteen years of a happy marriage, Carl died. Nothing seemed of value anymore. My mind space was filled with hatred. I was driven to seek revenge and punish the thief who stole my happiness. All roads led to George. He was the thorn in my flesh. He was the stalking beast that I needed to kill. The hunter became the hunted.

After I buried Carl, I sold my Doncaster home and moved to Sydney. There I bought the biggest mansion I could find. I tried to find happiness. But all my grief had only compounded into a cyst of regret. I still squirmed at the mention of George's name. And when my mother said that she loved him, she became complicit in his perverted crimes. For a season, I hated her.

My life was a falsehood. No one saw the cracks in my soul. Grief cast a mighty shadow over my mind. This was reflected in my lifestyle and in my writing. I hated myself and my world. I hated everybody. Everybody was complicit in George's crimes. No one helped me. No one cared. I felt so much hate toward the world and to myself. Someone once told me to fake it till you make it. And so I overcompensated. I paid for my friends to have a good time. I was generous to a fault. All was simple and unblemished in my endless stream of parties. I falsely presented love and peace, when all I felt was bitterness and emptiness. I was the black-soul widow.

And just as a good debater can confidently present views they don't support, I could write fairy stories that I never believed in. Every one of my fictional characters lived the high life. They all found the elusive pot of happiness at the end of the rainbow. While eager readers were titillated by my love scenes, in reality I harboured enough hatred to destroy a city. In the chasms of my mind, in the ramblings of my high intellect, hatred abounded. I was a dangerous woman of substance. Revenge was brewing in my soul.

For a while, I enjoyed a lavish lifestyle of a rich widow in my Sydney mansion. I drank excessively and entertained a stream of lovers. I appeared happy. Yet, my innards screamed with sadness and grief. I wrote about the simplicity of love. I wore the best clothes and jewellery. I dined on mince and slices of quince wrapped up in a million dollar note.

Haha.

Truth be known, I wore a mask. It was not a Spider-Man mask, but a B.M. Rising mask. I was the prominent, successful author. In reality, I was a fraud. I did not feel like a prominent or successful person, in any capacity. They were merely the labels my readers and publisher attached to the mask I donned. The real 'me' felt weak and afraid.

My pain had compounded after Billy and Carl died. I was like an empty shell or a tricycle with a missing wheel. I did not know who I was or where I was going; especially since my mother would never discuss my father. This mystery was the bane of my existence, and added to my sense of estrangement. I was like a ship without a rudder.

As a result, my life was still full of questions, angst and confusion. And my stubborn mother would never disclose her past to enlighten me, even when I was an adult; even when I had the right to know.

However, when she visited me in Sydney, I tried one more time to get the truth out of her.

"Kellie, you never need know these things," she insisted, as we sipped vodka in my trendy lounge room. "This is such a beautiful house that you live in. Are you happy here in Sydney, away from Melbourne?"

"Yes," I mumbled, feeling frustrated by her stifling attitude.

"Then you don't need to know things about my past. I just want to forget about Russia. We are in Australia now. This is the safest place for us. And you have never gone without anything."

"But, Mama," I protested.

"Shsh," she sighed. "I travelled to Sydney to spend quality time with you. George sends his regards. He is busy with some business venture or other in Melbourne. Tonight we are celebrating your latest book launch. I am so proud of you. And I am sure Billy and Carl would also be celebrating with us, if they were still alive. You have a wonderful life. You don't need to wreck it with too many details."

Her response, or lack of, infuriated me. My heart was racing.

"Who is my father? Why won't you tell me?"

She shifted in her armchair. "Kellie, I do not want to have an argument with you. There is just no point in digging up the past. I don't need all this pressure. I said that I don't want to talk about such things, and that is the end to it. In all fairness, I am happy to meet with you here, and I love you very much. But some things do not concern you. They are strictly my business." She stared me down. An icy wall of indifference now separated us. "Drink up, Kellie."

"Ok, Mama. Cheers," I said, as I touched her glass with mine.

"That's right," she said, as we sipped our highball drinks. "That's how I want it."

I often wondered about my father's identity. Was he a soldier? Or perhaps he was in the Bolshoi ballet. Or maybe he was a poet or author, like me. Was he also passionate about the 'philosophers of old'? Was he always seeking answers to questions that evade the common man? Did he have other children? Who were his parents? Who were my grandparents? So many questions. Too many truths that would never be told.

Oh, Mama. Why won't you tell me?

So I hid behind my author mask. I smiled as I mingled with the educated and wealthy. Yet, all the while, I felt like an imposter. Who was I really?

Carl Jung aptly said that each of us has a *shadow*. This is distinct from our *persona* or the image of yourself that we present to the world. In line with his thinking, my shadow comprised of hidden anxieties and repressed thoughts. As a child in Port Melbourne, I had to play happy families. But all the while, I felt hatred toward my evil stepfather, and disappointment with my mother.

24

The High Life

In Sydney I lived the high life. I laughed on the outside but cried on the inside, as I went from one party scene to another. I likened myself to a muted piece of soap, shifting from one soap-smeared dish to another and then another. I secretly hoped that someone would see through my charade. But they never did.

My books were more popular than ever. I thought my readers wanted to escape their dull reality; that they wanted to enjoy the grandeur of one-dimensional characters who graced mansions and palaces. So I wrote about larger than life people who found true love in fairytales. My glamorous heroines lived in opulence and self-indulgence. They lived the lifestyle that the poor could only dream of. But those fake stories would soon die a natural death.

Behind closed doors, I struggled to make sense of life with all its social snares and shortcomings. The world was devoid of safety nets for the wounded children, like me. At times, I dwelt on my former life as Kellie Earl. As explained, *Earl* was the surname my mother gave us after marrying Ryan Earl. She thought 'Earl' sounded regal, unlike the creepy thief whose surname we carried. Please note that I mean no offence to anyone who carries this surname.

I could not forget how George had abused me. It sickened me. No amount of scrubbing in the shower can erase the pain and filth I felt. I felt like soiled goods that no one wanted to buy. At times, I despised myself. When I saw my mirror reflection, the chasm between the innocent child and the glamorous woman was insurmountable. Where had I gone? Where was the child who read 'John and Betty' books?

I always felt Billy's presence. It was the ghost of a murdered child waiting for someone to bring the killer to justice. For decades, George had gotten away with his crimes. I was still a powerless woman with a powerhouse of hate. It was the perfect storm.

But I had to be patient. I had to wait it out. I had to be content owning the Bridge Street house. After all, I won the first battle. Following that, I had ample money and several published best sellers. But fame and fortune didn't diminish my pain and anguish. It was then that I knew I had to take action. I had to take the law into my own hands. *Tit for tat*. But is revenge ever sweet? Unlike me, George had no moral compass. His sociopathic world hinged on his twisted ego. Like King Richard, he had a twisted spine. I noted the way he taunted and controlled people. I watched the way he used money to buy himself out of every tricky situation.

He became my role model for evil. He showed me how to mastermind the perfect murder. It was all about deception and public image. Of course, no one suspects a philanthropist. And just as he got away with murder, I knew that I could do the same. One day, I would kill him.

25

Reminiscing

For several years, I lived in comfort in my Sydney mansion. I occasionally revisited my tatty, old teenage diaries. They were full of the literary gems of youth. In my confused adolescent mind, I had written down all my thoughts about Ian and Craig, and even about the school girls who turned nasty on me. I recorded how I felt when I lost everything that was important to me; how all my dreams turned to dust, so to speak.

When my tears caused some of the ink to run on the pages of my diary, I simply wiped the soggy paper with a tissue, or smudged it with the palm of my hand. I empathized and sympathized with the innocent child whose soul was crushed by a paedophile. I wanted to reef Kellie Earl from her lost world and give her a word of advice. How many of us wish we could give advice or console our younger self?

I promised myself that when Kellie Earl finds peace, I too would find peace. Although I was B.M. Rising, a published author, I was still the grieving child. Kellie and I were one and the same. She is the painful part of me that I tried to abandon. And I realised that she is more than blurred words on a piece of paper. Sometimes, she was the monster in my head.

Although I adorned myself with jewels and fine garments, I would always be the wounded child. Kellie lingered in the recesses of my mind with the lamb lost in the wilderness. She was the drowning kitten dying before it had a chance to open its blue eyes; or the abandoned, wide-eyed puppy in the dank, dark cave. She is the drunken socialite with her head in a toilet bowl.

I only had to read my old diaries, and I was *in situ* with the abused child I used to be; the girl I left behind. It's reminiscent of time travelling. Kellie's exquisite words relay sadness of a bygone era; my bygone era. My life. These were the sad seeds that George planted.

Although I was no longer a child, I felt Kellie's struggle as she tried to open her wings and soar above her mundane world. I felt her anxiety and regret, as she searched for the pinnacle of hope that she could only find in her fictional mountain-top experience. John and Betty were fortunate. Kellie was not.

I used her pure words to infuse freshness and naivety into the flailing characters that B.M. Rising created. By doing so, I was not breaching copyright laws, for Kellie's words were my words. I was that terrified child who panicked and fretted for someone, anyone to save her from the monster in her head. B.M. Rising was Kellie Earl.

It is difficult for adult writers to capture and authenticate the visions of youth. Thank God for my fading diaries. They captured it all: the dreams, the disappointments and the fears of adolescence; along with the nightmares-without-hope that Kellie endured.

In the intensity of my teenage moments, I had scribbled my scrambled thoughts into my blessed diary. It was a simple act that saved my life. It gave me something to aspire to. Writing a book and shining a beacon for other lost children, became my salvation; my light at the end of the tunnel.

Kellie's tears found their way into B.M. Rising's popular stories. Readers understood the girl I used to be, sometimes more than I did.

And when I felt as if I were abandoned on a desert island without connectedness to others, I sensed my readers reaching out to me. In my imagination, they hurled fresh fish onto the hungry seas of no-return. They cracked coconuts on a desert island with me. They laughed with me when life was too absurd for words. They hung on to my every word.

We all crave for, and sometimes pity, the child we used to be. But that child is always there in our mind. Ageing merely renders us as a compilation of adult and child emotions. Our body withers. But not our memories.

'Where do you go to, my lovely?' are words from a famous song that could easily be mine.

Children wrongly assume that when they become adults, they will suddenly become wise. They think all their pain will fade when they sit with the elderly in bingo halls. But this is a falsehood that only adults realise, for nothing changes.

Freud aptly named it Id, Ego and Superego. Although we achieve adult status, we are still vulnerable to our childhood insecurities. Changing one's name through marriage or dead poll, doesn't erase memories. Even a pen name doesn't delete the real author from the equation.

Each one of us is prone to disappointments and the joys of love. We still laugh and cry with the same voice of childhood. Although we are unique, we are basically carbon copies of each other. We all cry and bleed. We all die. We all have mountains to explore and sandpits to dodge.

Maslow's *Hierarchy of Needs* is a relatively good explanation for people's condition. For one to feel complete, different needs must be met. Maslow visualised a pyramid that formed a hierarchy of needs. He placed the most basic physiological needs, such as food, water, warmth and rest, at the base of the pyramid. This structure supposedly gave people stability.

Notably, if you leave an egg out of a cake, it will not bind. And if you leave love out of your soul, you will never find happiness at the peak of life's pyramid. According to Maslow, all your needs must be met if you are to reach the top of your pyramid and gain 'self actualisation'. This is where a person becomes the best possible version of themself. I call this 'my mountain-top experience'.

In hindsight, I was in the world but not of the world. My thoughts often floated in the celestial realms of creativity where I disassociated from life's traumas. I was untouched by whatever fate threw at me. I withdrew into my creative world on the mountain-top. I escaped life's darts. Sometimes, I returned to reality to drink myself into a stupor. But when I found life too painful, I retreated into my literary universe and wrote another book.

26

The Reckoning

A reckoning occurs when people's actions are judged as being good or bad. They are then rewarded or punished. According to one's beliefs, the reckoning can occur either on the earth or in the afterlife.

Earthly judgement is dealt by the legal system. Rules are clearly defined by the judiciary. Then punishment is measured by the extent of the evil actions. Some crimes against humanity are considered as being more evil than others. And there are discrepancies between war and peace times. For example, murder during peace times was once a hanging offence. But it may be considered as downright bravery during a war.

However to further confuse things, intentional killing of civilians or prisoners in a war is considered as a war crime. Rape, pillaging and the conscription of child soldiers is illegal. But we all know that these things readily occur. And how do soldiers know if the civilians and children are carrying weapons which they intend to use? How much trust is evident in a war zone? None! Absolutely, none. Civilians get slaughtered during wars, regardless of the rules. At the end of the day, the changing Law is the ultimate enforcer. The concept of punishment is a slippery slope.

However, not all villains are caught, and survivors scream out for justice. Their only consolation might be their religious belief that the criminals will be punished in the afterlife. According to some religions, hell provides a fiery home for the infidels. They will not escape judgement. They will be punished by a greater force. According to this theory, the survivors of a crime have to wait till the perpetrator dies, before they get justice.

It's all very confusing. I tried to rationalise all the theories on crime and punishment. But after years of abuse by George, I reckoned that it was time for him to receive his just punishment in the here and now. I did not believe in the afterlife, and was not prepared to wait for him to die and go to hell. Besides, I wanted to see him suffer and squirm in the here and now. I wanted to inflict maximum pain and degradation. And I wanted a front row seat to the spectacle.

As you know, my life was a stream of parties after Carl died. I tried to project the image of the happy party girl. But all I felt was anger. No amount of pills or alcohol could erase the pain within my soul. I had no time to wait for God to punish George. And I didn't believe in hell anyway. As explained, my life was already hell on earth.

Since I wanted to gain control over my downward spiralling life, I figured that there was only one course of action for me to take. George had to die.

***

I'd spent many nights thinking about the best way to kill my nemesis. I fantasised about boiling him alive in a geyser, or running a stake through his vampire heart. But none of these options were practical. Fortunately, I could go to the local pub and get hold of a

Glock pistol. Yes, that seemed simple enough, and it would easily fit in my handbag.

By chance, my mother invited me to holiday with them in their Albert Park terrace house. They were so proud of the permitted improvements they'd done to their home. And when I arrived, George was adding the finishing touches to the electrical wiring in their sparse kitchen. My mother was shopping at the time.

George had no idea that he was about to die. His judgement day had already occurred. Now he would be punished. He would be punished for taking Billy and my childhood. He would be punished for destroying my peace and equilibrium.

I never liked waiting for my birthday presents. And I certainly wasn't going to wait for George's death to see him punished in eternity.

"You're dead, George." And he was.

Fait accompli.

27

Persistence

Regardless of being in the sandpit or on the mountaintop, I had to mend bridges with my mother. I mean, I killed her husband after all; and that is not something to be taken lightly! I never said "sorry" to her. Truth known, like Ryan's rissoles, we never discussed *George* again. And neither did she say that she was sorry for bringing him into our home. And I don't think she ever will.

Never. Ever.

I realised that my killing of George did not produce my anticipated peace and stoic equilibrium. Instead, it gave me no joy. Committing the perfect crime was as tasteful as drinking flat beer. I had challenged the *logos* of our planet. As stated, I played God for a while.

'So what is *logos*?' you may ask. According to Aristotle, *logos* is the capacity for us to differentiate between good and evil. Some philosophers consider it a divine reason that gives order, form and meaning to life. It is the mind of God. Heraclitus saw reality as an attunement of opposites.

Perhaps it's the glue that holds life's jigsaw in place.

However, I have my own 'fishbowl' analogy of life. It's how I see the social order. For instance, have you ever watched fish swimming in a fish bowl or tank? They just go round and around. Sometimes, they bump into each other. Sometimes, they blow their air bubbles and stare at you from the other side of the glass.

And sometimes, I think some people swim in different fish bowls. Not everyone seems capable of obtaining peace, reasoning or harmony in their fish pond. As explained, there are different definitions of *logos*; just as there are different definitions of truth, murder and punishment. And at the end of the day, like George, some prefer hostility over peacefulness. They don't want harmony or stability in the world order. They refuse to follow the rules. Neither do they want to see a balance between the forces of good and evil. Instead, they are like fat pigs wallowing in the mud; indulging their evil thoughts and despising all that is good and pure. They avoid metaphorical mirrors and dark glasses that reflect their true identity. I mean, how many of us want to see a video of ourself in our darkest moment; even though it may be an eye-opener or wake-up call?

Therefore, I ask if sensitivity is innate or socially instilled, as John Locke implies in his *tabula rasa* theory? Are some born inherently evil whilst others exude kindness? Or are we all innocent babies; blank slates waiting for our environment to mould our personalities? You only have to watch toddlers to see their evil personality traits forming. You have to teach them to share their rattles, and not hit each other over the head.

28

The Blame Game

To set the record straight, please understand that I do not want to paint my mother as being complicit in George's crimes. Like me, she was a victim of circumstance. She had her own demons to contend with. I watched her struggle. I know she grappled with some of the simple things in life; such as looking me in the face and telling me the truth about my identity. I always felt her underlying resentment of me. But why?

However, I have fond memories of our time together on the wide balcony of my Sydney Harbour mansion not long after George died. I consider our brief time together as a major turning point in my life. My moment of truth.

For most of the day, mother and I had pleasant talk about nothing in particular. She spoke about the way Melbourne had changed since I was a girl. And I told her about how happy I was living in New South Wales. As we sat together, sipping champagne at my imported Italian coffee table, a warm harbour breeze licked our faces. We had a clear view of the iconic Sydney Harbour Bridge and the Sydney Opera House. It was wonderful.

Over our lives, we had countless experiences; some too salacious for this book. And we didn't need to air them to each other, as we sat on my balcony. Best to *let sleeping dogs lie*. Instead, midst my healthy potted succulents and bamboo plants, our private memories remained such.

On that glorious afternoon, we watched numerous boats sail across the smooth, clear waters of the harbour. The world seemed peaceful as tourists made their way onto a ferry. We sat on my balcony like two contented seagulls basking in the sun, just watching the waves lap onto the shore. I instinctively felt the walls coming down between us.

Midst all the pleasantries, I tried to push aside any bitterness. I tried to forget George and the damage he caused. I tried to forget that my mother brought him into my Bridge Street house. George was gone. No one suspected me. All that mattered was the moment.

"Kellie, my dear," she said nervously, as she clenched her fists. "I need to tell you something." Suddenly, she looked tired and worn as she fidgeted with her bulky opal and diamond ring. "This is the last time I will travel here."

She sounded resigned and calm as she looked into my eyes. "My time has come, Kellie. It comes to all of us. I am grateful for the time I have had. I am blessed." And then she took a sip of her champagne.

"What do you mean by saying that your time has come?" I quizzed. "This is a glorious spot here, and I love having you visit."

"I am old," she continued with reserve, "and I guess my vodka and cigarillos finally caught up with me. My doctor said that I have incurable liver cancer. He advised me against too much exertion."

"Oh, Mum," I said, as tears welled in my eyes, "this can't be true."

"Yes, I saw several doctors. They said that I have three years left, at most. And please don't bury me in a box. I've paid for my funeral plan, and want to be cremated. Just scatter me at sea, down at Port Melbourne."

"Oh, Mum. I can't even think about such things. You'll live forever.

"Let's just enjoy our time together, for as long as we have. But you are always welcome to come and visit me. My new home in Armadale has many rooms. A community nurse visits me regularly, to check up on me. They don't want me travelling to New South Wales anymore. But there is no way I would miss coming here today, for one last time. I am proud of your achievements."

"And I am so glad you did," I replied, almost choking with tears.

"Now that George has gone, I come and go as I please," she continued. "And with whom I please. I am a free woman. But it is sad the way he went. Such a shocking way to die. He should have known better than working on exposed wires. He could have paid an electrician. George was not trained. He just liked to do everything himself. So reckless." She sighed and shook her head of glossy, grey-streaked hair. "I guess all the Ouzo finally got to him. He got a bit forgetful as he got older. So stupid of him."

She forced a smile and said, "But now it is my turn to go. I want you there with me, Kellie, when I take my last breath. Yours is the last face I want to see before I leave this world. You are my beautiful girl. And I love you very much."

Her words ripped my heart out. My body went numb. A wave of grief consumed me. It couldn't be possible that she was dying. I held her soft hands in mine. I desperately needed my mother. We were two ageing women adorned with priceless jewels. We had gained much in the way of riches, yet lost everything along the way.

For the first time, she no longer seemed the strong woman who defied the jealous gossips in Port Melbourne. They sought to bring her down. Because of her stylish dress and exquisite make-up, she never seemed to fit in with other housewives in her neighbourhood. She was too big for their fishbowl.

But I considered that she was a strong woman. Despite her flaws, she always held her chin high. She defied the vicious rumours that circulated about her. Some called her a mail order bride or a prostitute. She ignored them. Instead, she put on her prettiest dress and sheerest stockings, and strutted down the streets. Her silky, black hair flowed freely about her perfectly formed shoulders. Her long legs rivalled those of Marlene Dietrich.

And she never joined the local gossip sessions, in order to defend herself. Why should she? She had as much right to be in Australia, as any of them. She was a survivor, and proud of it. And neither did she need her critics' friendship or empathy. She had her beloved vodka and fond memories of her childhood in Russia, to keep her warm.

But now she was a broken, old woman whose days were numbered. As she sat beside me on the balcony, I was gripped with lingering fear. How could she leave me when I needed her the most?

"Yes, I will definitely visit you in Armadale," I said, feeling shocked by her news. I suppressed my stubborn tears. "We have so much to catch up on. And I can't wait to see your new house. But it just doesn't seem fair that you are ill." I paused. I held back my tears. "We will have to squeeze everything into such a short time."

"But it is never too late," she said, and lightly squeezed my hand.

29

The Truth

"I know you have been very depressed since Billy died. We all have," my mother said, as she leaned back in her chair.

Suddenly, my stomach tightened. The memory was still raw.

"Yes, I really lost the plot when Billy went," I said. "My world fell apart. We both seemed like lost migrants who never fitted in."

She nodded. She shared my anguish. Suddenly, my body ached with an urgency for the truth. Who was I, and why had my life gone belly up?

"Mama, who is my father?" I pleaded. "I need to know before it is too late. Please tell me."

"Kellie," she said nervously, fiddling with her crystal flute, "he was a bad man. When I was a young woman and escaped to England, he was sent to bring me back to Russia. It was before Billy and I came to Australia. Your father was such an evil man. A trained killer for Stalin. That is why I would never talk about him. They never give up on those who escape. He threatened to kill Billy. He called him a bastard child."

Her hands trembled as she remembered stories of the million Russians who died under Stalin's Great Purge. "Mass killings and genocide," she uttered the words as she bowed her head. "He raped me! Stalin's henchman raped me."

She fought her tears. She placed her trembling hand across her lips.

"He raped me," she blathered, fighting her tears. She placed her trembling hand across her quivering lips. Her unique rings caught the sunlight as tears trickled through her fingers. "And I took a loaded gun from that pig's army bag, and pointed it at his head. I hated him. Oh God, I hated him. I would never return to Russia. I would have only died in a Gulag, along with millions of my countrymen."

"And you killed him, Mama?"

"Yes," she said defiantly, as she wiped her tears with her hands. "Yes, I killed your father."

"And Billy's father?" I persisted. "Who is he? We don't look anything alike."

Her flushed face had many frown lines, as she mustered the courage to continue her story. Although it was painful for her, it was necessary for me. My belly ached and my soul screamed out for the truth.

"Kellie, I loved Billy's father, Alexei Popov. We were engaged before the war broke out. We went to Art school together in Moscow. But he was sent away, and died on the battlefield."

Tears flowed from her tortured soul. She loved Alexei with an undying love. He was her soul mate. Her beautiful eyes reflected her pain and indemnity. Midst her anguish, she explained that she had tried to find the best path in Australia for her little family. All that really mattered to her was that she had enough food for herself and her children. And that is why she tolerated wealthy George. George was a means to an end. She thought his wealth would enable her to give us a better life.

How wrong she was.

As we sat together on my balcony, enjoying the harbour view, the sunlight shimmered across the waters and warmed my body. I rose and lovingly placed my arms around my beautiful mother. Thank God she was alive.

30

Fish Bowls

On that blessed day, I could not bring myself to tell my mother to her face, that I killed her husband. She would not understand. The echoes of her widow screams were forever etched into my memory. I remembered her downtrodden appearance at George's funeral. It aroused the sympathy of those who attended. But not mine. His death was a necessity. I thought I did everyone a favour.

So why was I still plagued by nightmares after he was eradicated from the face of the earth? Why did his face taunt me at night? His insidious words screamed into my sleeping hours; waking me in a cold sweat. It was as if he were in my room; in my bed. Before my confession to the police, his ghost haunted me. I was desperate to silence it.

Carl Jung, one of the great psychologists of the twentieth century, would have said that my recurring dreams were of great significance. He believed that dreams have to be understood because they are relevant to someone's psyche and mental health. Keeping this in mind, since I was constantly plagued by hideous images of George, I needed to 'talk it out'. But I couldn't tell anyone. I suppressed my crime and the hideous images, even to my detriment.

But after my heart-to-heart with my mother, when she told me the truth about her killing my father, the balance in the scales of justice shifted. I became entangled in something much wider than myself.

Several murders had occurred, both in peace times and during the war. My mother had seen it all. All the while she was protecting me from the truth; the harsh reality of the human spirit. Mostly, she feared that the KGB would track her down, and we would all be killed like countless others. That said, maybe I was protecting her by not telling her the truth about George's abuse of me.

Obviously, my mother and I swam in different *moral fish bowls.* Whereas she could live with murdering my father in war times, I could not live with killing a paedophile in peace times. My conscience got the better of me. Maybe that is the difference between peace and war times. *Killing* is normalised when countries embark on war. And when the white flags are waved, we are expected to drop our weapons and all get along, as if nothing had happened.

At the end of the day, my conscience was always the elephant in the room. It was an overriding force in my character. Although I killed a heinous villain, I always felt guilty. I was constantly plagued by nightmares that only drugs and alcohol could alleviate. I was faced with an eternal punishment in a lose-lose situation. All the money in the world could never alleviate the trauma that enveloped me.

So I beg the question: was it my mother's fault that I murdered someone? Did I inherit her 'murder' gene? Or was it George's fault? Or maybe it was the sea that constantly lapped against the unassuming sands of time; uncaring of the abused children who drowned in its waters.

When my mother shared her miraculous story of escaping the KGB, everything started to make sense. I had a light bulb moment. Suddenly, I understood my place in the big picture. All the jigsaw pieces fell into place. Knowing who I was enabled me to take ownership of my actions. I no longer had to fear retributions from the law, for I had a higher calling. I was unique.

After my mother revealed that she was a murderer, it was time for me to confess to murdering George. Not directly to her, of course. She would read about it in the newspapers. Also, I wouldn't reveal my suspicions of George murdering Billy; not till I had enough proof to have him charged posthumously. I concluded that there was no need to further upset her with my unproven notions.

Once the truth was out, surely she could not judge me. We had both killed our rapists. And just as she had made peace with herself, I had to be true to myself. I did not want to spend the rest of my life living a lie, and wondering if the police would ever charge me with George's murder. There's nothing worse than constantly looking over one's shoulder.

31

Enough Is Enough

In movies, the 'bad guy' always gets caught. That seems to be Hollywood's natural order. And that is why I needed to confess to the perfect crime. I wanted mine to be a credible story. Everything had to finally make sense. For too long, I was overcome by all the confusion and secrets in my life. But one secret would have to stay as such. I could not tell my mother about my suspicions of George murdering Billy. I had to have absolute proof before I opened Pandora's Box. I would have to sit on that secret. Hopefully, not for too much longer.

Over the course of a sunny afternoon, as my mother peeled back the layers of her identity, I started to understand who I was. Her confession gave me the key to open the door to my soul. I felt like an orphan who finally found the identity of their birth parents. Like piecing together a broken dish, I hoped to put my life back together; if I may loosely use that phrase.

As mentioned, I became a blank slate or *tabula rasa*. Just as John Locke believed that when we are born we are influenced by our environment, now I was going to be influenced by the *whole truth and nothing but the truth*. I would become part of the 'truth cycle'. And that meant confessing to murder.

Unlike Humpty Dumpty, I did not have king's horses or king's men trying to piece me together again. And that didn't work for him anyway. I concluded that my mother's fears had transferred to me whilst in her womb. I became the frightened refugee who didn't know where their last meal was coming from. I felt the biting chill of winter in the displaced persons' camp in Sweden. I hid during the day when the enemy planes flew overhead. I heard the screams as the innocent Belarusian children were hanged, for giving food to the starving partisans.

And then I became the face of the man whom my mother hated the most; her rapist.

As we sat on my harbour-side balcony, on that monumental afternoon, the balance was shifting in our 'mother daughter' relationship. For the first time, I felt connected to her. Despite the circumstances surrounding my conception, she birthed me. She gave me life. She tolerated and nurtured the child who resembled her cruel rapist.

Although the truth about my conception was painful, I appreciated hearing it. I felt like a chicken that just stepped out of its eggshell; frail and vulnerable. My legs shook as I emerged into a cruel pecking order in the henhouse. For the first time, I was ready to take on the world. I was ready to confess to the police, and face the consequences. I needed redemption.

***

The next day when my mother returned to Melbourne, my house felt empty. I dreaded the thought of losing her. I dreaded not being able to call her or gossip over a glass or two of vodka. But I was resolute. Now I knew exactly what had to be done. Just as my mother confessed to me, it was my turn to confess to the police.

I could no longer stand the shackles of malice that bound my spirit. My hatred of George had become an entity that lived in my heart. By holding on to the terrible memories of my childhood abuse, I was simply empowering George's stranglehold over me. Enough is enough. I had to confess.

The world needed to know who George really was, even if it proved painful for my mother. It was time for her to fall from Humpty Dumpty's wall, and face reality.

C'est la vie!

32

Baked Beans

At times, I wondered if my beauty and youth lured George to my side. Did I betray my mother by sleeping with her man? So many painful questions for a little girl. I was full of self-doubt. More often than not, I felt guilty. Was it really my fault after all? As a child, I could do nothing. I suffered in silence. I seemed to have no rights. No voice; just a festering hatred.

Why me? I thought. Did the gods hate me? Did I kill a black cat in a previous life? My mind was racked with endless possibilities, both real and imagined.

As a child, I could have told my mother or one of my teachers about the abuse. I could have gone to the police station in Bay Street to report George. There was no need to hold on to hatred for decades. No need to harbour murder in my heart. However, I was scared; too scared to say a word.

Any victim of sexual abuse knows that this crime is not only physical. One's soul and emotions also get shredded when they are raped. Most of the carnage is in a place where the eye cannot see, nor do others perceive. You are muted by fear. It is impossible to tell anyone. You become Humpty Dumpty sitting on a wall, waiting to be pushed to your death.

It's as if the victim's life is a sheet of glass that is shattered on the rocks of time. Pieces and slithers of glass prove too fragile and sharp to ever piece together again. Even if one attempts such an act, there is a high probability that their hands will be sliced open. And this will only cause more pain.

At the end of the day, I seemed to survive the rapes; though the word 'survive' has many nuances. I hid the shattered pieces of myself in the pages of my novels.

As promised, I had kept George's secret. After all, I owned the Bridge Street house. And when I became an adult, I accrued much wealth of my own. I told no one about the assault. Not even my mother. And no one had any inkling. There seemed to be no need to wreck everyone's life.

Besides, I lived a luxurious life that most people only dreamed of. My Sydney Harbour mansion had million dollar views. My plush furniture was imported. And my A list of friends was to be envied. I had ample opportunities to move on with my life. I was no longer the frightened school girl. I was stronger. But the death of George was not the happy end to my story. I still tried to find answers to the myriad of questions that only existed in the matted fibre of my subconscious. He was the eternal monster in my head. And it didn't matter where I lived.

I felt compelled to make amends for something that was already concluded, done and dusted! I committed the perfect murder and left no clues. George was a noxious paedophile, and I was his silent victim. Now he was dead and buried; but not his memory. It trailed me in the nights when I went to bed. I was tormented. I desperately needed to find peace.

One nagging question remained: was killing George my only option? Could it have been avoided? Had I brought the whole tragedy upon myself? Then again, why did George single me out and turn me into a murderess? Or maybe it was simply destiny, or a stroke of the pen in God's master plan? I was destined to be a killer.

All the while I was the famous author, B.M. Rising, who was adored by her readers. Everything had gone according to plan, in relation to George's murder. But unlike George, my conscience seemed to be my undoing. Or maybe it would make me a better person. But Billy was dead, and that was my reality. I was never going to bring him back, regardless of where the blame lied.

And one day when I was home alone, nursing a hangover from the previous evening, I sent my confession to the police. I told them that I was wracked with guilt over the murder of my step-father, George Spiatis, and needed to set the record straight. I gave them explicit details of his death; details that only his murderer would know.

By confessing, was I simply mimicking a cat that drops a dead mouse at its master's back door? Is that what I was doing? Did I want to drop George at the foot of the police station, to be rewarded for killing a paedophile?

My life turned totally upside down; another seismic shift. I had hoped for redemption and liberation from the pain that followed me like a shadow in the night. But confessing didn't restore that which the beast had taken.

And then the police sent me to prison. It was inevitable. I was not rewarded. The news of the murder was plastered all over the front pages of the newspapers. My mother was mortified. My fans were horrified. How could such an accomplished person like me commit such a heinous act? It just didn't make any sense.

I was fully aware of the consequences of posting the confession. But I had no choice. I was compelled to exchange my seemingly comfortable life in a Hollywood-style mansion in Sydney, for a paltry, bricks-and-mortar prison existence in a jail cell. By so doing, I went from riches to rags; like Buddha's journey of enlightenment and self-flagellation. Or *Opus Dei* as I nailed my soul to a crucifix. Peace carries a cost.

Although countless people had admired me, the evidence against me told a different story. I was not the sweet and innocent socialite that I appeared to be. I was an iron butterfly. By my own words, I was a cold-hearted murderess. I turned on the electricity while George worked at exposed wires. I stood by and watched him die. I made no attempt to phone an ambulance.

The police said that George's murder was planned to perfection. And there was no way that I was deranged or mentally impaired. I was a clever deviant who almost got away with it. Put simply, I was a 'nasty piece of work'. A femme fatale.

Or was I?

Following this, my life became a series of court trials, sessions with lawyers, and countless hours with psychiatrists. I 'slipped and slid' from one court scene or doctor's couch to another. Everyone wanted a piece of me, or so it seemed. All the while no one knew the real me from a bar of soap.

I felt like a tin of baked beans being spilled open, with my contents spread on a kitchen bench for all to see.

Oh yes, I was the personification of a psychology manual. And the clinical psychologists hung on to my every word. They tried to find a pathway into my mind tunnel. Mostly, they blamed my mother and my father whom I never met. They kept digging and digging into my subconscious, until they found a shred of sanity that hadn't been tainted by George's abuse. Perhaps they should have simply read one of my novels.

PART TWO

33

Raw Dialogue

When I first arrived at the prison, I had my guard up. I blocked my ears when I heard the prisoners crying at night. Elements of regret made them miss their lost children and the shreds of family they forfeited. I had no children. I had no living family, except for my self-centred mother. Once the truth about George's death was in the media, she never contacted me. She was already dead to me. So I had no reason to cry for anyone.

At the end of the day, I cannot cast judgement on others, for I am ravaged by my own foibles. So in order to protect myself from further contamination by prisoners, I mentally detached from my overbearing penal surroundings. I avoided the power games some of the prisoners indulged in. I was with them, but not one of them. I was merely a spectator.

I heard them whispering that I was a murderer. I guess I was a novelty to them. Some women had never read a book, let alone rubbed shoulders with an author. And others respected me for boldly taking 'their hatred' to the ultimate level of murder. I committed the act that they had only thought about. I killed the paedophile who represented every evil trait of manhood. George was the monster in all our heads.

In hindsight, although I thought myself above them, I was truly a criminal. I was the worst of the worst. Evil is evil, whether it is clever or stupid, planned or random. I brought a whole new level of insanity into Fairlea; murder by the rich and famous. By definition, a murderer is someone who takes another's life. Dictionaries don't care if killers are geniuses or street sweepers. They don't compare wartime killings with peacetime violence. A life is simply snuffed out when someone is killed. A killer is a killer. But, dear Reader, good wins the day. The peacemakers inherit the earth. Isn't that the way a good story goes?

I had many ideals competing in my fuddled brain as I peeled potatoes in the prison kitchen. But one day, my attitude changed. I suddenly realised that my fellow prisoners were more interesting than anticipated. Each of them had a unique story to tell; something I could gratuitously capitalise on. Therefore, it was to my advantage to engage with them rather than being isolated.

As the saying goes, *A burden shared is a burden halved.* Together we became the naughty children who were exiled to the sandpit. We bonded. The prison sandpit became functional. And those who knew that I was an author drew to my side. They eagerly 'spilled their guts'. I gave them a voice.

In jail I heard the raw dialogue of the bleeding souls of inmates. In my quiet moments, I tried to artistically and sensitively capture their teardrops in my words. I was aware that many people love to read about the journey of the underdog and the misfortunes of others. They want to join the jigsaw pieces of the criminal mind. Tales of 'wrongly accused criminals' also make the best seller list.

I just wanted to write their stories.

34

Fairlea Women's Prison

It felt as if I'd returned to the Dark Ages. My dank jail cell was far removed from my lifestyle in trendy Sydney. Ironically, the prison world reflected my true inner self. I could remove my mask. To give further insight into prison life, I will share some of the history of Fairlea prison: the unlikely place where I met my soul mates; the place where I played mental ping pong with some of the most heinous criminals; the place where I sharpened my wits and softened my edges. Ultimately, it was the place where I felt accepted and began to heal.

The infamous prison was built in the 1950s during a time when we were recovering from World War 2. It was a time when women did not have equal rights with men. For example, the average yearly wages for a male factory worker and clerk were $592.33 and $866.40, respectively. The average yearly wage for a female factory worker and clerk were $294.40 and $325.06. Mind you, a loaf of bread only cost 8 cents in those days.

They say that *hell hath no fury like a woman scorned*. And that is so true. Having a group of us impounded and living side-by-side in a prison, even during times when women began to have more equality, was the unforeseen compilation of misadventures. We were a tapestry of failure and hardships; a highball cocktail of white-collar and blue-collar crime; a group of hardened petty criminals; a turbulent sea of high tides and low tides being manipulated by social forces. Mostly, we were a bunch of feisty chicks who did our best to 'keep it together' and survive.

Naturally, every stone at Fairlea was imprinted with stories of fury and rage, as women tried to take control of their destiny. They wanted to push their heads above their torrid waves of misfortune. They endeavoured to seize what was stolen from them by treacherous lovers, business associates or greedy friends and families.

I was intrigued by their actions. I recorded many of them in my diaries. As mentioned, diaries have been more-than-useful to me over the years. As I mingled with the other prisoners, my prison uniform not only stunk with the wafting tobacco haze that filled their idle moments, but also with their decomposing dreams that emanated from their dying souls. They wandered the prison yard as they smoked and nattered. Sometimes, they spoke when nobody cared to listen. At other times, they shouted and fist-punched the sky. Some hated everyone and everything. Life was meaningless.

Since I was trying to inject positivity into my life and ultimately into my writing, I kept my distance as much as possible. I watched their brooding, dark moments as a sinister aura of contempt and unsuspecting loathing gripped them. I cringed when foul words spewed from their cursing lips. I sensed their inward skirmish as the forces of *good and evil* battled for supremacy.

They wanted to strike at humanity; at the social order they once threatened. Now they had nothing to lose. They were empty shells. On the outside, most of them had been beaten and ransacked by drugs and alcohol. They were the walking wounded. Their skewbald tattoos told uncanny stories.

Yes, I kept my distance.

During the night, their cries reminded me of the death rattle of a blowfly sprayed with toxic Mortein insect spray. The annoying insect makes its final dive to mother earth; then dies the sordid death that we humans anticipate. And that is what happens to a defeated human spirit that is sprayed with vile hopelessness, isolation and condemnation. They crash and die on the inside.

In a musty prison where souls were laid bare, some of the women feared me. They sensed my inner force. Although I looked so sweet and innocent, my innards were vested with insurmountable rage. I was a murderess. I had profuse contempt toward the society that let me 'fall through the cracks'. I hated my perpetrator, enough to kill him.

But I found my true self in that primal, penal environment at Fairlea. I found freedom through the 'world of books' in the small prison library. I spent my stolen moments reading about the old philosophers such as: Seneca, Aristotle, and Heraclitus. I read about the existential nihilist, Friedrich Nietzsche. His belief that life is meaningless and humans are insignificant, helped me to understand the thoughts of some of the women. By contrast, I even enjoyed reading an old leather-bound Bible. God knows who put these books there. It was like finding a pearl inside an abandoned oyster.

The 'fifth column' is another idea that caught my attention during my prison reading. The ancient philosophers considered it to be a destructive force. This word occasionally appears in modern newspapers or spy novels. It refers to a clandestine group that infiltrates a community, to spread fear and lies. The 'fifth column' also employs espionage and sabotage. A modern comparison could be 'white anting' or sleeper cells. You will note that I occasionally refer to this concept in this book; especially, in relation to George Spiatis.

Over all, I used the philosophers' eclectic wisdom to draw on my inner resources. I became stronger. I vowed to never be abused again. I would heed the warning signs. Trust had to be earned. And no one would get the better of me. I would never suffer in silence again.

To outsiders, I had the face of an angel, and the hands of a killer; a total contradiction. My complexity befuddled the inmates. Some hated me with such fury, that they reminded me of George. Others considered me as being a useless snob. Maybe they were all right.

Meanwhile, others called me Miss Zed, out of respect for my writing talents. They were fascinated by the way I was able to readily convert my random thoughts into glossy novels. They said that they couldn't string two words together. Instead, they wanted to tell me their stories. Bingo.

In effect, I was the queen bee of literature, and they were my drones. They knew that beneath my unruffled surface, my brain was constantly ticking; always looking for adjectives, metaphors and similes; relentlessly conjuring poems or fascinating story lines. I didn't need a shovel to escape from Fairlea. Literature was my escape tunnel. They liked that about me, and wanted to share in my liberation.

35

Rand Lourdes

The prisoners who shared their stories with me were redeemable souls. Throughout their lives, they had too much 'shit' thrust at them. Some were denied an education, which seemed the least of their worries. Many came from broken homes filled with abuse of the worst kind. Instead of rising above their dire circumstances, instead of finding a mountain-top where they could bask in the glorious light of hope, they succumbed to their weaknesses.

Wanting revenge, they were fortuitously dragged into lives of crime. Like true nihilists, they believed in nothing and had no loyalties. They had no purpose other than an impulse to destroy. Like hungry flies attracted to sticky fly paper, they were stuck to their sad future. They had no escape from life's dung heap.

Some prisoners resented me. They objected to other inmates telling me their stories. They saw me as an intruder in their harsh terrain. Maybe they saw me as 'the fifth column'. They loathed my polished appearance that was a bi-product of my privileged life as a wealthy banker's wife. Mostly, they lacked the insight to see beneath my gloss and veneer. They didn't know my struggle-story. They didn't hear the voices in my head that plagued my quiet moments. And neither did they care.

Instead, they focused on their own hardships and imperfections. Their rough external features contrasted to my well-groomed image and poise. I saw the hatred in their eyes. I felt their strong shoulders that deliberately bumped me out of their way. Their *bully power* sometimes scared me.

Out of all the prisoners, Rand Lourdes hated me the most. She was a thickset New Zealander, being a good six centimetres taller than me. And she was built like an ominous army tank. Her jet-black, unkempt dreadlocks hung about her coffee-coloured skin and broad nose. Most of her body, apart for her angry face, was covered in tattoos. At a guess, she was in her early twenties.

I was told that she was a descendant of a Maori chief, and that she was used to being in control. She was doing a jail sentence for stabbing a police officer in a Melbourne night club. Overall, she had no filters and lacked empathy. She never apologised for her crime, and never would. With a sense of self-entitlement, she considered herself as being above the law. Rumour had it that Rand kept a voodoo doll for her enemies.

At Fairlea she shared a cell with her prison wife, Tanya Drinkwater. Tanya was a plump redhead who was just as tough as Rand. With her violent fits of jealousy, she threatened and bullied anyone who got too close to Rand. And Tanya was willing to attack or even kill anyone who offended her wife.

One Tuesday morning as I was on my way to the prison library to read about Plato, I was confronted in Cell Block C by Rand and Tanya. They were looking for a fight.

"Out of ma way, bitch!" Rand exclaimed, with a broad New Zealand accent. "Ya days are numbered."

Snarly Tanya pushed me hard against the wall. I was winded. Then I felt her sharp fingernails scratch my arm. Her flaming, green eyes glinted with rage as she bared her missing teeth. I felt her hot breath on my face.

"Scum bitch," she said, as she pushed me away.

I felt sick with fear.

Then Rand and Tanya laughed like circling hyenas. I winced as I looked into their shark eyes. I tried to find a glimmer of humanity; a ray of light in their dark souls. But I only saw a black abyss of moral depravity.

Rand spat in my face. I let her warm saliva settle on my flushed cheek. I didn't challenge her. Instead, I looked away. I was not in the mood for a cat fight, especially when I was outnumbered.

"Ya gutless piece of shit!" Rand said. "A bloody author! Ya coudna write a book if ya arse was on fire."

"Let's do it, Rand," Tanya said, sinisterly. "Let's set her arse on fire. I got matches in my cell. Or let's stick a live one in her honey pot."

"Na. Got betta things to do t'day," Rand said, as she patted my bottom. "She'll keep. We'll get her. She'll keep till then."

With that, they turned away. I heard their hyena laughter echo as they did a victory lap along the corridor. I breathed a sigh of relief. Today there was no more fun to be had at my expense.

As my silent rage boiled, I had a flashback to the times George raped me. Now I wanted to run after those two feline thugs and vent my rage and indignation.

Come back ya toothless weaklings! I wanted to scream. *You wanna pick a fight with me? Don't run away ya cowards. You haven't got the brains to defeat me.* These fighting words rattled in my head. I ran my trembling fingers across my mouth. I was slipping to their level of aggression. My lower nature was getting the better of me. They were getting the better of me.

But I thought better of it. I had heard stories of women being accidentally sliced with knives by Rand and Tanya, when they were on kitchen duty. Others were scarred by serious burns in the laundry room. My cellmate, Lucinda Phymms, had her left ear sliced off by Rand in a kitchen fight.

Now as the two bully women disappeared out of sight, I took a deep breath and steadied my nerves. With my shaky hands, I straightened my hair. Although I was terrified, I would write my feelings down. Now was not the time for aggression. I would remain silent.

This incident in the corridor changed my thinking. I realised that if I didn't get out of prison soon, I would do something I regretted. I knew that I was capable of murder, if pushed. And my clock was ticking. I was a middle-aged woman, and time was not on my side. I couldn't waste my energy on prison brawls. Besides, I had books to write.

Although I wanted to make a couple of prison friends in order to hear their stories, I feared that I may not live long enough to publish my books. So I promised myself not to walk alone and be vulnerable. I vowed to follow all my lawyer's instructions. He said that I should keep to myself and 'not mess' with the other prisoners. He also said that I had a good case for my early release.

At my next court trial, he said that I should plead 'diminished responsibility. Then I could have the murder conviction quashed on the basis of post-traumatic stress disorder and 'Battered Woman Syndrome'. That sounded fine to me.

Ultimately, I decided to tread softly, softly. I would follow his sound advice. I would go home soon. Besides, I only needed a couple of good stories from the prisoners. I could invent the rest. Yes, I had a good imagination. I could imagine several dark scenarios. There was no need to risk my life for my craft.

Also, I feared that if I stayed too long in Fairlea, I'd be carried out in a box. I might succumb to the hatred manifesting in the rocky hearts and steely stares of the women. As mentioned, I mostly feared Rand Lourdes. And I wanted to stay alive with both ears.

I concluded that there is no way she would ever become my friend. She would never share her steely story with me, over a cup of coffee in the prison dining hall. Anyway, she was one-dimensional with no depth. She was all front. Just another stereotypical bully. A murderess if given half a chance. And I wasn't taking any chances.

Although I initially wanted to confess to George's murder, with the possibility of being jailed, now I wanted to escape. I longed for the luxurious lifestyle I had forsaken. I hated living in a small prison cell. At times, my nerves were frayed. Although going to jail sounded romantic and Bohemian, it was a living nightmare. I'd been punished enough.

I longed for the freedom I left behind.

36

On The Inside

Since Rand was unpredictable and violent, I wanted to steer clear of her. She probably meant what she said about, "setting my arse on fire". Yes, her threats intimidated me. And I didn't want to push any of her buttons. Or mine, for that matter.

And then the writer in me surfaced, and I wondered about the plot of her story. Since she seemed to hate me with a burning passion, I was curious to know why. But I knew she would never open up to me. Hers would be an incomplete chapter in this book.

Although she was only in her twenties, she was an old soul. I surmised that she was once an innocent, little girl swimming in a New Zealand rock pool. So who poisoned her well? In the end, she became glued to the sticky fly bait; just like me. *Why, oh why, Rand?* Now I was intrigued.

Then I wondered about the overall downfall of all the prisoners. I heard that before incarceration, some of the hardened ones had tried to relieve the compounding, nasty voices in their head by using drugs. But once they were trapped in jail, drugs were not as accessible.

Within the prison walls, the prisoners had to face their demons 'head on'. This proved insurmountable for some. Instead of improving their lives, they lived in a downward spiral as they detoxed. Their negativity increased when they were trapped with the worst of the worst. They lashed out. They were brutal. And all the flies would die together.

By contrast, some used the system to their advantage. Because they wanted their prison time reduced, they became model prisoners. Some converted to Christianity in the prison chapel. Others completed university courses. Overall, they changed direction and dodged the sticky fly trap of longer jail terms. They vowed to improve the society that previously rejected them.

In hindsight, freedom is unattainable in a prison where stony-faced guards control your every move. They tell you when to shower and even when to *shit,* more or less. In fact, there is no modesty in either of these acts. There are no blind spots in prison cells. And you have to get used to your cellmate using the toilet, a few feet away from you.

Freedom then becomes something that is highly valued. That random walk along the beach, or stroll through the city, becomes a wish that was never appreciated until it's denied. Going to the cinema, or hopping on a train-to-nowhere, is simply a dream when inmates are shackled to their prison sentences; when their feet are glued to the sticky fly paper.

On the inside, many lose hope. Or maybe they never had it to begin with. They feel like they are trapped on an escalator going nowhere. Neither do they want to be converted or educated by the prison system. They just want to get out of jail.

Instead of attempting to improve their lives with a whiff of redemption and salvation, they curse their harsh reality. Entrapment only adds to their resentment of the society that birthed them. Hatred erects more barriers in their mind; more Humpty Dumpty walls to fall off.

Revenge often smoulders on their lips. Like me, many hated their mothers and absent fathers. They cursed their own existence. They blamed their disappointments on others. Blame shifting became their way of life.

Meanwhile, others gave little thought to the incorrigible seeds that others planted in their deprived lives. They'd leave all that psychoanalytical shit to the therapists. All they knew was that they survived all the 'shit'. One day they would be free and able to take care of any unfinished business. Look out world!

But not all the prisoners could plan their future. Not all could imagine being free again, if ever they were. As mentioned, the mental shackles one throws over their own mind are more claustrophobic than the musty prison cells of Fairlea.

In desperation, some self-mutilate. They want to relieve their insurmountable tension and stress. They want to feel pain, just to know that they are still alive. They tear at their flesh with whatever blunt instrument they find. Dripping blood and broken bones herald their harsh reality. Pain invigorates them. It confirms their humanity. In the end, they might get a short stay in the public hospital. At least, it's a break from the prison system; and a return to the real world that never understood or wanted them.

But by doing so, they simply compound their problems. After getting stitched up and mended, they are returned to their prison cell. Nothing has changed. Physical pain was merely added to their mental anguish and morbidity.

Some prisoners were deemed by authorities as being beyond redemption; too poisoned with hate and rebellion to be rehabilitated. They were shifted to the higher security at Barwon Prison. They were immobilised by the fly trap that swung in the breeze of retribution.

37

The Fly Trap

Dear Reader, my time at Fairlea was not wasted. And your sympathy is not needed. As you will see, many valued thoughts crossed my mind during my prison stay. Ironically, if I had remained in my Sydney mansion, I would have never ventured to a library to read the works of great philosophers. Amazingly, reading them added nuances to my logic. It gave me an edge. Learning about their antiquated societies helped me to knit together my piecemeal, modern-day existence. Although the shattered glass of my life would never be mended in a flawless fashion, at least it flashed rainbows in the sun.

Now I like to think of myself as a sweet wine maturing to perfection. Doing prison time has not made me grow weary. Instead, the prison environment released my creativity. It added credibility to my real and imagined characters. And somewhere in the mix, I inserted my own insecurities. My poignant words found direction and purpose in print. *Fait accompli.*

Realistically, it is not easy to write a novel. Sometimes, words evade the author, regardless of their literary brilliance. And when one is way-loaded by life's catastrophes, how do they invent credible stories with a happy end?

When one lives in a state of constant instability and flummox, how can they draw constant energy or 'pulling power' from a waning mule? If you only focus on your pain, you can't infuse true joy into your stories. Mostly, how can you write about the world at large, if you live in a hermit's vacuum? Sooner or later, you must release the painful memories that cloud your daily existence. You need to view the world from a different perspective. Mix with others, and kick the sorry-state mule into mobility.

Writers know that we need to regurgitate our memories, if we are to share the chafed fibres of our existence. Good and bad; all these events define who we are. We cannot pick and choose happenings that are outside of our control. Good and bad memories all form our stories. They are the seeds of our existence; be they defined by the gods, destiny or our own wilfulness.

When all is said and done, I did not choose for George to come into my life. I would prefer that he hadn't, even if it enabled me to write a gripping first-hand experience of rape. Neither did I choose for my brother to mysteriously die in a tragic car accident. Also, I certainly did not choose to become a widow at a tender age. These are all cruel parts of my life that I wished had never occurred. But all the emotions associated with these memories add brilliance to my writing. They made me who I am. Now I understand pain, rejection and loss of a loved one. In fact, I understand the loss of oneself.

To write a novel, one must embellish their stories and characters with some first-hand facts. And I have ample facts in the chasms of my soul. After all, how can one write a gripping story if they do not encounter real, interesting people and authentic, challenging situations? A writer can only write from their personal knowledge base. At day's end, we need to be aware of the universal and celestial voyage, and the carnage of transitioning humanity. That's how we find the words to fill the pages of our novels.

Words become the vibrant burst of colours of butterfly wings; or the putrid stench of a bloody war zone; or the screams of the desperate in a burning building. They have the power to make us laugh or cry. They can be kind or cruel. They can transport us to times and places that only exist in the author's imagination. They are the flashing rainbow of colours on the shattered piece of glass.

Maggots and grubs are creepy, crawly creatures. Yet, they evolve into celestial, aerial flyers that surpass even the most trained pilot. Every summer the aeronautical skill of flies-and-mosquitoes outwits tourists and beach wanderers. They are rulers of the skies. Although we are at the top of the food chain, bugs eat us. Ironically, we need to protect ourselves with insect repellents. We are the victims of flies and mosquitos. We are their food source. Are we therefore caught in their fly trap?

Ultimately, these are factors that writers need to consider above inspiration and case studies; above maggots, flies and other vermin, both real and imagined. When one writes, they wonder what others will think of them. Their words become very personal. Strangers will know that they have insecurities similar to their own. Authors give their audience a window into their soul.

And if an author can convincingly portray a grisly and shocking murder scene, readers may also wonder about what is going on in the author's mind. How could someone who seems normal and bespectacled, invent such horrid stories? What is amiss? Is there such a thing as 'The Mad Writer Syndrome'?

And just as his contemporaries judged Seneca the philosopher for his hypocrisy, when he relished the lifestyle of being rich while professing detachment from such, I also had a 'divided self'. Therefore, some may consider me as hypocritical. Yes, I am an arrogant grub turned into a beautiful butterfly. And I have all the negative emotions in the kaleidoscope of literary debauchery. I have a trillion words at my command. I am a writer after all.

38

Prison Stories

Overall, prison was a closed society that sought to wear me down; to drive me to repentance. But I did not submit. Instead, I developed a harder emotional shell. I would not fall off Humpty Dumpty's wall. I became less sensitive to life's knocks. I was ossified like a bone. Also, I stopped wearing my heart on my sleeve. I grew stronger. Like a bold caterpillar crawling to the end of the branch, I was ready to burst into flight as a butterfly. I would never let Rand or Tanya wear me down.

Thankfully, I was able to write the prison stories in a blank notebook. As mentioned, I infused them with the brilliant analytical reasoning of past philosophers and prophets. Their ancient wisdom gave me insight into the human condition. I could, more or less, understand people like Rand and Tanya. But I still avoided them.

Other prisoners' stories fired my spirit; too many to share in this novel. Their truth surpassed fantasy. Or maybe their stories were merely imaginings and rants that they shared with me. They tried to make their lives sound more heroic and interesting. Sometimes, their truth and lies overlapped. And then I added my descriptive nuances. The truth became buried somewhere between heaven and hell.

As mentioned, 'truth' can be a slippery concept that has many definitions. We all know that witnesses to a car accident rarely agree.

Still, the prisoners' stories both excite and chill my soul with their varying degrees of truth and lies. They are intriguing anecdotes that mesmerise me with their complexities and contradictions. Many blockbuster movies are based on the lives of women, such as these.

39

Lucinda Phymms

The prison stories teemed with *amazing histories*. Many were the prisoners' hodgepodge and mishmash fantasies. A few of the women were wary of what they disclosed to me. They feared that it could end up in print. And they didn't want their prison sentences extended. However, two of them, Lucinda Phymms and Ruby-Rose Wickham, drew close to me. Both of these women were in their early twenties. They were like chalk and cheese, both physically and mentally.

They eagerly shared their riveting stories with me, as we walked the concrete yard that was the size of a tennis court. Sometimes, we chatted in the dining hall. Since Lucinda shared my prison cell, she had the lion's share of my time.

These women appreciated my interest in their lives. They needed to offload the pain they had suppressed for many years. In effect, I became a medium for the stories they wanted to share with the outside world. I gave them a voice. Within the prison confines, they randomly shared snippets of their tragedies. And when I listened, I felt ashamed of how they'd been thrust into a jail cell at such an early age.

As mentioned, glamorous Lucinda shared a prison cell with me. This gave her the opportunity to divulge many of her salacious and hair-raising stories. I'm not sure how many were entirely true. But she was good company, and we seemed to get along.

Lucinda had a deep-olive complexion and the most glorious, golden-brown eyes. Her scraggy, ash-blonde hair highlighted her pretty face. She said that when she left the prison, she would be a movie star. She bragged that she'd once been shortlisted for a role in a feature film. Now she was confident that a director would select her. She just needed a second chance.

Lucinda said that her parents told her that she was a descendant of a beautiful Indian princess called Janaki. The story was that when Janaki was young, her father betrothed her to a prince from a distant land. She strongly objected to this, and ran away. Devoid of her fine clothes, jewels and palace staff, she went into hiding.

Janaki married Lucan and lived the simple life of a farmer's wife. Her parents never chased after her. They promptly betrothed their youngest daughter, Fatima, to the foreign prince. They wanted to maintain favour with their wealthy neighbours.

Like me, Lucinda had a penchant for the finer things in life, such as jewellery, furs and speedy cars. She said that she had the heart of a princess, and should have lived in a castle. That was the life she was entitled to. She cursed her great-great-grandmother for marrying for love instead of wealth.

It was Lucinda's lust for jewels that landed her in prison. She told me that, over the years, she was invited to many high society parties in Europe. Being light fingered and ambidextrous, she stealthily robbed many wealthy ladies. It was her insatiable impulse. It was her due.

"Their wall safes were ripe pickings," she boasted.

However, she insisted that she didn't like being labelled as a cat burglar or kleptomaniac; thinking the terms too grubby for a royal descendant. At times, she seemed ashamed. She thought Janaki would never approve of her granddaughter's criminal career.

All the while she sought her regal relatives. But to no avail. Feeling disappointed, she returned to Australia. There she bought a dream apartment that overlooked the Royal Botanic Gardens in Melbourne.

She could have lived comfortably, if only she didn't get greedy. But she wanted to do one more job. One burglary. It was a sure thing. And she had itchy fingers.

The prominent jewellery store in Toorak Road had no cameras. Under the cover of night, Lucinda easily slipped in and out. She was super proud of her multi-million dollars haul. And just when she thought she'd committed the perfect crime, an undercover male detective befriended her in a trendy Toorak bar. After sharing too many drinks with him, she bragged about her cache of jewels.

"If you don't believe me," she teased, "come back to my place. You won't believe your eyes."

He eagerly went to her apartment to see them. He ran his hands across the necklaces and diamond rings that she spread out of the bed.

'Gotcha!' he thought to himself. His eyes glistened with joy. He knew he'd get a big promotion for catching this notorious thief.

40

Ruby-Rose Wickham

The second story of interest is that of Ruby-Rose Wickham. Her plight is far removed from that of a misplaced princess, and even that of a Ten Pound Pom. Although we ended up in the same prison, we travelled along different paths to get there. Different seeds. Different players. Yet, the same outcome. And that, dear Reader, makes the telling of her story more compelling.

Ruby-Rose readily formed an attachment to me in Fairlea. I say 'attachment' because she followed me as much as possible. She seemed to be always popping up in my life; be it in the small yard or in the dining area. Sometimes, she visited my cell.

In Fairlea she regarded me as somewhat of a mother-figure and counsellor. I didn't mind, for I was eager to glean interesting details of her torrid story. Like all the prisoners, she wore denim overalls over her grey t-shirt. She seemed friendly enough. But her story was harrowing. And I am eager to share it with you.

Unlike me, Ruby-Rose was dumpy in appearance. She wore her coarse, ginger-grey hair in two twisted plaits that dangled down her porcelain-like face. She had a broken front tooth from when she got into a fight with scruffy Tanya Drinkwater, the notorious prison bully.

Ruby-Rose only had a stump for her left hand. She explained that when she was a child, she set fire to her hand by holding it over the flaming stove in their kitchen. In her twisted reasoning, she wanted to know what it felt like to 'burn alive'.

Although her story shocked me, I was fascinated. Why would someone do such a thing? What drove her to harm herself in such a brutal fashion? Throughout my time in prison, we had plenty of opportunities for her to share snippets of her story with me.

One day in the crowded dining area of the prison, Ruby-Rose sauntered next to me and handed me a fresh cup of tepid coffee. The broad smile on her cherub-like face indicated that it was a gesture of kindness. Not needing permission, she sat beside me on the wooden bench.

"How are you Ruby-Rose?" I routinely asked.

"Good, good, Miss Zed. All good. Is your cuppa good? I like bringing you a cuppa. I used to do that for my mother, you know. She liked hot chocolate. I always gave her hot chocolate at night-time, you know."

"Yes, I know. You've told me the story many times."

She sighed wistfully. "I suppose I have."

I sipped my coffee. She had forgotten to sugar it.

"This is exactly what happened, Miss Zed," she said enthusiastically, as she nudged closer to me. "No lies. This is my full story. Please put it in ya book."

Over the following months, she told me her tragic story. It goes such:

Somewhere in country Victoria, quaint, fifteen-year-old Ruby-Rose proudly did the unthinkable. She followed a master plan of revenge and murder, as set out by her boyfriend, Travis Oandia. She meticulously spiked her family members' hot chocolate night-cap with strong sedatives. Travis stole them from his father's pharmacy.

It was a glorious home that Ruby-Rose lived in with her parents, Patrick and Tilly Wickham, and her three younger siblings: Bethany, Claudia and baby Angus. It had once featured in the Port Phillip Herald. But Ruby-Rose wanted to destroy it with her fire. No regrets. In fact, she felt excited as she started the lethal house fire. She simply rolled up an old newspaper before lighting it at one end with a match. She used it as a flaming torch to set alight the downstairs area of the upmarket, weatherboard house. Too easy.

She was mesmerized as the fire quickly took hold. Its fiery fingers greedily consumed the lower part of the two-storey wooden house. The ferocity of the wall of flames energised her, as she watched it roar and make its way to the upstairs rooms where her family slept.

She felt energised as shadows flickered on the white walls of the historic house. She was warmed by the crackling flames that curled along the blue-velvet lounge room curtains that had been her mother's pride and joy. The fire was a vision to behold. It resembled a red and gold sea of fiery destruction.

Ruby-Rose smiled as the flames engulfed the wooden staircase that led to the upstairs bedrooms. As smoke filled their upstairs rooms, her siblings were fast asleep in their beds; snuggled between fresh cotton sheets and pure woollen blankets. Their deep slumber was ensured by the sleeping pills she had put in their hot chocolate night-caps earlier.

By contrast, her distraught parents were awake in their Queen Anne bed in the nearby master bedroom. They silently screamed. They were paralysed; unable to rescue anyone. After all, she had spiked their beverages with a different type of drug.

Under the cover of night, Ruby-Rose fled the fiery scene. The fire crackled behind her, as she sped on her pink pushbike across the open field at the rear of her house. She headed toward the Wences' neighbouring farm. The fire afforded her enough light so that she did not steer herself into a soft patch in the newly-dug soil.

She felt no guilt as sweat poured down her blackened brow. She felt energised as charcoal creases formed across her skinny neck. Her scraggy, red hair was matted with smoke. It swept across her ashen face; the face of an arsonist; the face of a killer.

41

Justification

A dull pain riveted Ruby-Rose's almost-flat chest. Anxiety rattled her. Would she exit her parents' property before the fire brigade and ambulance arrived? Would the police know that she started the fire? Many doubts and endless possibilities stirred her mind as she pedalled across the field. She suppressed her fears. She had rehearsed her story. Now she was confident that she would hold-up under pressure and police questioning.

She breathed deeply. She pedalled harder and faster toward her new future. She assured herself that her siblings were better off dead, than being reared by two emotional cripples such as her hypocritical parents. And she despised the way they were brainwashing her four-year-old brother, Angus. They seemed to be turning him against her; turning him against the only rational being who lived in their mansion on the hill.

Ruby-Rose was unwavering as she darted through the field. Five hundred head of cattle were being prepared to graze there. Her wealthy father had paid top-dollar for them at the Flemington Market. Healthy, prime beef with dewy eyes and silky, soft coats would soon feed on the lush grass. They would be fattened and sold at New Market for a high price.

But that was never going to happen. None of her parents' plans and dreams would reach fruition. With a box of matches, she had ended them. Instead, a greedy fire engulfed their envied outback home that many *city slickers* longed to acquire and turn into a fashionable guest house.

Fiery plumes emitted into the hazy night. She heard the crashing of timber. She smiled a victor's smile. She pedalled so fast that the soles of her feet felt as if they were burning. The dusty air covered her in a fine film. She could hardly catch her breath.

"Faster. Faster," she told herself.

She ignored the tangled hair strands that irritated her reddened eyes. Her focus was on reaching the fence at the end of the field. There she could easily open the wooden gate that separated the Wences' property from hers. Then she would ride along the familiar dirt road that led to their modest farmhouse.

The Wences had been active dairy farmers before their retirement. Now they were happy to sit at home, waiting for the occasional visit by their family. Their five children and twelve grandchildren lived in Melbourne. Occasionally, the Wences gladly babysat Ruby-Rose and her siblings.

Now as the savage fire took hold of the Wickham mansion, the night air became thick with smoke fumes. The tightness of Ruby-Rose's chest hardened to a stabbing pain.

"Breathe, breathe", she told herself, as she pushed on the rubber-capped bike pedals.

Behind her, billowing smoke plumes blackened the sky. Scorching flames encased the two-storey weatherboard mansion.

As Ruby-Rose pushed forward with the ferocity of a killer shark, she imagined the drama that begat her family. She imagined the excruciating pain and torment that consumed her parents as they lay in their bed. They were wide awake, yet paralysed.

Inside her desolate throat, Tilly Wickham made no sound. She was immobilised by Ruby-Rose's pills. She gasped for breath. Her silent warble emanated into the last wafts of smoky air. Her pretty face contorted. She was in agony as the flames scorched her legs. They curled along her pink, nylon nightie as it melted onto her skin. Stupefied and sedated, Tilly lay beside her husband of twenty years. She was burning alive.

In his mind, Patrick struggled to reach his agonised wife. He fought his pain as the angry flames licked his body. The ginger hairs on his legs were blackened. He wanted to rescue his wife. He wanted to be a hero. But his muscles were powerless. As the angry flames raced across the bed, his life was ending.

Despite his age, Patrick had always maintained his health and fitness. He could outrun or arm-wrestle any teenager who dared to take him on. Now he couldn't wink an eye as his life flashed before him; as torturous pain riveted his sinews and athletic form.

Years ago when Patrick was imprisoned in a Japanese prisoner-of-war camp in Borneo, he valiantly arm wrestled his fellow soldiers. It was just a bit of fun; their way of distracting themselves from the inevitable death that stalked them. But he was a survivor. He survived the starvation and mental anguish of the war camp.

After the war, Patrick was called a war hero. But he considered himself a fraud. Mostly, he knew that the war had made him crazy. Sometimes, he had strong impulses to 'lash out' and kill someone. At other times, he wanted to plunge a carving knife into his own chest. All the while he resisted a strong urge to crash his car into a tree, or run down a group of school children. He was no longer the high spirited young man who donned a soldier's uniform and marched off to war.

Many of his friends died in Borneo, without laying hands on their posthumous medals. Patrick's grief at their senseless death was too deep for him to handle. His war medals didn't alleviate his remorse and survivor's guilt.

He constantly wondered if there were anything he could have done differently to save his mates. Could he have taken on the enemy with his bare hands? Maybe he should have been beaten and locked in cages with his mates.

Maybe. Maybe.

42

The Room

After the Borneo battle that many labelled as 'unnecessary', Patrick invested in the cattle farm that he inherited from his wealthy parents. In their heyday, Mr and Mrs Wickham Senior were wealthy cattle exporters in Victoria. They were much respected. And young Patrick had followed in their tradition.

Investing in the future, Patrick renovated the mansion. At times, this task also proved a battlefield, as he tried to overcome the harsh winters and sweltering Australian summers. During his sobering time on the farm, he had killed countless rattlesnakes and put out many spot fires caused by lightning sparks. His neighbours held him in high esteem. But now all that bravado meant nothing. He was being consumed by flames. He was seconds from death. Strength, beauty, wealth and hope were about to be cremated by Ruby-Rose's fire.

Like his helpless army friends who fell prey to an unrelenting evil, he was now being dealt a cruel blow. In a twisted way, he thought he deserved to die. Like his dying fellow prisoners, Patrick had no time to say 'goodbye' to his family. Instead, his mind was in a haze as shock engulfed him.

He was unaware that three of his beautiful children had already died peacefully in their drug-induced sleep. The children had no chance to challenge and confront death. They could not escape the fire. They had no voice. Once they placed their heads on their soft, feather pillows, they never saw the light of day again. In their deep sleep, they never felt the flames.

Ruby-Rose and Travis planned the fire as a way to claim insurance money. Travis promised that they would run away together and live in Queensland, once she killed her parents. She believed him.

But Ruby-Rose was not entirely evil, for she loved her siblings. She thought they would be better off dead than living with their evil parents. In her mind, their death was an act of kindness. She didn't want them living as orphans. This was her justification for their murder. In effect, she wanted to tie off all the loose ends in one fell swoop. She had reasoned it all out with her fifteen year old wisdom.

But mostly, Ruby-Rose did not want to have to further suffer the humiliation of 'the room', as she and her siblings called it. This musty room at the top of the stairs was the bane of her existence. It was a small, dark room that a visitor could easily overlook, unless it was specifically pointed out. In effect, its sliding wooden door simply looked like another panel in the wall.

Over all, the room wasn't much bigger than a cupboard. And that's what it should have been used for. But instead, it was the hideous place where Patrick locked his four children, from time to time. It was a form of punishment for their imperfections. Being locked in there was horrendous and did irreparable damage to them. It induced claustrophobia and severe panic attacks.

Whenever Patrick considered that any of his children disobeyed him, he would lock them in *the room*. To them, it was like being hurtled into a pit of snakes or a den of lions. It was a living nightmare; worse than being burnt alive.

But Ruby-Rose's fire destroyed the insidious room. Just like the Battle of Jericho, the walls *came tumbling down.* Never again would children be locked in there like battery chickens. No more solitary confinement.

She pedalled across the fields, as the fire ruthlessly destroyed the mansion and its occupants. No frantic screams were heard. Patrick's tears of absolute agony were immobilized. He was a prisoner in his own body; frozen in fear whilst burning in agony. This time, money and eloquent words could not save him from his vindictive daughter. She had out-witted him.

Without warning, the fire ravaged their home and destroyed their envied life. The wooden embers crashed and fell about him as his ten-bedroom house was reduced to rubble; Ruby-Rose's rubble. Ashes to ashes.

"Pedal, pedal, breathe, breathe," she chanted, as she crossed the field. "Go! Go! Go!"

Fait accompli.

43

Lovestruck

Although I was appalled by what Ruby-Rose had shared with me, a couple of weeks later I caught up with her again. I needed to hear the end of her story. This is how it went:

As the fire roared, Ruby-Rose pedalled as fast as her skinny legs and dusty boots would take her. She soon reached the Wence's farm house. In the distance, she could hear the wail of a fire truck. She hoped her parents would already be shrivelled to a black mass. She tried to imagine her brother and sisters quietly sleeping somewhere in Neverland happy at last. She thought she had done the right thing for them.

She pretended that the death of Bethany, Claudia and Angus was not final, and they would all meet again. Since she no longer believed in heaven, she had no idea where they really were. Maybe there was a beautiful waiting room for good children. Not a prison cell, like the one her deranged father dragged them into. Her siblings would now be playing in a room filled with soft toys and bags of lollies; a cross between the Land of Oz and Disneyland. Yes, she had done them all a favour.

Despite what the church told her about heaven and hell, she thought that hell was in 'the room'. She didn't have to wait till she died, to experience sheer torment. She already knew the horror and torment of Hades' Inferno.

But now she would be safe. Travis was her saving light. He rescued her from 'the room'. She thanked her lucky stars that they met at a church picnic along the Yarra River in Melbourne City. It was the typical boy meets girl scenario, on a pleasant Sunday afternoon.

"Would you like to sit on my blanket, Ruby-Rose?" Travis asked her. "There's heaps of room on it for both of us."

How could she resist his innocent charm? She was flattered. And no one was watching her. Her father was busy supervising the drinks table. Her mother was chasing after little Angus, to make sure he didn't jump in the river.

"Yes, thank you, Travis," Ruby-Rose replied, as she grabbed a small plate of food.

With a vegemite sandwich and a piece of rainbow cake, she sat beside her new friend. She was intrigued by his confident flair. He was two years older than her, and seemed very mature for his age. He was attentive, and said how lovely her pink-gingham dress looked. She told him that she liked his haircut. He said that his aunty who lived in Glengarry, did it with her new scissors. She always cut his hair.

Then Travis asked Ruby-Rose about school and what she wanted to be when she grew up. She said that she hoped to move to Melbourne, and do a secretarial course at a business college. He told her that he wanted to be a chemist like his father. Or maybe a rich lawyer, like his Uncle Stan who lived in Brighton.

She felt strange tingles when their hands briefly touched. It felt nice. She moved closer to him. Not too close, for she didn't want to stir her father's disapproval.

Midst the euphoria of first love, the bells of nearby St Paul's Cathedral rang. Ruby-Rose battered her thick, ginger eyelashes in response to Travis's loving gaze. They sat on his blue, tartan blanket that was spread on the lush, green grass. They quietly ate their lunch. All thoughts were on each other. They were oblivious to the banter of the other church goers.

Ruby-Rose and Travis's eyes locked euphorically. Instant attraction. Instant trouble. They were consumed by a passion that would never kowtow to social graces. They were kindred spirits. That day the seeds of rebellion were sown. Their deadly pact began.

As they sat on the blanket, they didn't make things obvious to the other church goers; and especially not to Patrick Wickham. He would be furious. His daughter having a boyfriend was not part of his plan.

"Let's catch up next week at church," Travis insisted, before they parted ways. He gave her a cheeky wink.

She nodded in agreement. She blushed with delight. The seeds of their deadly plot were planted. There was no stopping it.

Unperturbed, Ruby-Rose and Travis enjoyed attending a midweek fundraising seance that was held in their local church hall. Although Ruby-Rose once read in the Bible that consulting with the devil's angels is sacrilegious, she didn't care. It appealed to her wicked side. Also, weekly Bible studies provided the young lovers with the opportunity to sneak out the back of the church hall; to have a kiss, cuddle and feel.

Together they would overcome any obstacle. Ruby-Rose just had to follow Travis' plan. During the week, she told her parents that she was visiting her school friends to catch up on homework. Instead, she rode her bike to Travis's place. Travis told Ruby-Rose when his parents would be playing Bridge with their friends in Toongabbie. This provided the perfect opportunity for the young lovers to pursue their passion in his single bed.

44

The Tryst

Having gleaned his father's medical journals, paying particular attention to female anatomy, Travis had an intense knowledge of contraception. He provided Ruby-Rose with contraceptives that he stole from his father's store room. Now that nothing was in the way of the young lovers, they could explore their wild passions.

In the stillness of his typical-boy's bedroom, with its Bristol blue walls and royal blue bedspread, Travis taught Ruby-Rose how to satisfy his primal instincts. He promised her that he would make her a woman. He said that her body was beautiful. He kissed the stump of her hand and promised to buy her a new one. She believed him.

But the young lovers weren't totally happy with their arrangement. His mother was losing interest in playing cards. And things were often rushed when the two of them met at the back of the church hall. Despite the constant fear of being caught by the church vicar, they persisted. Perhaps the threat excited them.

Yes, Travis had everything planned. All the while he promised Ruby-Rose that her father would never find out about their tryst. She was safe with him.

"I'll look after you from now on, Ruby," he whispered, as they snuggled in his bed. "Nothing will ever come between us. Nothing."

He kissed her face and willing lips. He stole her heart. She trusted his pledge. She believed that his words would blossom into a beautiful tree of love. She enjoyed the intimacy of being loved by a boy.

For months the young lovers glided under the adults' radar. They shared their stolen moments between the church bushes and his single bed. The seeds of passion blossomed. Ruby-Rose's cheeks even seemed to have a dash of colour. Her step was lighter. She felt more love towards her school friends and towards the world at large.

None of her schoolmates knew her secret. And she planned to keep it that way. She knew how easy it is for young girls to 'dob' each other in when they are pressured by parents. Under a veil of secrecy, Ruby-Rose trusted no one except Travis.

Travis became the centre of her life. When they were apart, she longed for the next time they would meet. When she sat at her school desk, all she could think about was Travis. Oh how, she wished that things could be 'proper' between the two of them; that they could tell everyone that they were madly in love.

But mostly, she wanted to tell Travis about 'the room'. So far, she was reticent on this subject. She didn't want to cloud their relationship with more barriers, more bad seeds and opposition.

But the pressure of silence became too much. During one of their intimate times, she shared her family's dark secret.

"He locks me in the cupboard if I don't get good grades at school," she sobbed. 'It's awful. I think I am going crazy. If it weren't for you, Travis, I don't know what I would do. Sometimes, I just feel like ending it all; by jumping in a dam or something. Or just run away into the bush."

"Don't do that, Ruby," he pleaded. "Just do your best at school. Our time will come and we will run away together."

He held her close. So close, that she thought she would dissolve into his chest; into his heart and soul. She loved the sound of his breathing. She breathed in his aftershave as she trailed her fingers across his soft stubble. It felt nice. Manly.

"Travis, what would I do without you?" she sighed.

"I'm here. You'll never be without me. We will always be together. Just the two of us. I'll get you away from your evil father. And your mother sounds pathetic. What kind of woman lets her husband treat their kids like that?"

"Yes," Ruby-Rose agreed.

"It's God's will for us to be together," Travis said. "He brought us together at church."

"God's will," she echoed.

In Travis's mind, he and Ruby-Rose were two autumn leaves blowing in the wind. He hoped for better times.

"I'll take care of you, Ruby," he promised, as he stroked her shiny, red hair. As they snuggled in his blue bedroom, he vowed, "I'll put an end to all the horrible things they do to you. Just cuddle me as close as you can, and don't ever let me go. I will always be here for you. Always. I love you, Ruby."

She believed him. For the first time, she felt truly loved. She eagerly kissed his moist lips. She felt his taut arms around her. They shared their private places. And then they vowed to take control of their destiny.

45

Found Out

Their secret was out. A church elder saw them canoodling at the back of the church. He immediately told Patrick.

"Thank you for passing the information on," Patrick said appreciatively. "I will pray for her soul."

But he never prayed. Instead, all hell broke loose at home.

"You defiled sinner. Hoar!" he roared, at Ruby-Rose.

She thought the windows of their showpiece home would shatter. As he exploded into a righteous rage, he resembled a blustering bull. His eyes bulged with poisonous outrage and contempt. He pushed Ruby-Rose up the stairs and into 'the room'. He scared her to the core. Her heart thudded like bullets hitting the tree trunk.

"Your smutty secret is out!" he shouted. "No more sneaking around behind my back! I will send you to a boarding school in Sydney."

"No, Papa," she protested. "Please don't. I want to live here."

He grabbed her by the scruff of her neck and slammed her against the wall. She thought her lungs would burst.

"You are an evil witch! I curse you. You broke God's laws!"

"I did nothing wrong," she sobbed.

"Nothing! Nothing! That's not what I hear."

"Nothing, Papa."

"You lied to me, for a start. You said you stayed at your girlfriend's because their car was hit. And you wanted to stay overnight and catch the bus home the next day. That's what you told us. But that was a lie! You and Travis slept under a tree near the church. And he made up a story about his whereabouts to his gullible parents. Now they've banned you from their home, their family and their son. My good reputation is in tatters."

The colour drained from Ruby-Rose's face as her father stepped closer. He emitted a graveyard cough. His face turned a shade of purple. He slapped her face with such force that she stumbled and hit her head against the wall.

"You will never see that boy again. Or else," he blustered. He shook his head. He pointed his finger in her face. "Or else."

Ruby-Rose clenched her fingers so tight, that she thought they would snap.

"I wasted all my good teaching on you!" he roared. "And now you resort to this sluttish behaviour. You do not belong in this good family. I disown you."

Ruby-Rose felt her heart beating like a drum.

"I will send you to a boarding school to finish your education," he threatened. "No more bloody boys! No more lies! Do you understand?"

He raised his fist to her face. Her warm urine trickled down her leg.

"Patrick, dinner is ready!" Tilly called from the downstairs kitchen. "I poured you a glass of wine."

Distracted, he turned away from Ruby-Rose. He closed the panel door of 'the room', locking her inside. He headed down the stairs.

46

The Plot

Travis knew a lot about medicine. Sleeping pills were his speciality. He'd been feeding them to the stray cats and possums. He gained his pharmaceutical knowledge when he worked in his father's chemist shop in the nearby town.

Travis figured out how long it took for someone to fall asleep, die or simply be immobilised. He knew which pills did what. He would use his knowledge to set his master plan in motion.

"I've got a plan, Ruby," Travis enthused, when he met her outside the school gate. He leaned his pushbike against the fence. "Let's run away together tonight. We could start a whole new life without parents. We can't go on like this. I think your father will kill you. He sounds like a psycho."

"But I haven't got any money," she sighed. "I've got nothing till they die. Then I inherit my share of everything: the farm, the mansion and all his life insurance money."

Travis ran his skinny finger through her hair. His greedy mind was ticking.

"We can get rid of your parents, and you can get the insurance money right now. I've got it all worked out. And I have something for you. This will help you."

With that, he pulled an envelope from his blazer pocket. He opened it to reveal the tablets inside.

"These tablets will immobilise your parents," he said, as he pointed to small, blue tablets. "Then you will be able to get the job done without interference."

"The job?" she quizzed.

"Yes, burn the whole frickin' house down with your parents in it. And get the insurance money."

"I can't do that. They will get out of the house. They will escape," she protested. "He will kill me."

"Not with these tablets," Travis assured, as he held one up. "You can put them in their nightcap. You know, make them think you are trying to be nice because ya feel guilty. And whammo! You bump them off. They will be awake in their beds, but be unable to move."

"What about my brother and sisters? What will happen to them?" she quizzed anxiously. "They will be put in an orphanage and we will never see each other."

"Then they have to go too. But in a nice way," he said, pointing to three large, white pills in the envelope. "These pills will put your brother and sister to sleep straight away! They will have such a peaceful sleep, and feel nothing."

"Nothing." Ruby-Rose smiled.

"And these are happy pills," Travis added, pointing to two circular, pink tablets. "These pink pills are just for you; to cheer you up till we get our plan underway."

She gingerly took the envelope. She studied its contents.

"When will we do it?" she asked.

"Tonight," he insisted. "Take a happy pill now. It will calm your nerves." She swallowed a pink pill. She liked the idea of being happy, for she had been sad for most of her life. "We've no time to lose," he continued. "We must tell everyone the same story about the fire. Tell them that you had no idea about what happened. You heard things crashing, and was choking on the smoke. You thought everyone had left the burning house. So you ran to the Wence's to get help."

"Yes," Ruby-Rose agreed. "I will remember all that. And I'll start the fire tonight, after I spike their drinks."

"Correct," he said, and gently squeezed her hand. "You okay with all this?"

"Yes. Yes. And thank you for my happy pills. I feel better already. I'll take another one just before I light the fire. I want to feel really happy then."

"Good idea, darlin'," he continued, with a smug smile. "And soon we'll cash in their life insurance policy. Lots of money for you," he laughed. "You can buy anything you want after they're dead. You can even buy a new left hand, if you want to. And we can come and go as we please. No more bullshit."

"And I want them to feel everything when they die," she enthused. "I want my parents to feel every bit of their body burning. I want them to cook like a boiler chook in a big pot."

"Sick," Travis said. His wicked grin broadened. "Good one, Ruby. They will suffer, big time. Your shit parents will be wide awake and unable to move an inch. Not even blink an eye. Cluck, cluck. Cooked chooks."

They both laughed. Their plan was hatched. Ruby-Rose didn't have to worry anymore. And if she had any doubts, the happy pills would see her through. Full of hope, she secured the envelope in her school blazer pocket. With a zest in her step, she ran to catch the school bus to go home.

47

The Plot Thickens

Ruby-Rose sat at the front of the bus. She tried not to look too happy, for her school friends might be suspicious. She thought about the plan as she clutched her school bag. Travis' plan made a lot of sense. She knew she could do it.

Ruby-Rose peered through the scratched windows of the rickety bus. For the first time, she felt free and happy. A weight had lifted off her shoulders. Her life would change forever. Revenge and freedom were within her grasp. She wanted her parents to burn. She wanted them to feel the fiery force of her justified wrath.

She was so angry with them. She hated the way they treated her. She hated their philosophy of life. She hated the way she had to be the 'good daughter', when all she felt was hatred and frustration. If she did not comply with their commands, she was sent to 'the room' for what seemed like an eternity. Now it was their turn to be trapped in a fiery room.

Her parents said that children should be seen and not heard. So Ruby-Rose was denied a voice. 'Out of sight and out of mind' in the dreaded room. Alone in the darkness, no one saw or heard her scream. Full of anguish, she scratched her fingernails along the wooden door. Sweat beaded her brow as she tried to claw her way out. She broke her fingernails. Her web of fear, hatred and revenge spun out of control. She emptied her soul of all its tears.

She considered that her heartless parents brought the fire upon themselves. They sowed the seeds of bitterness, and would suffer the consequences. She would kill them in the evening. Oh, how she wanted her parents to feel the excruciating pain of being burnt alive. She knew what it felt like, having burned away her own hand. It was agonising. Now she wanted them to suffer the same pain all over their bodies.

But she wanted them to be conscious throughout the whole experience, as she had been. No pain. No gain, she thought. She wanted them to watch their twisted world collapse about them, one wall at a time. She wanted them to feel helpless; just as she had felt. And just as they had prepared the cattle for slaughter, she prepared their death.

Travis masterminded the entire elaborate plot. She loved his stroke of genius. He provided the pills that enabled the means to an end. And she could hardly wait to reach the end. She felt excited. Elated. Everything would work out.

She sat plumply in the rattling school bus as it headed home. She ignored all the chattering students at its rear. What would they know about true love? She felt special. Appreciated. She touched the envelope in her pocket. This wasn't just a dream. Then she thought about Travis' plan: first, make sure she had all the materials to light the fire; then put the pills in the hot chocolate. After she pedalled to the Wence's farm, she would tell the police that she thought the others had already left the house. She had no idea that they were still in the burning house. And lastly, she had to collect the insurance money. Then she would be free to live with Travis, happily ever after.

But what about the cattle in the field? They should be alright, she concluded. They were a fair distance from the house. And what about her sisters and brother? Shouldn't she look after them because she was the oldest? What would they think of her plan? Would they want to die in the inferno, just to get revenge for their big sister?

A tear crept in her eye. She hoped no one would see it. She had to pull herself short. She knew that she couldn't entertain such emotions or regrets. She had to be strong if she wanted to carry out the plan. Otherwise, she and Travis could never run away together. And 'the room' would always be the bane of her existence. Now it was all about her survival; forget her siblings and the cattle. She would never survive living in Sydney away from Travis. And that's all that mattered.

She breathed slowly. She breathed deeply. She needed single-mindedness to carry out their plan. She had to push aside any concerns for her siblings. The fire was the best thing for them. This was her last chance to kill her insidious father. She had to block out any doubts. She swore that nothing was worth tolerating his cruelty. Nothing.

She knew it would be easy to light a fire. She'd helped her mother light several barbecues. And since their National Trust house was mostly made of wood, she knew it would be easy to set alight. Too easy. It would go up in a flash, along with all the horrid memories.

As the school bus approached her home, the prospect of a fire excited her. She hoped Travis would be able to see it from his house, a couple of miles down the road. She felt happy as the bus stopped at her front gate. Now she could boldly carry out her murderous plan. The happy pill was working.

48

Mrs Wence

Having achieved the first half of the plan, Ruby-Rose pedalled furiously along the dirt track that led to the Wence's farmhouse. Behind her, smoke and flames filled the night sky. Her fire was a ferocious beast. The fire fighters and townsfolk would not be able to put it out with their buckets of water and hoses. Its intense, glowing heat would prevent people from entering the burning house. Like her parents' dreams, the house would go-up in smoke.

"I hate you!" she shouted into the smoky night air, as she remembered all the pain they had caused. Her hatred propelled her to pedal faster and faster. Harder and harder she pushed down on the pedals. Her body was red with exhaustion. But she couldn't stop now. No going back. No regrets. She soon reached the Wence's wooden verandah. It ran along the entire rear of their double-fronted farmhouse. She hopped off her bicycle, and propped it against the wooden handrail. She felt exhausted. Weak. She wanted to cry, but held it all in. No time for tears.

To feel stronger, she swallowed the last pink pill. Then with all her might, she pushed open the house's wooden back door. It swung wide.

"Ruby-Rose!" chubby Mrs Wence shouted, as she raced down the hallway as fast as her arthritic legs would carry her. "Thank God you're safe. You poor child."

Mrs Wence held Ruby-Rose against her broad chest. "I heard all the commotion. My hubby is already over there. He must 'ave just missed ya."

"Yes. I was scared, and just raced across the backfields. I wanted to be here with you. I wanted to feel safe. No one came from the burning house when I called out. I thought they were all safe and over here."

"Oh no, dear child. No-one's here," Mrs Wence said, as she stroked Ruby-Rose's matted hair. "Come inside, and we'll get ya cleaned up. It must have been ter'rble for ya. All that smoke and fire. It's a miracle ya go out."

"Yes, m'am," Ruby-Rose agreed. "It was God's will for me to escape."

"Let's go into the kitchen and I'll make us a pot of hot tea. My husband's already over there, trying to put out the fire."

Mrs Wence placed her arm across Ruby-Rose's shoulders. They walked into the large, warm kitchen that was in the middle of the farmhouse. The smell of freshly-made fig jam filled the room.

"I didn't know what was going on," Ruby-Rose said convincingly, as she sat on a hand-carved, wooden chair at the kitchen table. "I just saw all the black smoke, and heard ever'thin' crashin' about me. I whipped on some clothes, and ran for ma life. I only just made it. I figured that the others must 'ave escaped too. I shoulda' gone back and checked, but then I saw nothin' but smoke. I heard no voices. It was too hot to do anything. So I just hopped on ma bike and came here."

"God bless 'ya, poor lass. I'll make that cuppa for us," Mrs Wence said, as she put the bright-red kettle on her new electric stove.

"Yes, thanks Mrs Wence. It will help to steady ma nerves."

Within minutes the kettle whistled. "Now that didna take too long." Mrs Wence smiled. She hobbled to the table with two cups of piping hot tea. "I'll talk to the p'lice and find out where the rest of ya family is. And when you get settled, you can tell them what happened." She promptly sat at the table beside Ruby-Rose.

"The p'lice?" Ruby-Rose gulped, as she sipped her drink.

"Yes, I suppose that's the order it goes," Mrs Wence sighed. "But we'll have to take you to the hospital first, and get ya checked out. Hubby will tell us all about what's going on with the fire when he returns. It's just awful. Too awful." She placed her wrinkled hand across her mouth to suppress her tears.

"Yes," Ruby-Rose whispered, as she fiddled with her tea cup. "Just awful."

After they finished their tea, Mrs Wence cleaned Ruby-Rose's face. Mrs Wence said that Ruby-Rose had certainly gone through a dreadful ordeal for one so young, and would be in need of some medical attention. She drove her to the hospital in her new Holden sedan.

The doctors at the hospital were amazed at how collected and calm Ruby-Rose appeared. She was grateful for the tablets Travis gave her. Fortunately, the doctors didn't do any blood checks to reveal the happy pills that were in her system. However, they gave her a couple of sedatives to swallow, and some sleeping pills to take home.

Before leaving the hospital, the local police briefly questioned Ruby-Rose. They grimly told her that her entire family died in the tragic fire. They spared her the gory details. When she didn't cry, they put it down to 'shock'. Or maybe, she was over-sedated with pills.

Overall, the police were content with her answers. Ruby-Rose's house was old and it probably had loose wiring. These things were, more or less, expected nowadays. There were many old farm houses in the region that had recently caught fire. While the wary farmers blamed arsonists, the force of nature, or bad wiring, the police simply called it 'an act of God.'

***

Nothing else was said for the next two years as the insurance company investigated the 'suspicious fire'. Ruby-Rose happily lived with the Wences. Everything seemed in order. The right order.

49

The Eagle-Lamb

Ruby-Rose confirmed my beliefs. Most of us wear a mask. We hide who we truly are. We fear rejection, or we fear exposure. Like a bleating lamb, some women wait to be rescued by a strong man who will imbue them with a sense of worth and power. And some men want to be controlling, like a powerful eagle that swoops in on the vulnerable. Of course, these traits are not gender specific. Women and men can be equally as ruthless and vulnerable. Fairlea testified to this.

I was intrigued by the calculated coolness of Ruby-Rose's story. The young woman who delighted in trailing the bluestone prison yard with me, had a dark side; even darker than mine. She reminded me of a placid, lost lamb bleating in the dark woods. And then a powerful eagle landed on the lamb's slender shoulders. Instead of the eagle sticking its claws into the lamb and flying off with it, to devour it in its nest with its eaglets, the eagle inhabits the lamb. Its stealth and might fill the floundering lamb that strayed from the safety of the flock.

The eagle and the lamb become one formidable force. The lamb that looks so soft and cuddly has the imbued capacity of an eagle. It will kill those who offend it. One day it will kill the rest of the flock.

Meanwhile, the eagle-lamb thrives on the best grass in the fields. All the other lambs recognise its supreme power.

"I always had to be perfect," Ruby-Rose said angrily, as we walked around the prison yard. "My hair had to be perfectly brushed, my clothes perfectly pressed, and my school grades nothing short of perfect. My parents set the bar too high for me. Maybe that's why I burnt my hand off. I was sick of being perfect. I didn't want to be the perfect daughter who they could show off at council meetings or church gatherings. I was their trophy daughter. What if I wanted to run wild and play with the boys? What if? What if?"

"So why did they insist that you be perfect?" I asked.

"Maybe they used us kids as a cover-up for their imperfections," Ruby-Rose stammered. "I know they had a thriving beef business, and their image in town was everything to them. Dad liked to preach, from time to time, in the local church. Since he just about paid for the church building with his donations, they let him preach whenever he wanted. I guess the local community fed his ego."

"Sounds feasible," I agreed.

She smiled and nodded to herself. For a second, her mind took her somewhere else.

"But why did my parents lock us in 'the room' when we were less than perfect?" she asked, with a puzzled look on her face.

"The room? That's starting to creep me," I said. "I will look into it. You said that your dad served in Borneo?"

"Yes, that's what all of his war medals were about."

"Leave it with me. I will check it out in the library."

***

Ruby-Rose gave me much food for thought. I came to the conclusion that hatred is a funny thing. It's something that one has no control over. It just sneaks up. It is unreasonable. One day you love someone, and then you hate them. There doesn't have to be an isolated incident to cause it, though that is what usually happens. And I knew how fickle teenage boys could be.

In the beginning, Travis sounded sincere. He was a young boy infatuated with a girl. He made romantic plans for the two of them to run away. Maybe he meant it, or maybe he didn't. Perhaps he was frightened when the reality of his plan took shape. After all, his parents had his life mapped out for him. And Ruby-Rose was not part of their plan.

50

Borneo

Over the next couple of weeks, I went to the prison library to read about Borneo. I learned that prisoners were locked up in punishment boxes in the P.O.W. camps. I shared my findings with Ruby-Rose as we sat in the dining area.

"The enemy put prisoners in stifling boxes, to turn them insane," I explained to her.

"Bastards!" she exclaimed, sitting upright in her seat.

"That's why many soldiers were mentally stuffed up when they returned home," I continued cautiously. "They survived, but didn't survive. Most of them had post-traumatic stress."

"Yes, I've heard about that," she agreed.

"Maybe your dad only wanted to push the horrid memories of being locked in a torture cell, to the back of his mind," I said, carefully choosing my words. "He might have found some relief by locking his children in 'the room'. You know, it's all about cycles of abuse. Abused children usually become abusers. And this could also be true with your dad. He was probably a teenager when he went to war." She nodded in agreement. "Though saying this doesn't help you," I said.

A heaviness descended on her.

"I am not sure," I continued. "But it is possible. War does strange things to people. Some people go totally mad. They never recover when they return home. Others just 'shut shop' and never talk about the war. They lose touch with reality and can't find the way back to sanity. There are no winners in war. They just kill and maim and..."

"Oh, shit," she interjected. Tears filled her eyes. "I think that happened to him. I heard him talk about it once. About being a prisoner in a box."

***

The next time we met in the dining hall, Ruby-Rose and I talked some more about 'the room'. It was a painful subject that Ruby-Rose wanted to discuss.

"I thought about what you said about the war, Miss Zed," she said, as she sipped her cup of coffee. "You know, Dad was only a boy when he went to war. And I thought some more about the box in Borneo."

"But what happened in 'the room', Ruby?"

She nervously bit her lip, and bowed her head.

"It's okay," I said, and touched her hand. "You don't have to talk about it."

"I want to, Miss Zed. I need to." She paused. "'The room' felt like a prison. Yes, my father made his own prison camp in our house. Oh, shit! He did." Her hand was shaking. She had a pained expression on her face.

"It used to make my skin shiver and have goosebumps," she continued. "Just being locked in there drove me crazy. Just a poky, empty room with no windows, at the top of the stairs."

"Like a closet?"

"Yes. And I cried and cried. And no one came. No one cared."

"Sounds awful," I added, and gently squeezed her hand. "Oh, Ruby. It must have been so awful."

"Because of 'the room', the hatred came into my life," she blustered. "It crept in through the door hinges. And when I sat on the floor, it started at my feet and crawled up my body. It found its way into my heart. My chest hurt so badly that I thought it would explode.

"I thought the fear would make me tear my fingernails out. But that was what my parents wanted. They wanted to break me, like a piece of hard clay. And then they wanted to make me soft and senseless, and mould me into the way they wanted me to be."

She took a deep breath, and continued with her story. "I remember that in our show-home mansion, my brother and sisters were miserable. They also hated 'the room'. They left their urine smells in the wooden floor. But I guess that was the goal of my parents. They wanted to make all of us emotional cripples, just like them. We had nice clothes. Nice hair. Beautiful on the outside, and rotten where it counts. We wore masks, if you know what I mean."

"Yes," I agreed. "I know all about masks."

Ruby-Rose pouted. She seemed deep in thought as she studied the stump of her hand. "Is that why I really burnt my hand off, Miss Zed? They were driving me crazy instead of perfecting me. They made me do it."

I shrugged. "It just means they got the job done. Didn't it?"

"Yes. They turned me nuts. And they covered it up, and said that I burnt my hand on the barbecue."

She finished her cup of coffee, and leaned closer. "But I didn't just hate 'the room', Miss Zed. I hated my parents so much more. Hate just ate me up. I was so angry. Maybe I should have burnt them on the barbecue. That would have fixed things right then and there. And I wouldn't need Travis' help."

"Hatred is a funny bedfellow," I thought out loud.

"I hated everything they stood for, Miss Zed. And now I am still locked in a room in this bloody prison," she grimaced. "I hated their hypocrisy; their masks." She hit the table with the stump of her hand. Her coffee mug jumped. "It made me puke. My brothers and sisters were better off dead. Everyone was better off dead and gone. Even the rats in the barn that burnt to a crisp were better off dead. They no longer had to live with the constant threat of bait or poison.

"But do I care?" She defiantly pushed her empty cup away. "Does anybody really care? The world evolves around money. Money bloody money. That's what Travis and I needed to escape our cruel world. I loved Travis. I vowed that I would never hate him. And now I wish he was dead too. He's just another rat."

51

Blamed

My imagination was captured by Ruby-Rose's story.

"And what happened to Travis?" I asked, the next time we met. "Did you guys end up running away? Didn't you live it up with the insurance money, or buy yourselves a nice house or two?"

"That's a joke. How do you think I ended up in prison?" she huffed.

"You don't seem the type to confess," I surmised.

"Right on. I didn't confess. But I was stupid enough to trust Travis."

"And?"

"And, nothin'. Mr Oandia discovered that his tablets were missing. Detectives were called in. He confronted Travis, who then broke ranks. He told a pack of lies about me, and said that I stole the tablets. Then his father got a hot shot lawyer from Brighton, and they pinned the murders on me. I was blamed for the fire."

"What!" I exclaimed.

"Yep," she hissed. "I kept the secret of our plot for ages. And then the insurance company got suspicious. They never like to part with their money. And the police put it all together."

"But it was all Travis' idea," I said. "He should be in jail. You were vulnerable, and he manipulated you. That's totally not fair."

"Yes. And Travis just couldn't keep his mouth shut about the plot. He said that I did it all. He lied."

"But what about his being an accomplice?" I asked. "He didn't 'act in concert'."

"What's that mean, Miss Zed?"

"That's the legal term for when they are there when a crime is committed. He didn't light the match or see you do it."

"His pills made me do it," she protested.

"He sounds like a control freak. A bit like Charles Manson."

"Yes," she said. "Travis planned everything. I did his dirty work."

"Yes. He knew which tablets did what," I agreed. "He knew which tablets paralysed someone and which ones just put them to sleep. There's no way you would have any idea about the strength of tablets. And how could you possibly access the tablets, in the first place? It had to be an inside job."

"Travis said I stole them. He said it was all my idea. He even said that he was scared of me. He thought I would burn off his hand if he said anything to his parents. I wish I burned off his little dick." She smiled devilishly.

"Ha," I laughed, as I patted her arm.

"No, Miss Zed. I mean it. At times, I wish I killed myself too in the fire. It's just not fair all this shit I have to put up with. He got away with it. His parents had plenty of cash to pay their bloody lawyers when the shit hit the fan."

"Hell. It doesn't sound fair," I sighed. "When I get out of here, I'm getting a hot shot lawyer to get you out of jail. You've suffered more than enough, girl."

"Girl?" she smiled. "I like being called a girl."

"And what about 'the room', Ruby? Didn't you tell the police about 'the room'?" I asked, as we eventually returned to Cell Block C.

"The room... the room." Ruby-Rose stared at the ceiling as we approached her cell. "They'd believe in the sky falling before they would believe that my parents had a torture room. I mean, Dad was a war hero and hot-shot preacher. All the townsfolk worshipped him."

"Street angel and home devil."

"Something like that, Miss Zed. You know what I mean."

"Yes, unfortunately. There was no specific room in our house. But my stepfather was also a two-faced piece of shit in every room. Even in the backyard."

"A piece of shit," she laughed. "I like that. I never heard ya swear. Why's that?"

"I guess I find other words."

"You are an author, so I guess you are a wordsmith."

I smiled. "I can wear that title." I gave Ruby-Rose a hug before she walked into her prison cell.

PART THREE

52

My Turn

After twelve months of prison life, I longed for my release. Meanwhile, I just had to bide my time and trust my lawyer. After all, he sounded extremely confident and was trying to arrange bale for me. All the while I engaged with my two prison friends, and listened to their stories. I was going to make the most of my prison stay, even if it killed me.

I clearly remember the times I spent with Ruby-Rose and Lucinda. Things had been relatively quiet, on that particular day, when the three of us chatted in the dining hall. We had just finished our work in the laundry, and it was time for us to 'touch base'.

"Ok, Miss Zed," Ruby-Rose said enthusiastically, as we ate lunch. "Your turn."

"Yes," Lucinda agreed. "We've shared our stories with you, over and over. And I want to hear your side of things. How on earth did someone like you end up in prison?"

"I can't wait to get ya book," Ruby-Rose quipped, as she rubbed the stub of her hand. "I'm dying to know everything too."

"Yeah," Lucinda cheered. "I want to hear all the goss."

'Well, when you put it that way," I said, rising to the challenge. "I will have to start putting all the pieces together myself. For a start, I'm not here because of a broken love affair, or even a runaway princess, like you guys. I don't quite know why I'm here. It just seemed like a good idea to confess to the police. I guess I was trying to get closure."

"Closure," Ruby-Rose repeated.

"The final chapter. The one the reader wants to hear," I added.

"Closure. Closure," Ruby-Rose sighed. "I like that idea."

"Just say it from the heart," Lucinda said, as she patted her left breast. "Put it in your words, Zed. You know, how you would say it in your book."

"Make ya story a glossy jigsaw," Ruby-Rose quipped. "Put all the pieces together for us. I just love doing jigsaws."

"Ok, now let me think," I said, as I scratched my head. "I'm not good at jigsaws. In fact, I detest doing them. They're so annoying. I can never work out what goes where."

"Just start. One, two, three," Ruby-Rose counted slowly.

I laughed.

"You can do it," Lucinda cheered.

Speaking out loud was proving more difficult than writing it down.

I cleared my throat. "Anyway," I said, carefully selecting my words, "let me first say that Kellie is not my original name. The one on my birth certificate is Akeila Zeneta Zirakov."

"That's why we call you Zed," Lucinda said. "So you're really 'Akeila'."

"Actually, I prefer to be called Kellie Earl. That's the Australian name that my mother gave me. The last man who called me 'Akeila', got killed."

"Holy shit!" Ruby-Rose said, and burst out laughing.

"We betta call her Miss K," Lucinda said, with a broad smile on her face. "Special K."

We all laughed till our sides ached.

"No, Zed is ok," I continued, when our laughter subsided. "I actually like being called 'Zed or Miss Zed' in here. It sounds kind of important."

"Well, you are important," Ruby-Rose said, as she patted my back with her good hand. "And I can't wait to hear your story. All the gory details. Right!"

"Ok, ladies," I said, as I gripped my coffee mug. "I will try to squeeze it all in, before we have to go back to our cells. And this is how my story goes."

53

My Story

"First, when I was young, I saw the world as being divided between good and bad," I said. "Black and white. Happy times and sad times. I called the good times 'the mountain-top'. I was always on a mountain-top when I was writing. It was the way I escaped from life's dramas.

"And I called the sad times 'the sandpit'. That's because when I was in kindergarten, my teacher used to put me in the sandpit every time I was naughty."

"Naughty in kindergarten?" Ruby-Rose asked in disbelief. "You little bugger."

"Yeah, you know; when you won't sit down quietly and listen to the teacher reading stories to all the kids," I explained. "I liked to get up and act the stories out. It was more fun. You know, hopping around like Peter Rabbit or plodding all over the room like a policeman."

"I can see you doing that," Ruby-Rose said, with a grin on her freckled face.

"Yes, I loved to disrupt and show-off. I guess I was always a bit of a show pony when I was young."

"Just like me," Lucinda said. "I'm still a show pony. We are a good pair." She smiled and tapped my hand.

"They woulda put me in the sandpit, for sure," Ruby-Rose bragged. "I woulda made a hell of a mess in there. Flicked sand everywhere from here to eternity. Just to serve them right."

"I'm sure you would," I agreed. "But I was a quiet sandpit dweller."

"And what happened between the sandpit and jail?" Lucinda asked eagerly.

"When I was around thirteen years of age," I continued, "my mother started dating George Spiatis. That's when my world fell apart. He was the most horrible man under the sun. My older brother, Billy, and I absolutely hated him. He was a bully and a sexual predator. He did nothing but belittle my brother. He went out of his way to provoke an argument with Billy. But Billy would never take the bait. He always shirked-off George's comments and insults.

"However, it was a different story with me. It wasn't so much about George's constant insults, but the sexual abuse. He would sneak into my bedroom and interfere with me. Or else, he would sexually abuse me in my mother's bed, of all places."

"Oh, shit!" Lucinda interjected. "Bloody awful."

"Yes," I continued. "I remember that she had a picture of the Bolshoi ballet, just above her studded headboard. And when he screwed me, I had all the bloody dancers staring down at me in their pretty, white fairy costumes. God, it was horrible."

Ruby-Rose and Lucinda looked visibly disgusted with my story. But they leaned closer, eager to hear more.

"Anyway," I continued, "this abuse of Billy and me went on for a couple of years. My mother just never took it in. She never seemed to notice. Or she chose to block it out. She often worked late in the evenings, and usually drank her vodka during the day. It was like she lived in la-la land.

"And poor Billy developed a harder shell. He had to, so he didn't take George's silly comments to heart. I admired Billy for that, amongst his many qualities."

"Did he know you were being assaulted by George?" Lucinda asked, with a tremor in her voice.

"No. I never told him. Mostly, because I feared that it would tip him over the edge; what with all the put-downs from George. I mean, it certainly tipped me over the edge. And I ended up in Fairlea for murder."

"That is so horrible, Miss Zed," Ruby-Rose sympathised. "Why didn't you say something about the rapes to your mother?"

"Ruby, I was a bit like you with 'the room'. I just didn't have the confidence to expose his crimes. I suffered in silence. And I wanted to wait till George married my mother, before telling her about the abuse. Then she could put him in jail, get divorced and get all his money and houses."

"Did they get married?" Lucinda asked.

"Yes," I said, despondently. "Just after Billy died. I definitely don't think she was thinking right, at the time."

"That's horrible about your brother dying. So shitty for you," Lucinda said, with heaviness in her voice.

"Did you tell her about the rape then?" Ruby-Rose asked.

"No. Billy died just before they planned to get married. It was in a tragic car accident. He went away with friends one weekend, and their car crashed on Ferntree Gully Road." I paused here. I felt incredibly sad.

"It's ok," Lucinda said, as she put her arm around me. "You don't have to go on, if you don't want to."

"I want to finish the story," I assured them. "You two have shared your stories. It's the least I can do. Gotta put you out of your suspense sooner or later."

But hearing the rest of my story would be later rather than sooner. We had to return to our cells.

***

The three of us didn't have a chance to get together in the dining hall, till the following week. And then my friends were all ears.

"So here goes," I said, as I looked at my pie and chips that were on my lunch plate.

"Ok, Miss Zed," Ruby-Rose said. "I'm dying to hear the rest of your story. I hope you haven't already told Lucy."

"No," Lucinda interjected. "Zed made me wait. Just cos we share a cell, doesn't mean she told me before she told you."

"Okay, girls. Don't quibble," I stirred. "Now returning to where I was up to in my story. Oh yes. It was when my brother died." I paused again before continuing. "Anyway, I went into shock when they told me about Billy's accident. Just terrible. And that put a hold on any plans to tell my mother about George. I was mostly trying to come to terms with losing Billy. I felt that watching my mother marry that devil, and then my going through the court system to jail him, would have been too much to cope with. I was only a teenager. And I was already way out of my depth."

"You could of told her," Lucinda said, as she sipped her coffee. "I bet your mother would want to know."

"I can sort of understand why she didn't," Ruby-Rose empathised. "I never said anything about my father hitting me and locking me in that room. When you are abused, your mind plays tricks on you."

"That's partly the reason," I said. "But it's not just about my lack of confidence. You see, there was a lot of money at stake. George inherited valuable properties when his mother died, and he was quite wealthy. I think that was most of my mother's attraction to him, in

169

the first place. I mean, how could anyone love that big, fat pig, other than for his money?"

"He sounds pretty gross," Ruby-Rose said.

"And I figured that George was responsible for killing Billy," I continued. "I worked it all out."

"Really?" Lucinda asked, intrigued by my story.

"The car Billy was in with his friends, smashed and killed everyone. But George owned the garage where the car got serviced. I reckon he tampered with the car."

"That's a bit of a stretch," Lucinda said. "Was he that devious?"

"And the rest," I quipped. "He singled Billy out, and picked on him. He just wanted to wear him down, and bring him down to his level. But Billy retained his dignity right to the end."

"George sounds like a total creep," Ruby-Rose speculated. "I reckon he did it, just out of spite."

"Exactly," I sighed. "But I could never prove it. I wish I could somehow. Maybe I will do it when I get out of jail."

"It's lucky you didn't tell Billy about the rapes, before he died," Lucinda thought aloud. "At least, he didn't go to the grave with all that shit in his head."

"I think he suspected something though," I surmised.

"Why do you say that?" Ruby-Rose asked.

I looked around the room. It was starting to empty. "Anyway, it's time for us to go," I said, as I stood up. "I'll continue the story next time we all meet here."

"Oh, no. What a tease," Lucinda objected.

"It's ok. Next time is ok by me," Ruby-Rose encouraged. "I'm hooked. I gotta hear this."

54

The House

Despite Lucinda's pleas to hear the end of my story, I made her wait. The three of us were in the dining hall, eating our lunch when I continued with my story.

"Not long before Billy died, we went for a walk down to Port Melbourne beach. That was something we used to do when we had time to kill; if you will excuse my pun. And anyway, it was not long after I had the abortion."

"Abortion?" Ruby-Rose asked, in disbelief.

"After I went to a house party and had sex with this really cute guy, Craig, who I never saw again, I got pregnant. I told George that I was pregnant and he was the father."

"Holy shit!" Ruby-Rose blurted, almost spilling her cup of coffee.

"When I told George that he was the father, he gave me money to have an abortion. It was a thousand pounds that he'd won at the races. And he gave me a house."

"A house?" Lucinda asked. "This story is improving by the minute."

"Yes, I blackmailed him into putting the 'house we once rented' into my name. In exchange, I would keep our dirty, little secret."

"Did it work?" Lucinda asked.

"Yes," I smiled. "He put the house into my name, and he never touched me again."

"So much drama," Ruby-Rose said. "So how did this tie in with Billy's death?"

"After the abortion, I wasn't feeling the best, and I was bleeding heavily. It had been really difficult explaining the huge loss of blood, to my mother. But I just said that it was hormones, and some of my school friends had the same problem.

"Anyway, the last time when Billy and I were on Station Pier, just hanging out with the fishermen and watching the latest boat sail in, Billy got suspicious.

"'You just don't seem yourself, Kellie' he said intuitively, as we walked along the rickety, wooden pier. 'What's going on, apart from us having to get George out of our lives as soon as possible?'

"Nothing, really," I lied.

"'That's crap,' he snapped. 'What's really going on? Now tell the truth.'

"I had an abortion," I said nervously. But I felt like a traitor. I wanted to tell him the whole truth.

"'What!' he exclaimed, almost tripping on the wooden walkway. 'Did it happen at that party you went to? Did you get pregnant there?'

"Yes," I half-lied.

"And it was only a half-lie because Craig could have been the father. But I didn't want to say anything about George raping me, especially since Billy and I were planning to move out of the house anyway."

"Do you think Billy believed you?" Lucinda asked.

"Probably not," I sighed. "He usually knew when I lied."

"And if George knew that Billy knew," Ruby-Rose speculated, "then that definitely gave George a motive for murder."

"That's a long stretch," Lucinda surmised.

"Not really," I said, saddened by the cold possibility. "If Billy knew I was pregnant, George could have been worried that Billy would dob him in to the police. You see, George didn't know that I had sex with Craig. So George could have easily killed Billy, just to silence him. I mean, you couldn't put anything past George. No sense. No feeling. Just a big, fat pig who I hated."

"Me too," Ruby-Rose interjected. "I want to fry his balls."

We all laughed.

55

Carl Bamcroft

Despite us sharing a cell, I refused to divulge any more details of my story with Lucinda. She would have to wait till we met up for lunch with Ruby-Rose.

"And what happened after Billy died?" Lucinda asked me, as the three of us sat together in the dining hall eating sausages and mash. "The suspense is killing me. I've been longing to hear how things turned out for you."

"Well, after Billy died, and my mother married George, I lost interest in school; despite having won a scholarship. Everything was too much, and I couldn't cope. And the irony was that Billy and I had planned to run away in a month's time when I turned sixteen. We had the bond money to rent a house. Billy had money put aside from his part-time job at the South Melbourne market, and he was going to rent a flat with me.

"I still had most of the hush money that George gave me. I was going to leave school, and get a job in the supermarket to help with the rent. I didn't tell my mother that I owned the house she rented. That was my secret. And I planned to go to night school till I graduated. We had it all worked out. And then Billy died."

"So he bought you a house," Lucinda recalled. "And you had to keep quiet about everything."

"Actually, he first bought it to control us. He said that he would kick us all out if we didn't do what he said. So I got ownership of the house, to make sure he could never throw us out on the street."

"Smart girl," Lucinda said, with a huge smile.

"But weren't you married to someone, at some point?" Ruby-Rose asked.

"Yes, I worked in a bank in South Melbourne, after Billy died. I ended up marrying the branch manager, Carl Bamcroft."

"Nice," Lucinda said. "I wish I married a rich man. You are lucky. But what happened to your husband?"

"Sadly, he died," I said, with a heavy heart.

"Oh, shit!" Ruby-Rose exclaimed.

"Yes, it was a bit," I said. "But I knew that my life was never meant to be joyful outside of the sandpit. It seemed that fate devised more cruelty for me. In hindsight, I stumbled through life when Billy died. I really lost the plot. Money meant nothing. One day drifted into another. It was all a haze."

"That's so sad," Lucinda said.

"Like I said, I lost interest in school. All my dreams of going to Melbourne University went down 'the gurgler'. I thought it best to work as a clerk in the bank, as lots of my school friends did. So I chose the South Melbourne branch because it was close to home. Carl, who was the branch manager there, took an instant shining to me; first, for being a clerk with a flair for the job, and then as the woman he seduced with romantic dinners, jewellery and holidays."

"Nice," Lucinda almost purred. "I like this part of the story."

"Yes," I agreed. "He ensured my happiness on every level. And we had the most beautiful wedding in St Paul's cathedral. Being Mrs Bamcroft gave me a new lease of life."

56

The Haunting

Ruby-Rose and Lucinda welcomed my reprieve. It was about time I had some good luck in my story.

"So nice," Lucinda said. "And then what happened after you got married?"

"Well, Carl and I bought a five bedroom house in Doncaster. And I got away from George. Carl was my shiny knight with his comforting, tall presence. Because I am so tall, I like a tall man. He ticked all the boxes. He loved his job, and was respected by all who knew him. He was very proud of my writing career, and always encouraged me to never let the ink run dry, so to speak. It was thin threads that enabled us to meet each other, in the first place. I loved him to pieces."

"So romantic," Lucinda said.

"Yes, it was," I agreed, as tears welled in my eyes. "With Carl, I lived the dream. He was a loving man beyond words. We made many plans for holidays and raising a family. We were in sync. For a while, the night terrors about George ceased. I pushed the harrowing thoughts of evil George out of my mind. When I snuggled against Carl's sturdy frame, I felt protected. At night, his soft breathing lulled me into sweet dreams. I had no fears, and only a bright future."

"Lovely, lovely," Lucinda said. "He sounds divine."

"Lucky you," Ruby-Rose said wistfully.

"But things suddenly took a turn for the worst," I said, holding back the tears. "I found Carl lying on the lounge room floor in our house. He was foaming at the mouth. It was just awful. I felt cursed. I blamed myself. I had brought this on Carl; just one bad thing after another.

"As he struggled for his life, everything I valued disappeared, like water down a plug hole. I trembled as I called an ambulance. I was shaking so much. The telephone receptionist told me how to do mouth-to-mouth resuscitation on him. It seemed to take an eternity for the paramedics to arrive.

"Oh breathe, baby," I whispered, as they used a defibrillator on Carl. "Hang in there"' I pleaded. "Oh, Carl. Come on. I love you so much," I said over and over like a mantra.

"My heart thumped. My head burned. I bit my lip so hard that I tasted the blood. I felt useless as my world collapsed around me. Carl was my world. And he fought valiantly to hold on to life.

"And when a paramedic slowly shook her head, I knew Carl had left. His battle was over.

"A tsunami of grief consumed me. Billy and Carl were both gone. Now my life had no meaning. No love. I felt the intense heat as a volcano of remorse exploded in my soul. My body burnt with fever. I wanted to die. All the energy drained from my body. And I collapsed on the floor."

"Oh, shit," was all Ruby-Rose could say, as she wiped her eyes.

She and Lucinda looked intently at me.

"After Carl's funeral, I was consumed by my utter hatred of George. It was as if my mind had done a seismic shift. I had no one to love; and only George to hate.

"In my waking hours, I could smell George's aftershave on my skin. I could wash and wash, but couldn't rid myself of the smell that rotted in my soul. I had recurring nightmares. At night when I tried to sleep, I still saw his ugly face. I was haunted by his squirming wolf-eyes and his spirit of a flaming devil.

"So I sold my Doncaster home and moved to Sydney. I needed a fresh start. But the night terrors resurfaced. My mind worked overtime. I thought I heard George's horrid voice. I imagined him standing over my bed; staring down at me with his muddy eyes. 'Look at me, Akeila. Look at me,' he ordered. I was frozen with fear.

"I heard his heavy breathing. I smelled his vile odour. The beast was within me. I remembered the pain when he brutally raped and sodomised me. The growing ferocity of the terror consumed my sleep.

"I woke in a cold sweat. Carl was not there to protect me. All the wealth I possessed, could not wipe away the memories of George's heinous face. It festered in my mind.

"I often lay in a foetal position, praying and hoping that Billy would return to rescue me. That he would be my big brother again. I think about him all the time. Part of me is still missing. He was my heart and soul. He was my hero.

"And maybe Billy and I would have written and illustrated books together, as was our plan. Although I loved Carl with a passion; nothing replaced Billy. Maybe I would never have killed George if Billy were still alive."

57

Killing George

The next time the three of us met in the dining hall, my friends insisted that I continue my story.

"And that's why I killed George and ended up in here. Now you know the gory details."

"You're not the only murderess here, Ruby-Rose," Lucinda teased, as she sipped her cup of tea.

"True," Ruby-Rose smirked. She turned to me and said, "Oh boy, I hate George so much. I want to smack him in the head. So how did you kill him?"

"First, you must understand that many moral issues surfaced when I killed him," I said. "It was as if I moved heaven and hell. And I am sure Justitia, or Lady Justice's *scales of justice* tipped both ways as I drove to his house."

"His house?" Ruby-Rose asked.

"Yes. He and my mother had recently bought a trendy terrace house in Albert Park. They invited me to come down from Sydney, and stay with them during the Melbourne Cup week. The day I arrived, George was renovating the kitchen with the money he won at the Flemington races.

"As I stood outside their Art Deco front door, I thought I saw shadows moving on the other side of the lead lighting. For a second, I felt sick. I wanted to run. I wanted to go home and forget my plan. But I knew that nothing would change unless I changed it. So I hugged my black handbag to my chest. I thought about the loaded gun inside it. I had to be strong.

"Anyway, I anxiously pushed the brass door bell. It chimed a bar of *Zorba the Greek*. I still hate that song. It reminds me of George, every time I hear that tune." I shook my head in disgust. "My heart missed a beat, as the front door opened. And George, Lucifer's servant, cheerily stood in the doorway of his gold-crusted mansion."

"What did he say to you?" Lucinda asked. "Did he suspect that he was going to die?'

"No. He just said, 'Hello, Akeila.' He knew I hated being called by my Russian name. And he had no idea of what I was there for. None at all. In fact, he acted as if he didn't have a care in the world. All the carnage he'd done meant nothing. He was simply wearing work overalls covered in paint. He had a big, lecherous smile on his face. He didn't give a damn about what he'd done to Billy and me."

"I don't know how you held out for so long," Ruby-Rose said angrily. She hit the dining table with the stump of her hand. "I would have bumped him off ages ago."

"No. That wasn't the plan," I said. "My mother had to get his money first. I had to make sure of that."

"So why did that creep keep calling you 'Akeila'?" Lucinda asked. "He knew it annoyed you."

"Exactly. That's why he did it. He just wanted me to suffer and keep hating him. Like rubbing salt into a wound. I hated being called Akeila. I didn't feel like an Akeila. I am Kellie Earl. He only did it to annoy me."

"And what happened when he opened the door? I'm on the edge of ma seat," Ruby-Rose said, as she finished the last of her coffee. The women were captivated by my story.

"'I see you got a taxi here,' he said, reminding me of Lurch in 'The Adams Family'. "You are much earlier than expected. I could have picked you up from the airport."

I didn't reply.

"'Jana is still shopping at the South Melbourne market,' he said. 'You know it is always her shopping day. But come in.'

"I kept silent as he escorted me along the wide hallway. I could feel my heart beating with each step. We soon entered the newly-renovated kitchen at the end of the hall. There was a strong smell of fresh paint and varnish. It mingled with my pain.

"A rainbow of colours flashed across the wide rear window that overlooked their landscaped backyard. I felt the warmth of the sun shining through. But it did not deter me from the darkness that permeated my soul. I was on a mission.

"'She should return soon,' he smirked. 'Friday is her market day. But you know what women are like when they shop.' I didn't reply. 'They buy this. They buy that. Just a lot of expense. But she will be glad you arrived. We haven't seen you for such a long time. Sydney is too far away. You should move closer.'

"I didn't reply.

"'I am just working on the wiring in the kitchen wall,' he continued. 'I've almost finished screwing everything... together. It's very important to finish as soon as possible, without crossing any wires. I mustn't confuse the colours. But when I finish, I will make a pot of tea for us.'

"*A pot of tea*, I thought. *I'd love to throw it in your fat face.*

"'Please sit down, Akeila,' he insisted.

"I hated him so much. I smelled debauchery oozing from his flesh. He hadn't changed at all since I'd left home. I remembered all the pain he caused me; all the sleepless nights and feelings of no self-worth.

"But I thought I had done the right thing for my mother and Billy, by remaining quiet about the rapes. Billy went to his grave none the wiser. And my mother was very rich. I'd accomplished everything I set out to do. Over the years, I watched George build his empire. And now my mother co-owned all his properties across Melbourne.

"But I was wrong to be quiet about the rapes. I should have said something. I should have told someone. The silence of my cover-up had shredded my being; ripped apart my soul. I was imploding, one day at a time. But on that day, as I stood face-to-face with my nemesis, the beast, the monster, I was glad I had a loaded gun. Justice would finally be dealt."

58

Fait Accompli

"George Spiatis had lived too long. He thought I had forgotten his evil. Perhaps a sick part of his brain thought I enjoyed it.

"But as I stood in his kitchen, his clock was about to stop ticking. I watched him standing at the wall. I casually walked to their large fridge to get a bottle of milk. My hands seemed unsteady as I poured myself a drink. All the while I counted the seconds till I would kill him. Hatred boiled in my veins. The man who lured my poverty-stricken mother into his bed, with promises of wealth, was about to die.

"I can still see him today as he stood before the exposed wires. He had an opened tool box at his feet. He dared to smile. 'I will make you a cup of tea, Akeila, when I finish making the adjustments on these wires,' he mumbled. "And there's some *honey-snap* biscuits there. Your favourites.'

"I quietly sat at the breakfast bar and sipped my cool glass of milk. My handbag rested on the bench beside me.

"'You don't look well, Akeila,' he observed. 'Can I make it better for you? I have the touch.'

"I said nothing. I stopped short of spitting in his face. I just needed more courage to kill him. I sipped my milk. My long legs were pressed together. My eyes trailed the patterns of the polished, black and white tiled floor. I felt flushed. I heard George rub his paint-smeared hands on his overalls.

"'Akeila?' he asked, with an irritating voice.

"I looked away. Although he stopped talking in Greek when his mother died, he had not lost his accent.

"'Akeila?' he repeated. 'Did you drink too much on the plane? You know, milk is always good for hangovers.' He smiled. I felt outraged.

"I had no hangover. My mind was clear. For the first time since he had imposed his presence on our family, I was full of clarity, purpose and resolution. The only thing that was wrong with me was that I had endured years of his abuse. I had watched him bully my beloved brother to death. God knows what he did to my mother behind closed doors.

"And then the abuser-I-hated was in the glossy kitchen with me, standing in front of a wall filled with exposed electrical wires. Too good to be true.

"'I will make you one when I finish these blasted wires," he blathered. 'Some wires are harder to screw than others. Something is wrong with them. I think they are loose. I will twist them together. They need a screw.' He smiled then gestured to the light switch on the nearby wall. 'Don't touch the switch, Akeila,' he insisted. 'The wires are live. But if you wait, I will make you a fresh pot of tea. In a minute. Just a minute.'

"I nodded. I smiled my milk-moustache smile. And then he turned his back to me. A fatal mistake. He whistled while he untangled twisted wires with his spanner.

"I had a huge adrenalin rush. I darted to the light switch. I turned on the power. It released a tsunami of electrical currents through his body. George shook profusely as his life escaped through his thick fingers. He gasped as he fell to the floor in a burnt heap. THUD! His head crashed onto the floor like a bouncing ball. Blood flowed from his mouth and nose. Victory. Victory, I thought.

"Then a deathly silence filled the room. As he lay on the tiles, I picked up my handbag. I peered inside at the loaded Glock handgun. I gazed at its shiny magnificence. No need to use it. George created his own murder scene; the perfect scenario. And killing him was too easy. No smoking gun.

"Now we were both finally free. *Fait accompli.*"

59

Shopping Day

"While my mother was shopping at the South Melbourne market, I had killed her paedophile husband. I watched his soft, stocky body shake and convulse as he was electrocuted. He tried to scream for help. Help? You must be kidding! I dealt his punishment. It was imperative for me to witness his death, to ensure he didn't return from the dead like a vampire. His putrid memory was more than enough for me to bear.

"The smell of burning flesh filled the house, just like a pig cooking in the oven. I stood over his body. He lay at my feet, like a dog cowering to its master. I peered through the pristine-clear windows. I admired the perfect garden. Perched in a blossoming apple tree, birds happily chipped. So beautiful. And then I took a deep breath. I studied the corpse at my feet. I felt nothing for George.

Nothing.

"In a trance, I walked into their lounge room. I sat on their new leather lounge. Immobilised. I was still holding the glass of milk. About an hour later, my mother opened the front door of her 'jewel in the crown' house. She winced. Panic gripped her. She immediately sensed the hatred and 'smell of death' that permeated her mansion. She had seen it all before in Russia. She had seen the light leave the hollow eyes of helpless children. She had seen their spirits crushed by a political force that was led by a crazed dictator. Yes, she had seen murder and smelled death.

"I heard her shopping jeep crash on the floor. And then her stiletto boots clicked as she raced along the long passage. She burst into the lounge room where I was seated. I was still holding the glass of milk.

"'What's burning?' my mother shrieked, though she instinctively knew it was the smell of burning flesh.

"I was immobilised. My lips were locked. My mind was somewhere else. A tremor shook my deathly-cold hands. My tongue was as dry as a bone. My heart thumped so fast that I thought it would explode.

"'Kellie, where's George?' she asked. Her voice was racked with urgency and fear. 'Kellie, where is he? Is he in the kitchen?'

"Yes,' I whispered. Or maybe I didn't say a word.

"I looked at my mother. I felt her penetrating eyes. Her poise was replaced by sheer dread. For a second, all was deathly silent; like being in the eye of a cyclone. She ran into the kitchen, like a frightened cat.

"'George! George!' she screamed. I thought all the windows would shatter. 'George! George! Please, dear God, no,' she sobbed.

"I imagined her cradling his burnt body. I imagined her tears covering him. The hairs on my arms bristled. I clutched my glass so hard, that I thought it would break. Or maybe it did.

"And then I stared at my bloodied hands; the hands of a killer."

60

A Stressful Life

"It seemed that I had gotten away with the perfect murder. The sweet and innocent woman that I was had destroyed a tyrant. Everyone believed it was an accident. *George forgot to turn-off the electricity before working at the wall. Lucky I didn't touch it. I could have been electrocuted too.*

"But when George died, I still held on to my hatred. Nothing had really changed, except that I had to carry my mother's grief. For many months, she was the perfect widow; wearing black clothes and keeping her head low. No drinking. No partying. No happiness. At least, I'd carried out my plan. But I had mixed feelings about what I'd done."

"Touché," Ruby-Rose said, as she rubbed the stubble of her hand. "I woulda felt the same way. You were all mixed up. And things just got the better of you. I can relate to that."

"Yes," Lucinda agreed. "And a great story, Zed. You are the best."

"Did you feel betta after ya killed the scum?" Ruby-Rose asked.

"I felt more confused than ever," I replied. "Now I felt both worthless and guilty. I was dying a slow death. I had to confess. Guilt ate me up. And that's what led to my downfall.

"After I confessed, I had more questions in my mind. Like, did I break the natural order of nature by killing George? Or did I wrongly change the course of destiny? Are victims supposed to find justice on earth, instead of waiting for God the Almighty to take revenge in hell?"

"God! Ha!" Ruby-Rose angrily spat her words.

"I don't believe in God or hell, either," Lucinda added. "So what happened then, Zed? How did you end up here?"

"It all went belly-up after George died. Instead of harmony, my inner turmoil increased tenfold. It was reflected in my novels. Wearing silk gloves hides the persistent sunspots that come with ageing. But nothing can hide the bitterness that seeps through my pores, and finds its way into my novels. Murder and revenge didn't change a thing for me. I had no logos. The characters in my books never got the justice they deserved. At least, that's how it seemed. And I thought my readers deserved better."

"Holy shit," Ruby-Rose said. "Readers? That is amazing. I don't know what else to say."

"What do you mean by logos?" Lucinda asked.

"The natural order in life," I replied. "It's an appeal to logic. In our library I read that Christians call it God."

"Oh, boy," Ruby-Rose said. "I am speechless. I almost shit myself, just listening to your story; logos or not."

"God? I don't know about God," Lucinda said. "But it's a great story anyway. I'm all hot and shaky. I can imagine George standing there, glaring at me. He scares the hell out of me. Not that I believe in hell. He better not appear in our cell tonight."

We all laughed.

"I love the bit where she fried him," Ruby-Rose said, with a cheeky grin on her face. "He had that coming. I wish I was there. I would have flicked the switch. God, I hate him."

"The point is," I continued, "that after he died, I had mixed emotions. Nothing went according to plan, except for his execution. I thought it would make me feel better. But I only felt worse. By taking revenge, I set off a whole new order in the universe. It's like, everyone has a time to live and a time to die. How do I know that it was his time? And it all backfired."

"I can sort of understand that," Ruby-Rose said. "It's like me getting revenge and putting Travis in jail. I just don't know how I would feel about that. Will it ever take away all my hurt? I have no family, and the Wences disowned me years ago. I mean, Travis did the wrong thing by making me take the blame for everything, while it was all his plan. The pills he gave me got inside my head. I would never have thought of burning the house down and killing everyone for insurance money."

"You still did it," Lucinda said. "He didn't hold a gun to your head."

"But you will get revenge, Ruby-Rose," I assured her. "When I get out, I will make sure of it. And you will get justice. I will get the best lawyer for you. Travis will get his just deserts. And it isn't really about revenge anyway. It's more about justice and going through the right legal channels."

"But you still killed your family, Ruby," Lucinda added. "What was that all about, if not revenge?"

"Yeh," Ruby-Rose sighed. "It was definitely revenge on my parents, I guess. But not on my brother and sisters. I am not sure what that was all about, really."

"Collateral damage," Lucinda concluded. "That's what they were."

"I don't know," Ruby-Rose said regretfully. "It seemed right, at the time. I thought I was giving my sisters and brother a better life."

"In death?" Lucinda quipped. "How does that work?"

Ruby-Rose was getting agitated by Lucinda's questions. "Travis convinced me that it was the best thing to do for them," she retorted. "I mean, I didn't want them going into an orphanage. And it wasn't my idea, at all. Travis was the mastermind behind everything. And you robbed a bank, Lucy. So you're not exactly sweet to the core."

"Not true," Lucinda snapped. "It was a wall safe in a jeweller's shop. He was as rich as anything, and wouldn't miss the money. He probably had it all over insured. Anyway, I think of myself as Robin Hood."

"But you kept all the spoils," Ruby-Rose replied. "Robin robbed the rich to give to the poor."

"I think I deserved the jewels," Lucinda said in her own defence. "After all, I am a royal."

"A royal?" Ruby-Rose laughed. "And I'm the pope."

"Now I'm feeling outclassed by you two," I joked. "But getting back to what we were saying, Ruby, your story is complicated. You were damaged goods. You really didn't have a chance."

"Thank you, Miss Zed," Ruby-Rose said. "At least, you know what went on."

"Things were going to go bad for you sooner or later," I empathised. "Your father would probably have killed you in that room. He sounds like a real psycho."

"Like George, killed Billy," Ruby-Rose concluded.

"Yes. That's what I think," I agreed.

191

"God, we have so many unresolved issues here," Lucinda said. "Just three of us. But look at the complications: lost brothers, lost wealth, and Zed's lost childhood."

"There's a whole prison full of lost shit over there," Ruby-Rose said, as she pointed to Cell Block C. "A whole heap of complications."

"Yes," I agreed. "You're not wrong."

"Anyway, let's get back to it," Lucinda said with some authority, as she stood up. "Back to our little shit piles of logos."

The three of us laughed and had a group hug. I felt their love. I felt their sadness.

61

The Conundrum

I enjoyed sharing my story with my friends, though I hadn't shared all the intricacies of my moral dilemma. I saved that side of my 'evolving personality' for this book. Shall we call it 'leaving the best till last'?

However, in my brief time in Fairlea, the stress of prison life quickly caught up with me. Although I had been a feisty woman of substance who was thrust into a dank prison cell, my emotional and physical strength soon wavered. Mostly, it was caused by the bullying and resentment that reared its ugly head, from time to time. After a couple of months, my overworked heart had a weaker beat. Also, I was not used to the manual labour and mass-produced food. And just like Oscar Wilde the playwright, jail took its toll on my health.

Mostly, I tried to survive the daily routine of prison life. I steered clear of Rand and her mob. Like Lucinda, I was a juxtaposition at Fairlea. I didn't fit the profile of the other prisoners. And I didn't really belong there; though some may argue that point.

Rand and Tanya made me feel like that dirty, unwanted teenage girl who was rejected by her peers. All the bitchiness reignited my insecurities that were caused when the girls at school ostracised me for sleeping with Craig. That sort of pain never seems to leave; even in adulthood.

62

Vices

Dear Reader, so far I have shared several tragedies. According to the educated, a 'tragedy' is supposed to depict the downfall of a noble hero or heroine, usually through some combination of *hubris*, fate, and the will of the gods. Whatever their goal in life is, the hero fails because of their human frailty. Some prefer to blame the gods, fate or nature, rather than themselves.

Aristotle says that although the tragic hero need not die at the end, he or she must undergo a change in fortune. In addition, the tragic hero might achieve some revelation or recognition about human fate, destiny and the will of the gods. Aristotle quite nicely terms this sort of recognition 'a change from ignorance to awareness of a bond of love or hate.'

And now you realise that what I laid bare in this novel, is only part of the tragic journeys of several women. It is the part we shared at Fairlea Prison as we waited to be set free. Or the part we shared as we sipped champagne on my balcony on a warm summer's afternoon. And who's to say if we became wiser or embittered? Did Aristotle become more aware of the power of love and hate?

My mother's fortunes definitely changed. She went from being a homeless refugee, to becoming a rich, enterprising widow who owned many houses. She found *true love* with Billy and me. Although her vices were sending her to an early grave, she refused to abandon them. Instead, she said that she would smoke and drink to the very end. At one point, she told me that she was advised by her doctors to continue smoking. Well, that seemed a bit far-fetched. But if she believed it, then who was I to quibble with someone who had survived world wars?

The lesson I learned as I got older, was to never judge another. Unless you walked in their shoes, you don't know what they endured. This is clearly evident in my life. People thought I had a good life, being rich and famous. But they never saw the real me. They didn't know my back story until now. And neither did they know the Fairlea women's stories. Some were too gruesome for this book.

Ruby-Rose was like a lucky dip. You didn't know what you were likely to find once you dived into her history bag. I know that she loved to chatter as we strolled together, round and round the concrete prison yard, or in the dining hall. Above us were pure, blue skies; around us, the bluestone prison walls.

To some, she was just a prisoner with a number; just another social failure. But to me, she was a beautiful person with the saddest story. She was a survivor. She knew how easy it is for love to turn into hate; like a pendulum swinging from one extreme to another. One minute Travis loved her and promised the world. In the next breath, he was nowhere to be seen. She was caught unawares. She didn't see it coming.

Before she fell in love with him, she thought life was about hatred and beatings in 'the room'. And then she experienced love and bliss with the boy of her dreams. But instead of being set free, she realised that it was all a nasty charade. The lesson was learnt. *No pain without gain.* And she resigned herself to knowing when to 'hold or fold' her cards. Don't waste your time by trying to swim against the tide of the gods. *What will be, will be.*

And Lucinda, who was usually within ear-shot, always seemed to be at war with herself as she battled her compulsions. She loved to natter with me during the nights in our prison cell.

She would lie in her top bunk, and say how much she wished she had a glass of champagne in one hand, and a string of pearls in the other. From my bunk below, I told her that when she got out, she could go to fancy parties with me. I would even drive her to auditions as a movie extra, if she so desired.

"Who knows where it could lead," I enthused. "You could become a famous Hollywood star." This fanciful notion put a smile on her face.

Lucinda was such a pretty, little thing. As such, she became acutely aware of the envy-laced-with-hatred that some women felt toward her. She was targeted by the bullies. In prison she seemed to drift from one tragedy to another. She considered me as being the safe port in the storm. On occasion, I saw her as a reflection of my younger self.

63

Gods or Fate?

So far, I have talked about war and peace times, and the associated differences in morality. This difference in morality was also evident in the prison population. Some felt no sympathy for their victims. Their only regret was being caught. They bragged about their list of crimes, in the same way that one would prepare a resume for a job. They were more than willing to do it all again. By contrast, others were ashamed of their crimes and wanted to turn a new leaf when they left the prison. They tried to understand the forces of evil that impacted on them.

All these women were once innocent babies. They were a *tabula rasa* or blank slate. A baby does not have any concept of greed or murder. So who should the Fairlea women point their fingers at when they fall short of society's rules? Did they have any options to a life of crime? Or was it their individual weaknesses, as Aristotle said, that catapulted them into a life of crime? And where did these weaknesses derive? Maybe it was the gods or fate that set them on an alternate path.

Now I ask, are we convicted prisoners the victims rather than the perpetrators of crime? Are we symptomatic of the loopholes in the social safety net? Therefore, should adults be punished for not protecting the children? Are they the real criminals after all? Should it be a crime to turn a blind eye when schoolchildren have no decent shoes or a cut lunch? If adults fail to protect children from sexual abuse, should all the adults be punished?

Therefore, I can only wonder about who or what is to blame when children become criminals. Are criminals born or shaped by society, as Locke predicts? Would we criminals have been pillars of society, if born into different families? In effect, who cast us into the sandpit? And do we want to get out? What is true for one may not be true for another. Unlike inanimate objects, people are unpredictable. Psychologists can only consider each case individually. So many universal questions with no perfect answer.

Ruby-Rose was an abused child. Like me, she rose from her victim status to become an avenging god. She took revenge on Patrick Wickham. She had the power over life and death. Like the weak lamb that was imbued by the eagle's strength, she murdered her family. She thought she was doing the best thing for her siblings. It was an act of kindness; like putting an injured pet out of its misery.

Then there was Lucinda. She reminded me of a dainty Chihuahua that never realised how tiny they are till they tackled a bull terrier. Lucinda lusted after life's elusive fineries. She had a sense of self-entitlement. She wished that her great-great-grandmother had stayed in the castle, and given her granddaughter the life of a princess. But what if all of this was a cruel lie that her parents fabricated, and there was no princess or castle? Did their lies cause Lucinda's downfall?

Overall, I have happy memories of the time I shared with Lucinda and Ruby-Rose. Both of them looked to me for answers. Did my two friends think that by writing this novel, I would unveil the secrets of their souls? As you can see, I still have many unanswered questions swimming in my brain.

At every opportunity, Ruby-Rose and Lucinda sided with me. They offered protection from the bullies. There is safety in numbers. All the while they asked me about the progress of their stories. It was imperative for them that their 'shit' was shared, as soon as possible. Perhaps they feared that they would not live long enough to read their stories in print.

But what about people who commit crimes and are never caught? Some people think they are above the law. Although they are never labelled as criminals, and their crimes are never uncovered, their actions define them as a murderer. This is true for my mother. However, it could also be argued that she killed in self-defence, so it wasn't really murder, as such; more so a shade of grey revenge. And who am I to judge anyway?

Perhaps if I had my time over again, I should have approached George differently.

"You murdered my brother, you arsehole!" I would shriek.

And then I would hit him so hard that he would fall over. Then I would demand all his houses. But instead, he was quietly electrocuted by me. Exterminated like a cockroach. And he never faced punishment before the courts. True Justice was never met for poor Billy, since George was never publicly humiliated and sentenced.

Now I pose the question: can murderers be reformed outside of the prison system? Can they rehabilitate themselves without going to jail? Can they gain a conscience? In effect, is going to prison superfluous? This raises the question: was my confession necessary, after all? Did anyone benefit?

And so you can see my conundrum. Before I killed George, I desperately wanted peace. Yet, I could not find it. I heard Billy calling to me from the grave, 'Kellie, Kellie get George. Make him pay. Please Kellie.' Sometimes, I saw Billy's face in my dreams, or in a crowded street. He was always there; always waiting for me to get justice for him. Murder was my only option. I had a clear path to follow.

But the death of my step-father did not eradicate my pain. I still heard George's dreaded voice and saw his heinous face as he raped me. My only solace seemed to be in confessing to his murder. At least, I would get some recognition for killing a paedophile. At last, his secret would be out. But did anyone really care?

I wonder if my mother ever thinks about my biological father. Maybe he wasn't that bad after all. Maybe he was programmed by the Communist regime to hunt her down. He may not have had a natural killer's heart. Or maybe, just maybe, he loved her and wanted her to return to Russia with him; to make a little Russian family.

Mother was tight-lipped about my father. Who was he? I needed to know. I wanted to piece together my jigsaw life. Was his name Boris, Alek or Vladimir? Maybe she already knew him in Russia as one of her ardent admirers. But my stalwart mother would never tell me the full story. She wanted to take her secret to the grave. And I could not blame anyone.

64

Wisdom

A philosopher once said that self-reliance that is independent of objects is vital to one's state of happiness. This is regardless of when or where they live. If we become attached to or dislike external things, we'll often be unhappy, insecure and anxious. The world will not be the way we want it to be. Some might label us as whingers.

When modern day cynics say, "Everything disappoints me", there may be a strong element of truth in that. Indeed, I find this to be true. And our greatest disappointments come when we attach our happiness to others. People rarely meet our expectations. They disappoint us when they 'fall off their pedestal'.

Gender differences might limit women's choices. Men and women may be pitted against each other for job opportunities. Throughout history, women have notoriously been underpaid and undervalued. The Suffragettes were tired of whinging, and successfully challenged women's 'right to vote' in 1903.

Irrespective of gender, we are restrained by our individual gifts, talents and shortcomings. 'IQ' becomes the term psychologists like to throw around. It is a number that labels us. It measures our reasoning and problem solving abilities. And we all know that Einstein's number was 160; though there are others who have a much higher number than him. To overcome discrepancies in testing, we label people as having different types of intelligence. Is this a true reflection of their personal worth?

People are so complicated and diverse. There is no blueprint for the perfect human being. We all have to accept each other and learn to get along. Sadly, many of us want people to change to match our expectations. If they were fatter or thinner, drank less or more, or followed our theology we might like them more. How many times do we hear young women say that they will change him once they are married? Does this ever hold true?

People come and go in our lives, like waves lapping on the sea shores. They follow their own tides. Accidental friends venture in and out of our journey. They show us the nuances of life. Their words resemble grains of sand blown across the beaches of our existence. People can be both cruel and kind, depending on what they are thinking and what comes out of their mouths. Words define their values and beliefs. Truth to one person may be a falsehood to another. Just as sand becomes shards of glass, so too, loving words can harbour deceit and hatred.

Life is marred by deception. A tranquil sea can have undercurrents of mishmash. And then you wade out in the luring water, and drown. Some people may be philanthropists who do good deeds. But things can go belly up, like a beached whale. And when those we rely on fall from their pedestal, we are painfully disappointed. We wanted to believe in the unattainable.

Perhaps we needed a reality check. There was a clash between fiction and fact. Our emotions altered our perception of the truth. And we are abandoned when we don't live up to other's expectations.

65

Deep In Thought

The physical world is tangible. Emotions are intangible. One can be touched, held in our hands and measured; whilst the other can't. But we've all felt the strong impact of our unbridled emotions. How many lives have been taken when jealousy gets out of hand? Haven't you heard of the expression 'lost in love'? It seems that the poets want us to draw a line between the two worlds.

Heraclitus said that everything is forever passing into something else, and has an existence only in relation to this 'fluid' process. And the same can be said for prisoners. They are fluid. Regardless of how much time they spend in jail, they leave the prison in a different state than when they entered. They are still tangible. But the intangible chip on their shoulder may have turned into a boulder. Prison changes people, both physically and mentally; and not always for the better. Sadly, some prisoners only leave the system in a body bag.

However, with hard work and effort, negative emotions might be replaced or overridden. Maybe we should all sing happy songs, as they do in musicals. I know that this logic is not feasible, since some of us are tone deaf. But in the same way that light chases away the darkness, a change in attitude can work wonders for one's self esteem. It can facilitate our appreciation of others, and even of life itself.

Yes, I changed mentally when I was imprisoned. I gained a new appreciation of life outside of my prison cell. I knew how it felt to live with the underdogs; with those whom society rejects and deems as unacceptable. I gained insight, empathy and sympathy for them. Although I became wiser, my health deteriorated. The stress of prison life took its toll on me. As mentioned, I wasn't as robust as when I entered the stony walls at Fairlea; and bullying impacted on me. I certainly couldn't sing my way out of that one.

Undoubtedly, it can be argued that I was never robust. I was always a soft grub crawling along a tree branch; impatiently waiting to be metamorphosed into a beautiful butterfly. Unlike some unfortunate prisoners, I had the opportunity to leave jail, to reform and change my life. And Ruby-Rose will be given every opportunity to leave her tree branch and fly through the trees with me, when she gets out of jail; when my brilliant lawyer finds the legal loophole in her conviction.

Unlike rocks, emotions cannot be weighed. There is no measure for the love or hate we feel for others, or even for ourselves. To further confuse things, people like Travis can love someone for one minute, and hate them in the next breath. Emotions, like objects, are not fixed in their form. Divorce courts typify this.

Over time, intangible public loyalties shift as famous celebrities, or world leaders, fade into obscurity. Kingdoms fall. Although pharaohs have long gone, tangible pyramids still testify to their wealth. Adding to this theme of 'the temporary state of objects', our possessions can be easily lost, as occurs in bushfires, floods or through bankruptcy. Heraclitus believed that everything is in a condition of flux. Like rocks and sand, things transform. Everything is forever passing into something else.

Heraclitus and Ruby-Rose discovered that fire is the essence of life. In line with this, the Stoics believe that the unity of the universe stems from the never-resting power of fire. One could draw parallels here with the ever-burning torch throughout the Olympic Games. Even in war times, warring countries are able to unite in sport. And perhaps the stubble of Ruby-Rose's hand is a constant reminder to her of the dominance of fire over human flesh. She then used the 'power of fire' against her parents. It was the only power she thought she possessed.

By contrast, Plato believes that the only constant in life is 'the world of ideas', and non-physical forms represent the best reality. In his 'Theory of Forms' he suggests that the world that is perceived by our senses is deceptive and changeable. I agree with this. In the long run, objects cannot guarantee eternal happiness or security because everything changes.

Life can go belly-up; just like our transient happiness that is dependent on others. Possessions can dissipate or vanish in the blink of an eye. A hand can disappear in a jet of fire. Therefore, our happiness must come from within. What is real to us becomes our reality. We must learn to grasp and sow the seeds of happiness, instead of hate. Even with one hand, as in Ruby-Rose's case.

I am guessing that many rich career criminals, like Lucinda, were born into poverty. They crave a better life and the comforts that surround the rich and famous. They think the rich have a monopoly on happiness. So they strive to become like those they set on a combustible pedestal.

Impatience might become the downfall of those who covet. Because of their greed and lack of foresight, they resort to crime and a quick grab at cash. Rather than going through the right and legal channels, such as studying and working hard, they want everything here and now.

So now I ask, are the ones in prison the strong or the weak members in the universal fishbowl? Are they removed from the free world because its occupants are afraid of the strength of those who are corrupt or mentally deranged? Like cannibalistic fish in the fishbowl, will they eat their neighbours in the night?

66

The Quest

After sharing my story with my two prison friends, I still needed answers. Who was I really? Yes, I was a product of rape. But knowing that did not answer my unflagging, universal questions. Why was I here? What was the point of life? Was I more than just a murderess? I needed to know my place in society if I were to ever live happily in it. So I continued to scrutinise the works of the great philosophers. I tried to get inside their heads as I pondered life's profanities.

Heraclitus said that reality is an attunement of opposites. It is a harmony of conflicting elements. I know that the human spirit can be simultaneously pulled in many directions. After I killed George, many doubts and insecurities surfaced. Did I do the right thing? Was I evil or good? And then I realised that we are all a mixture of good and evil. As Ruby-Rose aptly said, I was all mixed up.

Good and bad impulses fuddle us when we are pulled in two directions; when we are of two minds. Yes, I have had many sleepless nights both before and after confessing. How does the saying go? *You are damned if you do and damned if you don't.* However, a rational person can choose which force dominates their life. Therefore, did I lack rationality? Was I to be cursed whichever choice I made?

Good and bad people coexist in all societies; like the weeds growing amongst flowers. Love and hate are juxtapositions on each other, like the red blood of a bleeding seal spilling onto a pristine-white snowfield. The goodness of people highlights the vileness of others, and vice versa.

A wounded soul is like a compass without a needle; a ship without sails, or a train without rails. It loses all perspective and rationality. It loses its direction. It is then that individuals need a guiding force, or a friend, to steer them through their troubled times. How nice it would be if we all had a shoulder to lean on; someone to offer us a hot chocolate on a cold night. But for some, that is merely a fantasy. They must be independent and draw on their own inner strength. And that, dear Reader, is a good description of me.

Although I hated George with a tremulous force, I also had the strong desire to love and be loyal to others. In prison, I offered friendship to Ruby-Rose and Lucinda. They saw me as the person they could lean on. Although I was capable of murder, I could also inject hope into outsiders. As stated, I was a melding of opposite forces. Whilst having a burning disposition to hate, I harboured a great capacity to love.

Sometimes, I was negative, believing that life is futile. I was like a flightless insect. At other times, I saw hope. Rather than just being a squashed bug on the footpath, I was the grub crawling along the bent tree branch, waiting to metamorphose into an elegant butterfly; waiting to be loved. I saw love and light in a kaleidoscope of colours in a butterfly's wings when is soared into the sun.

So much imagery. But what did it all mean? I still had many questions stirring. Like Icarus, my wings were clipped. I became a flightless prisoner by my own doing. And no one melted wax to glue my wings back together. So I walked instead of flying. And others walked beside me.

Many questions teemed in my mind. Seeking more answers about the nature of humanity, I was compelled to keep studying the words of the ancient philosophers. As mentioned, I read Seneca's engaging story that teemed with hypocrisy, lust and his eventual demise. Although his life supposedly evolved around the degradation of the wealthy, he had a penchant for their lifestyle; much like Lucinda. While he proposed that one should not be attached to earthly goods, he harboured greed for the finer things in life. He lived extravagantly. He had five hundred identical tables of citrus wood with legs of ivory, on which he served banquets. It was also reported that he was a loan shark. One could say that he was the personification of hypocrisy: *Do as I say, not as I do.*

Seneca reminded me of Patrick Wickham; both were full of hypocrisy. While Patrick preached the necessity of living a sinless life, he committed the ultimate sin against his children. While he preached a philosophy of 'loving thy neighbour', he nurtured a spirit of hatred amongst his family. The nihilists would say that his values were simply worthless lies.

Patrick hated those who abused him in wartimes. He sought some form of retribution, at his children's expense. He obviously did not read the part of the Bible that says to forgive your enemies. Needless to say, his children were not his enemies. And after the war, his only enemy was himself.

Heraclitus saw all life as being governed by justice, harmony, logos or reason. Other philosophers believe that by focusing on the inner goods of virtue, we can become one with the ebb and flow of the cosmos. We accept whatever happens to us as the will of the Logos.

67

Que Sera

I tried to apply all these theories to my situation. I concluded that what will be, will be. *Que sera*. Each of us swims in a fishbowl of our own making. Although we may not control the environment, we can partially control our emotions. As mentioned, we choose to be good or evil. I am sure I could have sent George to jail, rather than kill him; if only I had the capacity to think things through rationally. I could have given the ultimate power of revenge to the law courts; or maybe left punishment to God or fate. The police said that I had legal rights. So I could have, or should have, used them. But I did not.

And this is where things become blurred, for emotions cannot be dictated. Not all of us are able to control our impulses. And that's why people end up in prison. Sometimes, our self-preservation instincts override our reasoning. It's called a *knee jerk* or *reflex action*. Things just happen. We lose control and strike back at perpetrators, without thinking of the consequences. Things may backfire on us. After all, it seems that even evil people have some rights. It's a bit like inverted justice. Then their victims have to 'just get over it' and move on with their life. There is no retribution!

After retrospection and a lot of introspection, I realised that I was full of contradictions and inconsistencies. I was like a jigsaw with missing pieces. Sometimes, I had flashes of brilliance as I wrote my novels. At other times, I took the law into my own hands. I masterminded the perfect crime, only to later throw myself at the mercy of the courts.

I was bad, not mad. I had meticulous clarity when it came to planning George's murder: visiting his home early so he would be home alone; having a loaded gun in my handbag; and then devising the ingenious cover-up about his electrocution; although electrocuting him was a spur of the minute thing. I could have turned off the electricity. I could have phoned for an ambulance. I could have saved his life. But I didn't. I made a conscious choice to watch him die. And that's why the police initially considered me as a cold-hearted murderess.

But when I was handcuffed and carted away by the police, my life was one of total confusion. People I'd once relied on abandoned me. They say that when you're down and out, you learn who your real friends are. And that was totally true for me. My real friends were my readers. They put their money where their mouth was, so to speak.

I can brag and say that I was a vigilante. I was an upholder of justice. But in reality, I was a frail butterfly whose wings were not properly formed. I was not in full possession of my senses. I still had the mentality of a grub crawling along the branch. On that fatal day when I walked into George's terrace house, I was in a trance. I acted in autopilot mode. I carried a loaded gun. All logic simply flew out the window, leaving me behind with my broken wings.

68

Battle Of The Forces

When things go wrong, we try to blame someone or something. But why do we need to blame anyone? We are outraged when heinous crimes are committed and justice is never dealt. Sadly, some sociopaths have strong networks and are too devious to be caught by the law. They don't care who they hurt, and only think of themselves. Ultimately, no one is blamed and punishment is never dealt. And the victims are left to nurse their wounds.

This controversy over 'laying the blame', raises the question: why are some born with a social conscience whilst others are not? Is conscience merely something that plagues philosophers and sensitive individuals, such as me? Why do good people frequently fail to live up to their own expectations?

There seems to be a fine line between bad and mad. At what point in a person's life are they declared insane? Are we all born with a clean slate, and society poisons our mind? At the end of the day, who should we blame? Even Charles Manson was once a suckling baby. What turns good people into hypocrites and babies into serial killers? Why can't they see the error of their ways and avoid a disaster? Overall, some people try to be good, yet ultimately fail. Why? Why? Too many unanswered questions for this book.

Aristotle said that *logos* is the capacity for humans to show their feelings. It is also the capacity for humans to distinguish between what is good and what is harmful. Therefore, I would ask if this is the quality that is lacking in those who are hypocritical or those who end up prison? Perhaps we don't have the capacity to reasonably think things through because we lack *logos*.

Some wild animals are considered as being born mostly 'good', whilst others are inherently 'bad'. In the wilderness, animals develop their own laws of survival. Their environment and needs determine their level of aggression. The *Law of the Jungle* has no moral rules. It's eat or be eaten. Animals kill to survive. Their personalities are not complex like humans. I mean, have you ever seen a crocodile smile?

However, domesticated cats and dogs that are brought up in 'good family homes' don't need to hunt for food. Accordingly, they should lose their 'killer instinct'. But cats still kill innocent mice and birds. It is their sport and blood lust. It is never bred out of them, regardless of how many tins of fish they eat. And have you ever been scratched by a cat or bitten by a dog when you tried to pat it?

Is that what is wrong with us prisoners? We were never domesticated. We were never petted by loving humans. But then again, some pets turn on their owners. They literally bite the hand that feeds them. And people reared in good homes, may still become criminals for no apparent reason. Wealthy kleptomaniacs enjoy the thrill of stealing. Oh, such a muddle!

Siblings can grow up in the same home, and one will be good whilst the other is evil. Looking at Ruby-Rose, I wondered if her siblings would ever have felt the need to burn down the entire house, in order to destroy the evil that was inherent in Patrick?

Further to this, was Patrick's need to establish 'the room' merely a projection of his time in a prisoner of war camp; a time when prisoners were placed in prison boxes as a form of punishment? Or was it just part of his evil nature? Was the enemy who built the P.O.W. camp the 'fifth column' in world peace? Or maybe they considered democracy as being the 'fifth column' in their social order. It then becomes apparent that different cultures pertain to different forms of the truth, with each country thinking that they are superior and right.

Psychologists say that under pressure, some adults revert to the negative behaviours of their role models. This is also referred to as 'cycles of abuse'. If children have abusive parents, they may also become abusers; just like Ruby-Rose. All of Patrick's anger transferred to her. She carried out the very behaviour that she detested. This is also true of George. He was an abused child who grew into an abuser. And I am making no excuses for him. I am simply trying to piece his psychological jigsaw together, in the hope of gaining closure for myself.

I now ask, who were Patrick's role models? Was it his parents or the cruel war lords in Borneo? And then who were the role models of the enemy that attacked Western Civilisation, and caused the imprisonment of thousands of soldiers, many of whom died? However, as wars progress and war strategies are employed, there are universal power shifts. In the end, he with the biggest gun rules. They are the moral rulers. And the winners write the history books. Or get the likes of me to do such.

Therefore, the defeated enemy is always portrayed as evil, or the 'fifth column' in the world's social order. They were the evil spies that tried to bring about the downfall of another nation. By contrast, the winners are always considered as being righteous and virtuous. But we know that evil still exists in the ranks of the winners. The 'fifth column' is always present.

In Fairlea I witnessed genuine love and compassion amongst the women. Just as soldiers unite in a common cause, bonds of friendships were formed amongst the prisoners. They cared for those nearest and dearest. In a twisted way, crime united them. They had a 'them and us' mentality against the warders. The prison system was the enemy to defeat. It was a reflection of the society that rejected them.

Tanya met Rand in prison. Their bond was unbreakable. Tanya thought she was doing the right thing by being her shadow. This was the only way she could show love. In reality, she was merely a lost and frightened soul who clung to the only love she knew. She feared losing Rand. Like the eagle-lamb, the two of them united in a powerful force of hatred and control.

However, I could be wrong. Tanya could be more insidious than imagined, and Rand may have feared her. I could have mixed up my 'dominant partner' theory. I know how my fictional characters tick, but understanding 'real people' and their absolutes is another issue. And I am an author, not a trained psychologist.

My psychological knowledge was gained through my prison reading. And since I gained no fixed answers to my universal questions, I will let you draw your own conclusions. Maybe it is much simpler than all the text books propose. Some people are just born evil whilst others are good. Some are genuine friends, whilst others merely want to undermine the stability in a group. It has nothing to do with which side of the street you're born on. It's simply the luck of the draw in the gene pool.

69

The Laundry

Although my mother's story is nearing its end, and Ruby-Rose's story is ongoing; Lucinda's ended abruptly. Despite the princess in my kindergarten stories having a dashing prince save them, if I wrote another book with a happy end to Lucinda's story, it would only be a lie. And I hope I will do her justice when I share the story of the demise of the estranged Indian princess.

Her life was taken too soon. And opinions are divided on who killed her? Beautiful Lucinda with only one whole ear, desperately wanted to be a star. She hoped for another opportunity; one more chance at Hollywood. But she never got to read another movie script.

Literally, prison life killed her. She was not ready for the rough women who bullied her and ordered her to move whenever she crossed their path. Not cowering, she stood up to their intimidation as best she could. She had the heart of Janaki the defiant princess. She would not kowtow.

"Piss off!" Lucinda would have yelled in the prison laundry, when they tied the sheet around her neck. "You bloody bitches can't draw shit. I'm glad I stuffed up ya paintings in ya Art class. And ya can all go to hell!"

Tragically, I walked into the laundry room too late. I found her small frame hanging from a sheet that was tied around the overhead pipes.

"Somebody help!" I screamed, as I tried to lift her small body. "Please, somebody!"

I was sick with fear and panic. "Please hurry," I cried, as tears streamed down my face. "Oh, Lucy. Don't die. Please don't die!" I screamed, till my throat went hoarse.

Within minutes, two prison guards, Trent Oliver and Nadine Triton, burst into the room like a pair of angry bulls.

"What's going on Earl?" Oliver said. His tall, commanding presence was immediately felt.

"Oh, hell," comely Triton gasped, when she saw Lucinda's limp body. She hurriedly pushed a table under Lucinda.

"We'll get her down," quick-thinking Oliver said, as he lifted Lucinda's body.

All the while I willed Lucinda to live as I steadied her body.

Oliver climbed onto the table. Being tall, he easily untied the sheet. Triton and I gently lifted Lucinda onto the floor. I grabbed a clean blanket from out of a pile of washing, and placed it under her head.

"Please don't die, Lucy," I sobbed, as Triton did mouth-to-mouth resuscitation on my dear friend. "Please don't go. Please don't go."

Oliver took Lucinda's pulse. He shook his head. "She's gone," he said, glumly.

A tsunami of grief flooded my soul.

"You did all you could, Earl," Triton empathized, wiping a tear from her eye.

"The women have been brewing for a while," Oliver added. "We should have seen something like this coming."

"Yes," I cried. "I was too late. I failed her. I should have looked after her. We just can't walk around alone. We have to stick together. I should have been with her. I was too late."

"It's the bloody prison system," Triton grimaced. "It's hard to keep an eye on everything."

"There's always some cat fight stirring in some part of the prison," Oliver added. "It's having all the women in close proximity. They can't help themselves." And then he called somebody on his phone cell. "Yes, come to the laundry room."

70

Romance

Dear Reader, so far I have omitted certain elements in this story; for fear they would alter the genre from one of drama to that of romance. But indeed, there was much romance in my tale. And it all began in the shower room at Cell Block C at Fairlea Prison.

As mentioned, I enjoyed the warm water and suds cleansing my body. On this occasion, I whistled a tune. Suddenly, the half-door swung wide open as Tanya Drinkwater burst into my shower cubicle. Whack! She hit the back of the head. She grabbed my hair and reefed me out of the shower.

"You stay away from Rand, ya bitch!" my attacker's words hissed into my ears. "She's my wife. So you keep ya dirty hands off her, ya bloody stuck-up piece of shit!"

Gruff Tanya Drinkwater now had hold of my throat. Her sharp fingernails dug into my wet flesh.

"I don't care how many fuckin' books ya write," she snapped, pressing hard on my throat. The smell of her stale tobacco filled my nostrils. The site of her naked body repulsed me."Ya no betta than us, ya la-dee-da bitch!" she screamed in my ear.

I saw stars. I felt faint. But she was too powerful for me to pull away.

"Miss Zed! Ya all right?" Ruby-Rose screamed, as she rushed to my side. She was already dressed.

With her good hand, she grabbed Tanya's hair and reefed her away from me. She pushed her against a shower wall with such force, that I thought Tanya's eyes would pop.

"I'm okay, Ruby," I said. "I'm fine. It's just a misunderstanding. Let her go."

I grabbed my nearby towel, as Ruby-Rose released her.

"I'll get ya, bitch!" Tanya warned under her breath, as she grabbed her towel and slipped away. I was amazed at how much strength Ruby-Rose had in one hand. My throat was aching. I shook as I dressed.

"Break it up!" Triton insisted, as she rushed into the shower room.

"You girls okay?" Trent Oliver asked. He joined the throng.

"Yes," Ruby-Rose and I said in unison.

"It's under control now, sir," Triton said. "Just another cat fight."

I felt relieved when handsome Trent Oliver came to my rescue. I remembered the way he tried to save Lucinda's life. He was as noble as they come. Some girls wolf-whistled him on their way out of the shower room.

"Just cut it out," he insisted. "No more fights here. Be nice, ladies."

I couldn't help but laugh. *Ladies?* I thought. Well, we were ladies. Just ladies doing it tough. Ladies-in-waiting.

I lingered as the women left the shower room. I wanted to stay in Trent's presence for as long as possible. I noted his sturdy manliness: his tall stature and piercing blue eyes; his strong arms. *My Robin Hood,* I thought; and the perfect height for me. His sharply pressed uniform accentuated his well-proportioned body. I was drawn to his rugged, boyish looks and Adonis body. I was like a fly entangled in his sexual fly paper.

"Are you okay, Kellie?" he asked, as he stepped closer.

"Yes, thanks warder," I said, giving him a sweet smile. "They get a bit possessive sometimes."

"Group dynamics and prison romances," he surmised.

I nodded.

Although he emotionally tried to distance himself from me, the trap was set. Both of us were caught in it. Whenever I saw him around the prison, my heart pleasantly fluttered. Call it chemistry, temptation or the forbidden fruit. But whatever it was, we both felt its power. Don't they say that a woman loves a man in uniform? They also say to be careful what you wish for.

71

Released

After eighteen months at Fairlea, plus time spent in remand, the judge deemed that over the course of my life, I had suffered enough. She released me on 'compassionate grounds'. The place that had been described by the 'Fairlea Five' as 'soul destroying and an institution rivalled only by something out of the eighteenth century', had served its legal and literary purpose for me. It was no longer my home.

Although I never met any of the five women who were imprisoned at Fairlea for eleven days in 1971, for objecting to boys registering for National Service in Vietnam, I met other interesting characters. I have shared some of their flagrant stories.

After my retrial, I left the prison that operated for forty years. Amongst the 18,000 inmates who spent time there, no doubt many friendships were formed. That was certainly true in my case. Also, stories of hatred and murder left their mark on the prison's history. Some remember the deliberate fire in 1982 that took three lives. Fortunately, I had been released by then. It was the third major fire at the prison, and drew attention to the inadequate training of some officers and the unsuitable condition of the prison. Hence, those inmates who were considered as 'dangerous or disruptive' were transferred to Jika Jika. But, dear Reader, that is another story. It could be the fibre of my next novel.

I recall that on the day of my release, midst tears and hugs, Ruby-Rose and I said our 'goodbyes'. She promised to write. And I promised to get her the best lawyer to get her out of jail. Except for a yellow taxi that I booked, no one was waiting outside. And that's exactly how I wanted it.

I took a deep breath as I walked along the corridor of C Block with guard Nadine Triton. I felt safe with her because she was a martial arts expert. In her black, leather lace-up shoes, her steps were exact. My new Roman sandals felt stiff. I knew that it was the last time I would ever see the locked doors of prison cells, or share the prison showers with criminals.

Truth known, I had never really started living till I was imprisoned. Indeed, I felt like a *tabula rasa*. The eighteen months spent in Fairlea, changed my life forever. It was as if my entire life was compressed into 912 days. For clock watchers, this included a leap year.

Overall, it had been a roller-coaster experience living with the women. Some of them were a reflection of me. They felt that life had robbed them of the happiness they deserved, or the person they loved. We all had our skeletons in our closets, so to speak. We all had to find sanity in our crazy world.

But as I prepared to leave the prison, fate took an unexpected turn. When I was only metres from the exit gates, my stomach had butterflies. I tugged at my grey-cotton pants suit that I bought for my first day of freedom. I smoothed the imagined creases in my silky, white shirt. I fiddled with its pearly buttons. All the while I clung to my black, leather shoulder bag that contained my credit cards. It had no gun inside.

"Let's make a move, Earl," Triton said, as she half-smiled at me.

We promptly crossed the prison yard, heading toward the exit gates.

"This is your big day, Earl. A return to the world out there," she said, as we walked along a bitumen path. She pointed to the exit gates and sighed, "I saw many prisoners pass through those gates. Some returned. A big mistake. Don't ever come back, Earl."

I nodded. We continued walking.

"Hey, Zed!" a booming voice called from nowhere.

I turned around. To my surprise, Rand approached me. Triton grimaced.

"Hey, Zed!" Rand called, waving a couple of sheet of paper in the air. "I got something for ya. It's ma story in ma words," she said excitedly, with a broad grin on her face. "I want to share it with ya before ya go!"

I was dumbfounded. She was the last person I expected to see.

"Your story?" I asked, as she approached.

"A nice touch," Triton said sarcastically. She took the papers.

She scrutinised them, and shook her head in disbelief. Then she passed them to me.

"Yes, Zed," Rand enthused. "After all, I did threaten ya. And if anyone gets to know ma real story, it has to be you. Youz the author," she smiled, revealing a gold tooth. It was the first time I had seen her smile. She was almost pretty.

"Nice tooth," I said.

"Yeh, ma bro punched ma good one out when we woz kids back home. We woz just messin' round, ya know, just havin' fun. Both drunk as skunks. Been all day at a party. And he woz telling a story, and he punched his fist in the air. Well, it caught ma face. Can you believe that? And I said, 'Man, you gotta get me a new, gold tooth!' So years later, he did. How good is that?"

"Stand back, Lourdes," Triton insisted, when Rand got too close to a yellow line painted on the ground, just near the exit gate. "You know you can't cross that line," she said sternly, pointing to the line.

Suddenly, I felt a surge of compassion for Rand. I almost cried.

"Step back." Triton insisted. "Talk to Earl from over there."

Triton pointed to a spot a metre away. I stepped closer to Rand. I was all ears.

"Rand, this is great," I said as I flicked through the pages.

"I trust ya," she enthused. "You'll spruik it up with ya magical words."

"This is so fantastic," I said, feeling the adrenaline surge. "Thanks heaps."

"It's got warts and all, Zed," Rand enthused. Her thick dreadlocks flapped across her dark face. "That's what ya like. I wrote it in my creative writing classes. The teacher fixed up the grammar for me. Not too much. It's my words."

"I'm sure it's wonderful," I replied.

"Ya know that I couldna be ya friend in there," Rand apologised. She turned toward the prison building. "It's the other women. I have a reputation. Ya understand?"

"Yes," I agreed.

"A bad one at that," Triton added.

"Well, Zed understands. Don't ya?" Rand said. She reached out to shake my hand.

"I sure do, Rand. I sure do." I firmly shook her hand and promised, "I will post you a copy of my book when it's finished. There will be a special mention of you in it; you know, when I thank people who helped me. You do understand that I can't use your real name in the story?"

"That's ok," she said softly. "I'll know it's me."

72

Rand's Story

Fortunately, the media didn't get wind of my release. Neither had I told my mother that I was getting out. She'd been very ill and I didn't want to further stress her. Besides, she'd never bothered to visit me in prison, so why should she start now? I would see her in good time. My time.

As I sat in the back seat of the cruising, yellow taxi that headed toward Melbourne's CBD, I eagerly read Rand's story. It went such:

'If you are reading this, I am dead. My name is Rand Viola Lourdes. I was killed by my enemies. Or maybe I just topped myself off in one of my black moods. I don't know exactly how old I will be when they find my body. But I am 25 as I write down my last thoughts.

My life was not easy. Neither of my parents liked me. And I didn't like them back. They never divorced. Because of their strong religious beliefs, they always said that divorce was a sin. They just hated each other and got into heaps of shit fights. You know, bottle throwing and hair pulling. Just the regular stuff fighters do. And a bit of punching and slapping added.

My brother, Bourke, was older by nine months. Both of us were always right in the middle of it all. Fights and more fights. Smashed dishes and broken promises.

As far as Bourke went, he was also a real pain in the butt at times. Although he started smoking when he was ten, he was six foot five inches by the age of thirteen. And he had huge feet. His mates in New Zealand liked him a lot. Well, kind of. He could have been a great basket baller, if only he didn't get in with the wrong crowd and do drugs.

At home, Bourke and I used to fight a lot about nothing and everything. He ran away when he was barely fifteen. The police found him hanging out with some drug dealers under the local bridge, and put him in a foster home somewhere in New Zealand. He broke my front tooth before he went. Just mucking around. We were both drunk when it happened. He always liked to swing his arms around when he told stories. And one of his big hands whacked my mouth.

"Ouch! Shit!" I yelled as the blood spurted from my mouth. "Ya'll pay for this."

I made him promise to buy me a gold tooth to replace the one he knocked out. One day he sent me the money to get a new tooth. I think he sold drugs to get it. That is the only way that someone like him could ever get that sort of money. At least, he did the right thing by me. I can't say that I ever missed him when he ran away. And I never bothered to track him down. Like me, he probably ended up in prison or dead through a drug overdose.

I had no friends when I was growing up in New Zealand. And my nose, which is abnormally large, was the first thing people noticed about me. Rednecks at school beat me up because of it. They didn't care that I was clever in mathematics and science. And I even won a scholarship. I never saw the money. My mother spent it on her bingo nights in the local scout hall. Lucky I kept Bourke's money to buy a tooth when I left home.

I hated everyone at school, except for Maroky Tiki. She sat with me in some of my classes in year seven. She had the whitest skin with freckles. Her streaky-blonde hair reminded me of beautiful, soft feathers, and her green eyes shone like opals. She was as clever as they come. And I think she was the first person I ever fell in love with, although she hardly spoke to me. That was better than the others who called me names about my nose, or beat me up.

In year nine she started dating Aaron Curseri, one of the boys who beat me up. I was shattered when I found out. Then one of Bourke's old friends, Jack Jackson, gave me heroin to make me feel happy. He organised for me to have sex with tourists to pay for it. Because I was tall, I looked a lot older than my age. I didn't like the sex. Just jigga jigga. Slam-bang.

But I needed my heroin fixes. And Jackson got plenty of customers for me. One day I casually asked him where Bourke was. Jackson said that he had no clue. And neither did my parents. But I think they all lied. But it didn't really matter cause I had the heroin to keep me company.

Heroin was my best friend, at first. You know, all the pain went away. I felt warm and fuzzy. Total bliss. And then I realised I could not cope without my mate. I needed more and more heroin. If I didn't get my fix, it felt like someone was cutting my veins open. The pain was so bad. But it was a good pain 'cause it took my mind off Maroky. I lost count of how many men I had sex with. The heroin made me immune to their dirty hands that groped me. Heroin took away my pride.

And then it took my sanity.

It was a dirty, evil killer that no one sees coming. It's a killer coming up from behind. It's like a killer wolf waiting in the dark places in your mind, just waiting for you to make one wrong move;

maybe your last. Your last fix. And then it pounces. It gets you when you're weak and broken. And that's how I was when I went down the beach during summer and saw Maroky with Aaron. I just fell to pieces. Then I hid under the pier, and injected too much heroin. I didn't care. I just wanted to block out everything. I couldn't stand the pain of seeing Maroky with that loser. I really wanted to die.

Days later when I woke up in the Auckland hospital, I was disappointed that I still had to breathe. I had no reason to live. It was all just shit until Maroky visited me in my ward with a bunch of pink roses. She held my hand and said that she dumped Aaron, and wanted to be with me. I believed her.

I had a wonderful week with her when I got out of hospital. It was the best week of my whole life. She was so kind and she had the softest lips. At the end of the week she asked me to meet her down the beach, just under the pier where I used to inject.

"Close your eyes," she said when we stood on the damp sand beneath the rickety pier. "Count to ten, and I will give you the best surprise of your life."

I counted to ten. And when I opened my eyes, she was standing there with Aaron and his cronies. They had chains in their hands and ugly sneers on their tattooed faces. I felt sick. I glanced at Maroky who was smiling at me. Not a real smile. But a warped, twisted mouth filled with hatred.

And then she winked at Aaron, and they all started beating me. Someone kicked me in the ribs when I fell on the sand.

"Ya dirty dike!" they called, as they kept kicking me.

And then I passed out.

I don't know how long I was unconscious. I lost track of time. When I woke up, the tide was in. My khaki pants and t-shirt were soaked with sea water. I was stinging all over, and could hardly open my swollen eyes.

"It's all your fault!" my mother screamed at me when I staggered home and climbed into bed. "Ya should never have messed around with that girl. And I know about ya prostituting ya'self. God will punish you." Her face was puffed with rage. I thought the blood vessels in her neck would pop with all her yelling.

"Ya bloody disgraced ya whole family with ya heroin," she continued, spitting her words at me. "I know all about it! I bloody know! I don't want ya anymore! You and Bourke are nothin' but trouble. I'm glad he left."

I pulled my blanket over my head, and decided to never trust another soul. I would keep taking heroin till it killed me, or until a miracle happened and I came clean. Either way I didn't care.

But now I am dead. And it is either an overdose that took my life, or else I fell for the wrong person again. Please place a rose on my gravestone. Not a pink one. I am sincerely yours, Rand Lourdes.'

I wiped tears from my eyes as I placed her story in my shoulder bag.

"Are you ok?" the concerned taxi driver asked.

"Yes, thanks, driver," I murmured. "Please just get me to Collins Street. I want to go shopping for some fashionable clothes. That's all I want."

73

Free Again

I spent over an hour shopping in Collins Street. I finally decided on a blue, pleated-belted shirt dress and black stiletto heels. It felt so good to be dressed up. So good to be free again. No rules. No guards. Simply splendid.

I appreciated my first day of freedom. I watched the city folk bustling about the city streets, pressing against me in their haste to meet their destiny; rubbing shoulders with me as they rushed to catch trams and trains.

I felt like an unsupported flagpole, tossed to and fro by the reckless wind as it waved its white flag. I seemed to have no resistance against the hurl and burl of modern living. Feeling edgy, I tentatively stood outside Myers Department Store and studied my tall and still-elegant reflection in the shop window. People once said that I was stunning, beautiful. Was that still true at forty seven years of age? I knew I was starting to show my age. My only consolation was that I felt empowered by all my experiences. And I was eager to write this book.

Myers simulated a Roman Empire with all roads leading to it. People pushed past me in their haste to snare another win in the Myers bargain basement. All the while I studied my reflection in the wide shop window. I despised the grey flecks in my hair.

Wanting to improve my image, I promptly entered a hairdressing salon in an arcade directly across the street. I would rid myself of my greyness. I would take control. I would go blonde, like Marilyn Monroe. Don't blondes have more fun?

Although I was smartly dressed in designer clothes, my eyes had an alien hollowness about them.

"I want a trim, please," I said to the neatly dressed, young hairdresser. "And can you make me a sexy blonde while you're at it? I want to look like Marilyn Munro."

She laughed. "For sure."

I sat before a brightly-lit salon mirror. I studied the middle-aged woman who was now me.

The sweet hairdresser smiled. "I have the latest colour in. It's called Harvest Blonde. Marilyn style."

"Will it make me look young and beautiful?" I teased her.

"You are already beautiful," she assured. "And it will make your hair a lovely blonde colour. I will trim around the edges too. You know, just tidy it up a bit. Maybe take off a couple of inches."

"Sounds great," I said with a smile. "I definitely want to be trimmed around the edges."

Two hours later, a transformation had occurred. I admired my reflection in the huge salon mirror.

"You look lovely," the hairdresser insisted. "Are you going somewhere special?"

"Not sure," was my reply. I took a credit card out of my purse.

She did not need to know the details of my life. She did not need to know why I didn't bounce out of her salon with my glossy, blonde hair in tow. She did not need to know my sordid regrets. I still felt ugly, despite my make-over. But I could not tell her.

74

The Penthouse

After leaving the salon, I booked into the penthouse of The Octagon Motel in Prahran, Melbourne. It suited me for a short stay. I knew I couldn't permanently live in Melbourne again, because I needed to escape the city of my perfect crime. Melbourne held too many triggers and bad memories for me.

Also, living with my estranged mother in Armadale was totally out of the question. Her frosty stare would make my blood freeze over. And neither could I live in Sydney because too many people knew me there. So I decided to take my time before buying a new home; preferably one in New South Wales.

Please note that after Carl died, I had given up on ever playing 'happy families'. At the end of the day, I hoped to find some interesting stories within the prison walls. Mostly, I had a firm resolution to find a happy end to my own story. And that was all that really mattered.

Yes, I had everything worked out perfectly; just like George's murder. When I left the jail, I would focus on staying as far away from trouble as possible. I would chain myself to my typewriter, if need be. So I don't know why I bothered getting dressed up on my first day of freedom. I had no one to please. And I had no intention of going to anymore parties. I was finished with that scene.

Wearing sunglasses and sporting my new hairstyle, I enjoyed shopping in Chapel Street. I felt safe. I was lost in the crowd of shoppers. Thoughts of Fairlea and handsome Trent Oliver were pushed to the back of my mind. But we all know that fate is fickle. It didn't matter how many plans I made, destiny would run its course.

Then quite by accident, I bumped into Trent in the middle of Chapel Street. What a surprise. Call it the gods or fate. Out of uniform he looked as handsome as ever. The rugged jeans and t-shirt look suited him. The shower room chemistry was still there.

"Kellie Earl," he smiled. "What a pleasant surprise."

"You too, Trent." I was taken aback. "I thought I could hide behind these sunglasses," I said, as I removed them.

He moved closer. "Kellie, I'd know that beautiful face anywhere. You look stunning without glasses."

"Sunnies are just part and parcel of everything," I said. "Gotta keep the press at bay." I replaced my sunglasses on my nose. "Now I can hide in full view."

"This is rather awkward," he continued, "I mean, standing in the street. Hidden in full view."

He smiled. He sensed that I needed much more than a chat and a handshake.

"I've got the penthouse in The Octagon Motel, if you care to join me," I said boldly. "Plenty of champagne."

"Why not break all the rules?" he teased. He took my hand.

Needless to say, we soon became two consenting adults in my penthouse. Together we would shake off the past ghosts of Fairlea. Love was in the air. Kisses, cuddles and romance abounded. He was everything I imagined and much more.

My life was in fast motion. Trent and I compressed our 'missed prison opportunities' into two glorious weeks. We enjoyed fine wine and dining at my expense. Midst pink champagne and black, silk sheets, we shared many deep and meaningful secrets. His past was just as complicated as mine. He had six children. Three to each of his ex-wives.

But I didn't care how many wives or children he had, for I had lots of money. I would buy a big house in New South Wales with ample rooms for all of us. We would become one big, happy family; the family I never had.

Trent informed me that he was quite an author in his own right. He told me that after completing a Law Degree at Melbourne University, he got bored with life and travelled around Europe. During this time, he did a bit of freelance writing. Then feeling homesick, he returned to Australia. He'd always wanted to work in the prison system, and had high aspirations of being the CEO of Fairlea one day.

We laughed as we reminisced about our time in Fairlea and our chance meeting. I told him that I had a massive crush on him. It all began in the shower. He smiled. He'd heard it all before from countless other 'love starved' women. But hearing it again was good for his ego.

As he slept beside me in my king size motel bed, I studied his perfect face. His breathing was a sweet lull. I closed my eyes and remembered how we first met. When our eyes and souls first locked in Fairlea Prison, it was like a rainbow breaking through a cloudy sky; or a welcomed ray of light showing a lost soul the way home. Both of us were smitten with each other from that instant.

I quickly forgot the red marks on my neck where Tanya had grabbed me. Now as Trent and I lay together, I forgot the fears and tears of life on the inside. Since I had no criminal record, it was perfectly ok for the two of us to liaise. At least, that's what Trent told me.

As I gazed into his alluring eyes, my surroundings became insignificant. I imagined us being in a regal castle. He was my knight in shiny armour. He had taken me away from my cold reality, and transported me to that ethereal place where only lovers go.

He became balm that healed all the hurt within my soul. Midst laughter and cuddles, spa bath and champagne bubbles in the penthouse, we plotted a movie script about a jailbird and her warder lover. It seemed like a winner. He was a winner.

Then one morning while he was having a shower, I dashed out to the nearby shops to buy some sexy lingerie. He told me that he preferred French lace. But when I returned, he had gone. There was no note. No hint that anything was wrong. So where was my Trent?

I felt numb with disbelief. "Trent, where are you hiding?" I called with a quivering voice.

Like a love sick fool, I looked for him in the cupboards. Empty. Nothing.

"Trent, this is not funny. Come out."

I checked under the bed. Not there either. I prayed that he was playing a practical joke. In desperation, I phoned the reception desk. The chirpy receptionist said that Trent left the building, not long after I went out shopping.

I nervously replaced the phone receiver. Tears filled my eyes. I felt like such a fool. I wondered how long he'd been thinking of dumping me? Was it a spur of the minute thing? Oh boy, was I angry. I was so bloody angry. I couldn't believe that he had left; and that I meant nothing to him.

Nothing.

I sat on the bed and cried. It hurt so much. He had said that he loved me. And I believed it. How could he fool me? Me? I was smart. I'd read all the prison textbooks on psychology and theology. And

I'm the one who writes the clever stories about abandoned women. I'm the one who makes my readers want to tear the heart out of the rogues in my novels. I know how rogues operate. I know all the signs of betrayal. I am omniscient. And yet I'd been taken for a fool.

I threw my new French lingerie in the bin. I should never have bought it.

C'est la guerre.

75

Ransacked

After being unceremoniously dumped by Trent, I spent many nights alone in the penthouse. I drowned my sorrows with the finest wine. I relived our conversations, over and over. I tried to pinpoint the exact moment when he decided to jump ship. I recalled that he had offered to help me sell my harbourside home, and live with me in New South Wales. I promised to pay for the production of our movie. "Great idea," he said. And then he made passionate love to me. He seemed forever grateful for my patronage.

I promised him many things. He seemed to want all of them. He promised to love me. I believed him. We laughed and giggled like teenagers as we drank the finest wine. We planned our future together. We hoped for an eternity. He was my salvation.

But he left without a word. And I could only wonder if I could have done anything differently. For a while I felt so hurt. I blamed myself. I doubted myself. And then I became angry. I wanted to shout at him and tell the world of his betrayal. He reminded me of the emotional looters who came and went in our Port Melbourne home; only there for a season and a good time with Jana. Now I knew how my mother had felt when love slipped through her fingers; when her lovers abandoned her after they'd satisfied their urges. They were all losers and users.

But I'd foolishly thought Trent was different. He wasn't a loser; and definitely not a user. I'd seen the kind way he protected the prisoners. Sometimes, he put in extra shifts just to help get the system running smoothly. He'd been the first one to help me if I were threatened by Rand and her gang. I trusted him. He'd said all the right words; till now.

The knight errant stole the princess's heart.
That wandering rogue with medieval poise,
Seized her treasure of teardrop pearls and sapphire emotions,
That she'd concealed in her jewelled box of passion.
Ransacked, plundered.
Laid barren in a sandy world of experience.
Now left with only her dewdrops of wistfulness,
To comfort her winnowing dreams.
Tramp, tramp.
She hears the marching soldiers outside the castle wall.
Tramp, tramp.
They vainly seek her evasive, youthful dreams,
That are cruelly scattered by time's cold wind.
The princess cries into her gold chalice.
She wrings her tears from her satin sheets.
She places her pretty head on her feather pillow of regret.
She frets. She cries alone. She sighs and moans.
Tramp, tramp.
The soldiers march along her mind wall,
Protecting her from the enemy without,
But not the enemy within.
Her treasure chest is empty.

76

Selling Up

I promptly sold my lavish Sydney home, and bought my ideal apartment in The Rocks. I'd finally found my niche. Now I could truly settle and tie off all the loose ends in my life. I could find the happy end that had eluded me.

I was fascinated by The Rocks. I always made time to casually stroll the streets, or nestle in a café; with a cappuccino in one hand and a pen and paper in the other. The Rocks is a place full of history. Many of the former buildings in this trendy tourist area were made of sandstone. This is how the area derived its name.

Like nearby Sydney, this area was once a penal colony. Sordid stories about convicts, soldiers, sailors, prostitutes and street gangs abound. These desperate people were shipped from their overcrowded London streets and jails to distant Australia. Like kids dodging *cat poo* in sandpits, on their journey across the sea they battled the rats and the thugs. They all fought for a space in the overcrowded, leaky boats. Heaven forbid.

Now I feel content as I head toward my twilight years, knowing that I acquired my inherent portion of wisdom. Perhaps it will be enough to see me through to the very end. Indeed, I will go to the grave wiser than before I began this journey. And I hope you have also been enlightened as I shared my story.

Yet, I am keenly observant of my surroundings. I know that the world is constantly changing, just as Heraclitus said. Everything comes and goes. Nothing is permanent. The beautiful countryside of Australia is occasionally devoured by bush fires or floods. Bankruptcy and corruption force institutions to open and close. Empires rise and fall. Politicians come and go. Attitudes evolve and sometimes regress. But who decides what progress is? And who decides the fibre of the sandpit, and who should dwell therein?

Although I feel wiser for what I endured in the sandpit, I know that new experiences await me. Nothing is static. Just when you think you know it all, you learn something new. And I've heard that fifty is the new forty.

As I sit at my desk, with a gold pen in my manicured hand, I gaze through the opened window of my New York style penthouse. The hardwood Venetian blinds proffer shade from the sweltering 33 degrees heat. After all, it is just a typical Australian summer day.

You may ask, 'Why am I attracted to the Rocks, a settlement established by convict blood?'

Don't forget, dear Reader, that I am also a former prisoner of the State. Obviously, this experience shaped my opinions on where I would ultimately live. We all know the adage of *water finding its own level*. I guess I felt at home as I lived amongst the history of displaced convicts; people like me who wanted to belong. I could almost feel their spirits encouraging me to write this book.

77

Competing Tides

Today I am drawn to moral conundrums, rather than 'the easy life of the nouveau riche'. I draw inspiration from flawed characters, like myself, people who can't quite find their place in society. Therefore, they endure a frustrated life of disappointments and angry outbursts. Nothing goes according to plan. As a politician once said, "Life isn't meant to be easy."

Dear Reader, now when I am alone in my luxurious apartment; when I take an honest look at my reflection in my French mirror, I see fine lines around my eyes. They indicate my frailty. My once beautiful face is showing signs of ageing. And my heart and spirit are also wilting like a fading rose. Said plainly, I am getting old. But not too old.

My books are still full of passion and contradictions. I notice that sometimes an aura of love and harmony soothes my literary world. As I write, I can almost forget my pain. But I never lose touch with the lost child, the bleating lamb, the drowning kitten, or the shackled mongrel dog alone in a cave. The shadow man is always lurking in the recesses of my mind.

To compensate, I splash my manuscripts with descriptions of soaring butterflies. They rise in the sky like a fleet of multi-coloured air balloons. Their images are reflected in the pristine lake in a river of colour. My readers are then taken to a happy place.

At other times, like competing tides that are stirred by the bad moon rising in the night sky, a fury of hatred spews within my soul. It is bile that fills my ink cartridge and implodes in my novels. Nothing can remove the indelible angst that consumes my protagonists. Ironically, this also appeals to my readers. They feel the pain of my characters. They follow their turbulent journey. Then they rejoice when they find closure and retribution. Yes, we all need a happy end to a story. I can only wonder if this is a literary device, or a moral obligation on my part.

Overall, my readers have evolved. They no longer want to read about fairy floss romances in palaces. Instead, they want the proven and tried reality of flawed people who battle their innermost *dramas of conscience*; people just like me. They thrive on tragedies. They want to get inside the minds of criminals who find themselves in crowded prison cells. And then they want to follow them on their tumultuous journey of recovery, as they find the true meaning of love and hate; even if it doesn't come till the last page.

As I sit at my desk, I realise that my gold pen is an extension of my inner self. Perhaps it is my true self. Sometimes, I insert myself in the confounding plots that my readers love. For example, they might read about an author who falls foul of the law and ends up in jail. Therefore, you might consider that I am a bit like Alfred Hitchcock making his cameo appearances.

As you scan the pages of my recent novels, and linger on my poetic words that are dipped in the blood of experience, your heart is stirred. Perhaps it is a coming of age. After all, how can one fully appreciate happiness, love and freedom, if they never experience grief and sheer terror? The world is not always a pleasant blue and green hue. Sometimes, black moods and red blood splatter across the landscape. Sometimes, air balloons explode.

You see, dear Reader, I was sent to prison because I killed my wicked stepfather. Indeed, his punishment and then mine, was long overdue. But you may argue that I had already been punished because I was a victim of his abuse. He mercilessly raped and battered my naïve spirit, like a stalwart fish monger gutting his daily catch. Disgraceful!

Today as a woman of incredible wealth and stoic discretion, I should be happy. However, I am not. Proving that George killed my brother is still my goal in life. I want to shout this out to all, "George is a murderer! He killed my brother!"

In my quiet moments, I relive every experience; trying to fit all the pieces together. I look for the clues that will confirm my suspicions.

But George is dead and I can't touch him. Because I live in New South Wales, I am unable to spit on his grave as often as I would like. All I have to compensate me is my house in Port Melbourne. It always has good tenants, and its value is ever increasing. It is my trophy. A constant reminder of how I outsmarted the beast.

78

Royal Blood

At times, I wonder if I should have remained silent about my crime? Was confession foolish? After all, no one suspected that I murdered George. There seemed to be no motive for murder. I had always played the role of the perfect step-daughter. And the police blamed the faulty wires in the old house he was renovating. It was simply a fatal accident.

So why did I confess to his murder? Why? Why did I trade-in my privileged life in a Sydney mansion where I wrote intriguing novels, for a life in a dank prison cell? Why, oh why?

I silently screamed when I showered with battle-weary women at Fairlea. I felt dehumanised. Was I one of them, after all?

Apart from tattoos, we all look the same when we are naked. So was I just as evil as them? Or are there degrees of debauchery? Are prisoners simply the walking wounded; unified in our personification of childhood abuse? We had no choice. No love. Was love the only thing that was missing in our lives?

When my prison cell door clanked shut, the only freedom I had was in my boundless imagination. Fortunately, Lucinda kept me company with her endless banter. Sometimes, she reminded me of the privileged life I left behind.

"How many parties did you go to in Toorak?" she once asked, from her bunk above mine.

"Oh, too many. Probably as many as the houses you robbed," I replied.

We laughed.

And then she looked down at me from her bunk and cheekily asked, "How many diamond rings did you own?" Her wide, gold-and-brown eyes earnestly gazed at me.

"Too many. You never got your pretty, little hands on them, thank God. They were all safe and secure."

"Mmm," she sighed. "I cracked many safes with my pretty, little hands. I had a cache of diamonds and rubies. Occasionally, I wore costume jewellery. None of those highfalutin snobs knew the difference between my two dollar fakes and genuine show-stoppers. It didn't matter. I figured it was about how you hold yourself. If you strut into the party like a movie star, no one guesses that you're wearing op-shop trinkets."

We both heartily laughed.

"After all," she continued, as she lay back on her bunk, "I reckon I was more royal that the whole lot of them snobs. None of them could boast about being the descendant of a princess. What do you think?"

"Yes, you're right," I agreed, as I turned over in my bunk to face the wall.

"I reckon I self-actualised," she teased. "Top of the pyramid." With that, I burst out laughing. "And I was the 'fifth column' in all those high society parties," she continued. "I was the intruder. And you know what?"

"What?"

"I'd love to write a book and *pumpify* those stuck-up bitches. And the politicians. All glitz and show, and no substance. Just a group of party baubles hanging round a goose's neck."

"Have you been reading my notes?" I asked. I sat upright. She had piqued my interest.

"I might have," she teased. "I mean, aren't I a *tabula rasa;* a blank sheet that needs to be filled in and enlightened by you?"

"Oh, Lucy you are so funny."

"But it's true. That's what you think of us prisoners. We never got our basic needs met at the bottom of Maslow's Pyramid. We were once mini *tabula rasas* running around. Just a pack of bare-bummed-babies-blank sheets till our families stuffed us up, good and proper. They filled us in with a heap of bad memories."

"That's quite a spin on what I wrote," I said, amazed by her explanation. I stretched out on my bed, and placed my hands under my head. "Basically, you are right. In so many words, that's pretty-much what they said."

"You see, Zed. I am not just a pretty face," she boasted. "Remember that I am royalty."

With that, she hung over the edge of her bunk. I turned to face her. She smiled at me. Her straight teeth were pearly white against her chocolate skin.

"I'm now a full-fledged Nihilist, thanks to you," she proclaimed, as she flicked her ash-blonde hair off her dainty face. "Yes, I am. There is no such thing as truth. Not in religion or society's rules. The only truth is the one I create."

"Wow, you have been taking it all in, Lucy. I am impressed. Maybe you should run some master classes in philosophy and theology."

"Huh," she laughed, as she placed her head on her pillow. "I think I have no logos."

"Now that's one for the books," I stirred.

"Yep. I can't tell the difference between good and evil. Isn't that what old Aristotle said?"

"Well, yes."

"And Heraclitus said I can't get all my opposite impulses together. And that's what's wrong with Rand and her mob too. They are all at war with themselves. No attunement for those ladies! Now how about that?"

"Yes," I agreed. "That's one way of looking at it."

"That's how you look at it," she added. "I read your notes."

"Yes, you did." I placed my head on my pillow. She had impressed me.

"And like you said," she continued, "some of us just don't want peace; like that Tanya Drinkwater bitch. I tell ya what, I reckon she drank much more than water in her time. She is just so repulsive. Makes my skin crawl. She and Rand are like two spiders in the corner of the room; always waiting to pounce. God, I hate this place. I really do."

"Hey, come on, buddy. You'll be out of here soon. Remember that I am going to get a lawyer to get you out. You don't belong here. You are too classy."

"Classy," she repeated. I know she was smiling.

"You also have all the makings of a great philosopher," I stirred. "You know much more than you let on. Must be all that royal blood in your veins."

"Royal. Yes," she agreed. "And you have such high ideals. It's all those philosophy books you stick your head in. And you have high hopes for me. But I think I'll just stick to becoming a famous movie star. Just stick to the script. Read the lines, not between them. And I can't wait to go to those auditions with you. I'll strut down the catwalk, and smile at the cameras. Imagine me in a sauna with James Bond, or what about in Psycho's shower? Dadadadada," she hummed. Her happiness lifted my spirits.

79

Socrates

Now as I sit in my cosy study, I know that Lucinda is a star in the sky. I see her twinkling at night when I gaze out of my wide windows. Sometimes, I blow her a kiss. I know she is no longer trapped inside her prison cell.

In hindsight, would Janaki have done things differently, had she known that her great-great granddaughter's life would end in such a tragedy? Would she have married the prince she detested, just to ensure a life of wealth for her descendants? Again, this is something we will never know.

And then I remember reading about Socrates being imprisoned before his death. The last extant words of him to his friend, Crito, were, 'Crito, we owe a rooster to Asclepius. Please, don't forget to pay the debt.'

Crito wanted Socrates to flee prison. Instead, Socrates walked around his prison cell. Instead of escaping, he waited till the poison the guards gave him numbed his legs and then his heart. But why did Socrates talk about a rooster, in his last breath? Philosophers note that Asclepius was the Greek god for curing illness. Therefore, they believe that Socrates was saying that death is the cure. It is the only way that individuals gain freedom for their soul, from their body.

Ironically, Socrates spent his entire life searching for a universal definition for moral virtues, only to face an immoral death. But did he find freedom in that death? And was Lucinda finally free? Sadly, only the dead can answer that question.

Oh dear God, I was too late to save Lucinda. Please forgive me. She could have been a beautiful movie star, if only. And now I am crying. Oh how, I miss the nervous energy and enthusiasm of my little cellmate. I hope she is free from her compulsions that caused her downfall. I hope she clasps happiness in the sparkling stars as she gazes into the moonlight. Oh, dear God, I hope so.

I remember our funny, quippy chats; especially the one where she found my notes about the philosophers and psychology. With her raw insights, she put such an interesting spin on things. She simplified the complicated. And she knew how to pumpify the philosophers.

Her death was such a tragedy. And I remember her brief and simple funeral. In the quaint prison chapel, we held a small memorial service for Lucinda Ixia Phymms. Since she was a self-confessed nihilist, we kept things to a minimum. Minimum tears. Minimum sentiments. Just what a nihilist would expect.

Her death proved painful for me; too terrible to comprehend. Although another woman promptly filled Lucinda's bunk, I didn't want to talk to her. I didn't want to get too close. I wanted to hold on to the memories of the wonderful friend I'd lost.

80

Hindsight

C'est la guerre. One should accept misfortune without being too upset by it.

Therefore, if my life is meant to be tragic, should I simply roll with the punches and take it on the chin? The Bible says that *I should turn the other cheek.* Is that true? Should I have given George a free pass, as the police had done? Would that have given me the peace that I desired?

As mentioned, are we born into the miserable role we must fulfil? We have no choice. Regardless of which family I was born into, was I destined to be a murderess? Is predestination true? Accordingly, should I simply say that I am doomed or cursed, and *just get over it. Just let George take what he wills and forgive him?*

Or do the gods sit up there discussing the future of mere earthlings? Is that how it all works? Although the fictional Oedipus Rex tried to flee the misfortunes that were predicted by the gods, he ran right into them. As prophesied, he married his mother, regardless of which path he chose. After all, that's what the gods foretold. Therefore, he shouldn't have been too surprised.

Contrary to this, should one seek *kudos* or public praise; simply turn away from dabbling by the gods and the possibility of misfortune?

Should we expect the best and go for it; seek to fulfil a goal, and get a pat on the back? Is that a better attitude to life's quagmire? Would this approach empower us? Is it true that our attitude can have a bearing on the type of life we lead?

At the end of the day, do we control our destiny? Or is it really in the hands of the gods? And who do we blame when things go wrong? If we believe that the gods control our destiny, then they are to blame when things go belly up. If man is in control of his fate, then misfortune falls entirely at his feet. He brought it upon himself.

Ultimately, what will be will be, whether it's gods or fate, destiny or self. So what does that tell us about conscience and perfection? Is our conscience predestined? Are some meant to be vile whilst others are pure? Why do some of us have a conscience and sense of justice, and others do not? Rogues, like George, Hitler and the mongrels who killed Lucinda, violate fellow human beings, without the slightest guilt pangs? Evil people seek praise and prestige through their evil deeds; like my fellow prisoners bragging about their inflictions on their victims. Is this a flaw in nature's grand design? Is this an inversion of the moral code?

On the tragic day of Lucinda's death, my soul bled as I cradled her lifeless body. I sobbed bitterly as she lay limply in my arms. Her spirit hovered above. I wish I'd arrived earlier to rescue her. I wish I'd uncovered the murder plot and saved her. Oh God, how I wish.

I always suspected Lesley Wando from Lucinda's art classes. But I could never prove it.

Whoever was to blame for her death, be it the gods or fate, it hurt like crazy. And that's the final sting of death. It is so final.

Regardless of how good you are, and how many times you turn the other cheek, evil people might cause you to suffer. Dear Reader, this doesn't seem rational in the grand design of things. Shouldn't humanity share our planet with dignity and nicety? What is the purpose of all this hatred and violence anyway? Why can't we all just get along and sing *Kumbaya*?

So I can only wonder if there is an element of truth in *functionalism*, where everything has a function or purpose in society? One could certainly argue that if we did not have *evil*, then there would be no such thing as *good*. There would be no baseline and nothing to compare evil acts against; nothing to balance according to Heraclitus's grand design. And the definition of 'evil and good' is open to public opinion anyway. It is subjective, in the same way that 'the truth' is open to interpretation, as Lucinda so aptly pointed out.

Bless you sweet Lucinda.

PART FOUR

81

The Rocks

Today as a popular author with the *nom de plume* of *B.M. Rising*, I freely move through The Rocks' bustling streets. As mentioned, using this name reminds me of Billy's favourite song, 'Bad Moon Rising'. I still visualise Billy living in his own world. He sat in his bedroom and painted glorious pictures whilst listening to the music of Creedence Clearwater Revival. He wore headphones to block the hideous sound of George's irritating voice. Nowadays, playing *Bad Moon Rising* whilst I write helps me to reconnect with my past; to remember Billy.

However, the fictional world I now write about readily becomes my real world. It is devoid of George and his wicked ways. My imagination stirs me in the middle of the night, and draws me to my typewriter; like a chocoholic seeking comfort food; or a child seeking his favourite toy.

It is an unrelenting unreality that evolves from my fanciful words. But it is my unreality; a place where I have total control. I am logos. I am the prologue and epilogue, and all the cliff hangers in-between.

In my novels, my decision is absolute. I can be both omnipresent and omniscience in my tangled web of intrigue. I am the sole driving force behind my best sellers. I see and know all. I am an unrivalled time traveller. I am everywhere in every century. I penetrate all my characters' thoughts and feelings. I am their past, present and future.

My readers can also go anywhere with me. They can understand things that the real world does not afford them. They can see the world through the eyes of the underdog: the bird with the broken wing, or the puppy that no one wants. Or even the philosopher who struggles to join the dots in life's grand puzzle.

But I can't always hide behind my typewriter. So when I am out and about, strolling along the cobbled laneways of The Rocks, visiting one of the numerous weekend craft stalls, the Museum of Contemporary Art or one of the historic pubs, I usually wear sunglasses and simple attire to avoid attention from an ogling public. And my shoulder-length hair is still blonde.

Overall, I appear nondescript and inconsequential. I am not consumed by the world that evolves about me. I observe the shoppers and tourists who amorously chatter over cappuccinos in cafes. They compare their baubles that they purchased from the numerous craft stalls. They are energised by their tangible world.

But my inner world resembles an alien creature that is consuming me in metaphors and descriptive passages. It seems that adjectives and images surge through my veins, in their quest to fill the blank pages that spew from my typewriter. They protect me from harm. They catapult me to the mountain-top; to that special place that each person needs; a place that provides shelter from life's storms, and offers sanity in a crazy world.

82

Rub A Dub

Before Fairlea, I published countless books and spoke at numerous book launches. But still, this question defied me: when one becomes a vigilante and takes revenge on a murderer, an eye for an eye, are both evil? Am I now as evil as George? Are both of us reduced to the lowest common denominator? This question is time specific because the definition of *evil* changes during war times. When nations war against each other, people act like wild animals that don't know any better. It becomes revenge on a grand scale.

Oceans and skies are filled with weapons of mass destruction, as countries storm into battle. Kill or be killed. Murder is rampant. Blood flows through the streets. Morals change. Therefore, instead of scientists and other brilliant minds focusing on ways to improve man's lot, they invent ways to eradicate each other.

Bombs explode and streets are littered with corpses. The seas froth with innocent blood. Definitions of 'good' and 'evil' shift, as surely as the rise and fall of the sun. During war times, those who kill 'the enemy' are labelled as heroes. Yet, the same act in peacetime is defined as a crime; just like mine was. Had I killed George during war times, I would have received a medal instead of imprisonment and a seared conscience.

Conversely, some still see my act of killing George as righteous anger. However if it is such, then why doesn't it proffer peace for me? Why didn't my inner war end and the church bells ring in unison? Instead of feeling emancipated, I was crippled by sordid images of his baboon body pinning me to my mother's bed. And then in my thwarted mind, I saw him sprawled across the kitchen floor, dead, burnt and charred like a cockroach incinerated with a blow torch. His eyes protruded from his contorted death-mask face. He personified the evil that lingers in my mind shadows. He is always there. Always.

I now realise that being a vigilante, did not release me from these debilitating images. It just put more disturbing thoughts in my mind. When I was in my prison cell, I still saw George's horrid, taunting face. He trailed me into Fairlea. Bad memories rose like a tsunami of fear. His words echoed in my mind when I lay in my prison bunk bed.

'Look at me, Akeila,' he commanded, in the recesses of my mind.

He forced me to look into his jelly eyes that stabbed my soul. His black-death pupils shred my heart. His eyelashes peeled the flesh from my identity, like a razor-Venetian blind. I screamed into the quietness of my mind cave. I was robbed of sleep. My spirit wilted like a flower devoid of water.

Being in jail, surrounded by brick walls and prison guards, did not protect me from my memories. The enemy was within me.

Since some people only believe a partial truth, are there also degrees of sanity? And just as philosophers highlighted the changing definition of truth, are there also changing concepts of sanity? Murder in war time is heroic and sane. Yet, in peace times, the same act is considered as a mental impairment. Oh, spare me from these social inconsistencies.

Sometimes, I wanted to scream in the Fairlea shower block. Life seemed so unfair, confusing and full of blaring contradictions. But as soapy water covered my body, my naked voice warbled in the back of my throat. I still felt contaminated by life's impurities. And nobody cared.

I mechanically spread suds around my body as I stood with other naked women in the prison shower. We all looked innocent and pure. None of us had any defining features. No one wore a 'murderess' or 'grand larceny' label. Therefore, I liked to think of us as a glorious piece of lamé, a piece of material with silver and gold threads woven into it. Yes, that seemed appropriate.

Naked, we were all stripped of our coverings. We were as bare as the day we were born. Pot bellies, bulging guts, bony hips, sagging boobs; all typified our criminal torsos. White skin. Brown skin. Yellow skin. Soft skin. Hardened skin. Scars. Needle tracks along spider vein arms and varicose legs. Tobacco-stained fingers. Blood-stained memories. Tears and fears. Sad and mad.

Shower time was a familiar routine for us. As hot water ran down my face and trickled along my slender body, I knew I had to accept my lot. I was beautiful and regal. However, no one cared about my sanctimonious urge to confess. I was simply a displaced piece of soap in a prison shower.

Rub a dub.

83

Brawn Over Brain

Overall, I consider that my *life journey* can be divided into two parts; the before and after my Fairlea experience. In hindsight, prison was the best remedy for my wayward life. I was verging on self-destruction. Alcohol and party drugs were my poisons of choice. Removing me from the vices that were destroying my soul was the best therapy. I received a second chance and a new start in life.

And once I was in the prison system, I had the resources to sort myself out, so to speak. Having time on my hands, I read and read. I familiarised myself with the classics and works of distant philosophers. I felt at one with their thoughts. How ironic.

In the dank world of criminals, I developed my inner resources. Midst the brutal humdrum of prison life, I took a serious look at who I was. Was I better than my fellow prisoners, or was I simply a snob who thought herself above their antics? In my mind, my inmates were not clever enough to evade the law. But then again, neither was I.

At Fairlea, I wore prison 'garb' and walked around a dusty courtyard with disgruntled fellow prisoners. We all looked the same. We all seemed to harbour antisocial sentiments. Miraculously, I bided my time whilst playing the submissive role of the perfect prisoner. I was cagey. One could say that I grew up within those prison walls, for it gave me something that eluded me in my wealthy social circles.

I formed friendships with the most unlikely people; those I would have never met on the outside. Bonds were formed when we were thrown together in the 'too hard' basket. And I became mentally stronger through my trials. Mind you, I would not have wanted to stay there long term. Eighteen months was long enough for me to benefit.

That said, prison life gave this grub some nourishing leaves. It gave me enough space to crawl along the branch whilst basking in the sun of discontent. It created the environment where the butterfly could emerge.

I gained self-respect, and started seeing myself in a new light. Having my life threatened by prisoners, made me want to hold onto it. Life became valuable. It was no longer a throw away commodity. In my harsh prison environment, I didn't have the time to submerge myself in my fantasy world. I was forced to mingle with others and enter into the prison routine. There were no wild parties, cork popping and pretentious banter. No vices to prop me up.

Instead, I could 'smell the roses'. Although there were no roses in prison, I could smell the wave of the second wind that was invigorating me; preparing me for my return to the outside world. The seeds of hope were planted in my psyche. In a prison of dying souls, I found life.

Like a gallant gladiator riding a spectacular chariot into battle, my thoughts catapulted across the desert plains of my notebook. Adjectives and metaphors flourished like seeds in a parched terrain of paper. I became ready for my return to my mahogany desk and pewter lamp in my home.

In prison, I found the light at the end of the tunnel. And that is what inspired me to write this book.

On release, my novels intensified. Therefore, one could say that my jail time was beneficial because I perfected my craft, therein. I became the diamond polished by the rough stone. My publisher considered that my writing had an added dimension and zest. I had changed from the inside out, and it reflected in my enhanced imagery and sensitive portrayal of humanity.

Now I write about the competing powers of love and hate, and the maelstrom they create. I write about the meaning and lack of meaning in life. I highlight both its delights and inconsistencies. Life is not so simple anymore. Love has hidden obstacles that my protagonists must overcome. They must draw on their inner strengths to achieve their goals. And they always do.

84

Flashbacks

Today my only consolation is knowing that George led a miserable existence. After all, he had to live with himself. When he sipped his short, black coffee in his favourite cafe in Beaconsfield Parade, he remembered the way his mother pandered to the local priest. He remembered her black stockings and dress, and the thick, gold cross she wore around her turkey neck; and the way she made him kiss numerous statues in their local church. He remembered the candles that were eternally alight on their mantelpiece at home. They formed part of a mini shrine for her deceased husband. He was George's namesake.

George Maria Spiatis had to bear that name throughout his miserable life. It was a cross he carried. He tried to find happiness at the racetrack. He tried to don a mask. He smiled when all he felt was contempt and loathing. He saw the love and happiness that Billy and I shared, and he wanted to destroy it. As mentioned, he was the fifth column.

But he could never escape his sordid memories. When he bought his regular short, black coffee in his favourite Greek cafe, his childhood ghost was always there whispering to him; telling him that he was a 'left handed' failure.

He remembered being kept in detention at school, for being left-handed. Whilst some of the pretty boys got special attention, he got extra one-on-one attention for using the wrong hand. Being left handed was considered disgusting. It was a curse. And the Christian Brothers would beat his left handed tendencies out of him.

No one would ever believe what occurred after school hours, inside the classroom he called 'the fortress'. Who would believe the word of a child over that of a revered priest? Thus, under the guise of being moral and upright, the priests had easy access to the young boys.

The only windows in George's classroom were at least 'ten feet above the quadrangle', by the old measure. You needed a ladder to look into the classroom from the outside. This prevented people being able to keep a watchful eye on the priests in the classroom. It also prevented the boys gazing out of the windows during class time. It made them focus on their classwork.

But George knew what would happen to him once the last school bell rang. He knew he would be forced to stay behind with the priest. During detention he was forced to sit at a school desk and write with his right hand. Meanwhile, the priest would fondle George's private parts.

If George dared to pick up a pen with his left hand, he would be instantly whacked with a wooden ruler. It stung like crazy. Young George tried to block-out being molested while he sat at the wooden desk. Instead, he focused on writing perfectly with his right hand; his good hand.

As an adult, when he sat in the seaside cafe, the chubby fingers of his right hand tapped on the table top. He breathed in the sea air. He heard the chirp of the scavenging seagulls.

For a split second, he accidentally picked up his coffee cup with his left hand. He trembled. He recalled the slimy priest fondling him. It sickened him. And then he awkwardly spilled his coffee in his lap. It burned his thighs. But he felt nothing. Nothing. Nothing. Nothing. Just a blank space in the part of his brain that once harboured remorse or regret.

But he still had one hope. He always relished the idea of his mother dying. He knew he would inherit her fortune. It seemed a fair trade off. After all, she had passed on her left-handedness to him. In his warped mind, she had colluded with the priests. She had readily sent him, the handsome altar boy, to his spiritual death at the church camp. There he was raped by the older boys. Because of her, he felt putrid and damaged. It was all her fault. She was to blame for everything that was bad in his life.

Emotionless, he sat beside her bed as she lay dying at home. He watched her gasp and turn blue. He would not call a doctor for help. Instead, he applauded the cycle of life that would soon take this female beast. She was the monster in his head.

He looked at the gold-plated cross above her bedhead. He almost believed that there was a God who delivered justice. She couldn't die fast enough. He hated her. All the while he resisted an urge to place a pillow over her contorted face. He would wait. He would let fate take its course. She would be gone soon. He counted her final minutes. He was grateful when his stubborn mother drew her last breath.

"Goodbye, mother," he whispered, as he pushed her sun-spotted hand away from his. He lightly patted the woollen blanket on her bed, as one consolidating their thoughts. *Please don't ever come back.*

He stood up and smiled. It was time to open a bottle of wine to celebrate. Now George was going to become rich. He was going to be able to gamble in style at the racetrack. Although he was headed for hell, he thought he could buy a piece of heaven.

I always wondered if Mrs Spiatis knew that she had reared a pig such as George? Did she wish that she had shut her legs and never birthed him?

85

Too Easy

But now in my luxurious apartment in The Rocks, I enjoy a slower pace of life in a popular tourist area. I am not as eager to seek out storylines in prison cells. I learnt my lesson. Instead, I let my stories come to me in quiet cafe settings, or even while I'm shopping. It's amazing, the amount of engaging snippets that I hear from the conversations of my accidental friends; strangers who go about their daily activities and think out loud.

Nowadays, I could be likened to someone who goes into a gaming room, watches people gamble away all their money, yet doesn't open their own wallet. That's what I do. I watch people. They fascinate me. It seems safer from a distance.

Dear Reader, this novel is almost finished. No doubt, you are still left with the question: why did I doubt myself? I was the woman who got away with the perfect crime. I was the envied author who seemed to have everything: money, beauty, adoring fans and men. So the riddle begins with me. Therefore, I will further enlighten you on what happens to a wounded child who kills her abuser, and then falls on her own sword.

Please understand that for each day that George lived, I lost a day in the life of my soul. And my hatred bled into my novels. At night when I lay in my bed, hatred bubbled through my veins. It choked the joy out of me. I longed for the day that I could release it and get the ultimate revenge. When all was said and done, that's why I planned George's murder. I was prepared to shoot him; to blast his ugly head off his shoulders; to blast the monster out of my soul.

But things took a turn for the better in George's kitchen. As surely as the sun rises and falls, he created the perfect murder scene. After all, I knew that I could never explain to the police how I accidentally shot George, point blank, in his head.

And then he turned his back to me while he worked at the wall.

"Don't touch the switch," he said. I patiently sat at the breakfast bar. I resolutely sipped my glass of milk.

Exposed wires. Simply brilliant. I leapt out of my seat. With one flick, I fried him like a pig. I watched him scream and writhe as the electricity seared his worthless flesh; as it shook and cindered his useless body.

I wiped my milk moustache with my trembling hand. I smiled as his flabby body lay on their symmetrical floor tiles. I picked up my handbag that had a loaded gun inside it. It was all too easy.

86

Justice For All

As you have read in the course of this novel, some of us have a higher calling than being mere bullies and murderers. We have natural gifts and talents. Some are blessed with a high I.Q. Others might have one or more of the seven types of intelligence. And others have a strong moral compass. Some call it a piece of God that is invested in us: the knowledge of good and evil. I like to call it 'the power of conscience'. As you have seen, we each have a moral code. And I consider myself to be moral. That is my calling. I believe in justice for all; both the living and the departed.

Some may consider me as foolish by confessing. After all, George was an evil man in his own right. However, this need to confess is not evident in everyone, as you saw in the case of my mother and George. Unlike me, they seemed to push their crimes to the back of their mind; to that place in the wilderness where they allow no compassion or remorse to thrive.

Of course, confession does not mean that I am weak or a failure. On the contrary, my publisher tells me how wonderful my work is. I am a successful writer turned criminal, turned author, turned multi-millionaire. In short, I devised a rat-cunning way to survive a system that wanted to break my spirit. I rose above the voices in my head. I rose above any public criticism.

I could argue that killing George was an act of self-preservation. I protected my hold on life itself. But one's soul does not qualify to the same extent as protecting land and nation. We can kill in the name of defending our shores. But killing in the name of protecting oneself in peace times, is a crime. I did not get a medal. And when I confessed to electrocuting him, I was simply called 'insane'.

Now I ask, is it insane to aspire to peace and sanity during peace times? I desperately needed to get George's voice and the cruel images out of my head. That's all I wanted. And who decides what is justified; if it is good or bad to murder? If it is heroic of heinous? From observation, any act of killing another had repercussions. We've all seen the dreadful impact of war on our returned soldiers. Don't forget how war impacted on Patrick Wickham.

Hindsight is wonderful. But as an abused child, my only thoughts were on eradicating George. I thought that once he was gone, my life would return to normal; whatever 'normal' was. After George died, I hoped to recover my lost innocence. Instead, I played the murder scene over and over in my flummoxed mind. I lost my way on destiny's cold trail. Going to jail seemed the logical way to 'tie off' the loose ends in my life.

Wrong. Wrong.

Before confessing, instead of sitting on Humpty Dumpty's wall, I built a strong, protective wall around the real me. My essence was divided between B.M. Rising the author, and Kellie Earl the frightened and confused child. I would not let anyone get close enough to me, to ever see the dark well behind my eyes.

I felt painfully alone.

I had outsmarted George, my mother and the police. I committed the perfect crime. But in my subconscious, I was always seeking punishment for myself. It was as if I were begging my Super Ego to take control of the wicked child called *Id*.

As stated, killing George was too easy. If my life could be considered as a plot, then it reached its climax too soon. There was nowhere for the storyline to go. As every avid reader knows, criminals never get away with crimes. Their punishment is inevitable and almost expected. That's the way a good narrative goes. And that's how I felt my life would play out.

It was only a matter of time before the detectives knocked on my front door to arrest me. That's what social justice is all about. I was merely a player in the game of inevitability. Sooner or later, I would be caught. And I was always plagued by an unrelenting sense of guilt. My conscience got the better of me.

So why did it take me decades to kill George? Why didn't I kill him the first time he raped me? I think you realise that, from an early age, I found a safe haven when I wrote books. It became a means to defer the inevitable. When I withdrew into my bedroom to write, I became the lord and master of my fictional characters. I deleted them, at will. I knew them before they were created; long before they appeared in print. I was no longer an abused child. I was B.M. Rising who lived on the mountain-top. But we all know that pride goes before a fall.

87

Timeline

Throughout this novel, I have taken you on my journey. At times I drew on the logic of philosophers. I tried to apply their ancient theories to modern man's conundrums. In the process, I have shown you much sadness. But don't despair, for the best is yet to come. Being true to the structure of a good novel, this one has a happy end.

Before incarceration, my home was a splendid mansion in Sydney. It was the envy of most with its Persian rugs, hand-crafted designer furniture and Tuscan mirrors. All furniture was original and exquisite. But after my release from Fairlea Women's Prison, I knew I couldn't return to my Sydney mansion. I was like Princess Janaki who fled the wealth of the palace. I needed a fresh start and a new identity.

The intense public interest in my murder trial impacted on me, both physically and emotionally. It was time to move to The Rocks – to obscurity, away from the limelight and media attention.

However, there is some justice in life. All is not forsaken, for I found much pleasure in the later novels I wrote. Nowadays, I find that a 'new suburb and identity' works like a charm.

Keeping a low-profile works best in my interests. There is nothing more conspicuous than a murderess living in your street.

And my former Sydney neighbours knew my story, only too well. They heard the wailing police sirens screaming along their one-way streets, as the gun-toting police came to arrest me. Then they saw the flashing cameras of the paparazzi who tried to take photos of me. My neighbours eagerly read about my ordeal, in the local newspapers. They knew that I confessed to the grisly crime. They also knew that I sought redemption. Indeed, they followed my tumultuous story of the abused child who grew into the killer.

They knew too much about me, but nothing from me.

Obviously, I had to move away from them. There is nothing more distracting for an author than having people stare and snigger when you pass by. And to think that some congratulated me for killing George. They wanted to shake my hand. Oh, spare me. Just tell that one to the judge.

Nowadays as a Harvest Blonde living in The Rocks, I inconspicuously glide amongst the multi-cultural home to thousands. I enjoy my café cappuccinos. Undisturbed, I draw on my bubbly environment for inspiration. No one knows or cares about a middle-aged woman who ingratiates herself in the hubbub of tourism. They cannot connect me with Akeila Zirakov, the murderess.

88

The Mountain Top

Initially, there was so much public interest when I went to prison. Everyone wanted to read about me. And there was quite a buzz in the prison too. Prisoners were fascinated by the idea of having a celebrity in their ranks.

Although I am no longer in the prison system, I don't forget the sordid memories of my prison time. They fester in the archives of my furtive mind. I remember the abusive inmates. I can still smell their stale breath and yellowed teeth filling my personal space. I feel their stares.

Now instead of flashing cameras and ardent paparazzi chasing me, a notorious criminal, a *femme fatale*, I need solitude to formulate intricate plots for future novels. Climbing to my mountain-top is sometimes strenuous. Therefore, I must sever myself from the draining dramas surrounding me. I must rise above the trivial humdrum moats, and create a new world. My imagination needs to soar.

In retrospect, you might consider that my mother caused me to become a murderess, since she had countless sleazy men sleep over in our Bridge Street home. Their presence poisoned me. And then there was George; the worst of the worst.

A shame, you whisper. *How could Jana Zirakov marry a man like George Spiatis?* Yet, she seemed unaware of what transpired in her physical and emotional absence when she, supposedly, worked nights in St Kilda cafes. She didn't really need the money, for George gave her ample. She said that she liked to have her own money.

As she tried to live in her world of fairy floss lies, she was always running away from her painful memories; always self-medicating with vodka. As mentioned, I felt her coldness toward me. And now I know why. My father raped her. I was not wanted. And she needed to escape her toxic secrets.

Mostly, she wanted to retain her pleasant memories of being a child ballerina in Russia, when she sipped vodka with her Uncle Ruri. She wanted to dance away all her cares. In her mind, she was still a beautiful ballerina graced with poise and charm, twirling her way out of disasters, as she frog hopped from one man to another.

I adopted her lifestyle after Carl died. My life was a continuum of brief affairs and one night stands. But it didn't erase my pain. And I know that my mother was never free of her bad memories either. She had to sort out her own problems. I was no longer attached to her bitterness by a placenta.

89

Billy's Death

My mother was never privy to Billy's pranks or the endless hours of merriment we shared. Instead, she lived in her fantasy world of romance and wine. She had a penchant for Russian vodka, saying that it kindled her alliance with her homeland. She had her own demons to fight. In Russia she had seen her Royalist family destroyed under the Communist invasion. The Communists hated anything that challenged their absolute authority. They tried to obliterate an entire culture, along with her family.

But, Mama, the Cold War was over. And I had a war in my own home in Bridge Street. We were invaded by George Spiatis. He was the fifth column. And I needed to wear full battle gear.

In my seared, disillusioned mind, devious George Spiatis had gotten away with Billy's murder. No one could explain the mysterious car accident that took the lives of Billy and his two best mates; no one except me. I pictured the scene: in the pouring rain, their tampered-with car was tearing along the Ferntree Gully Highway. When the bonnet smashed back into the windscreen, they had zero vision. Then their car spun out of control and slammed into a tree.

BANG!

All occupants were killed on impact; including my Billy.

I was told that Billy felt no pain. That is my only consolation. His death was sudden. Petrol, smoke and fire instantly snuffed out his precious life. Flesh had no protection against the cold steel and shards of glass that crushed him, like a soft peach smashing against a wall.

But my heart eternally aches for Billy. I feel his pain. Justice was never dealt. And George was his murderer. Before George came into our home, my mother had already much to contend with. She tried to forget her former life. And I am grateful that she shared her sad story about Russia. But George simply added to her misery; to our misery. And Billy's death was the last straw.

Ironically, I was a product of rape by a Russian spy who chased my mother half-way across Europe to Britain. He proudly believed that she had an allegiance to Russia. Her soul belonged to Communism, and her flesh belonged to him. He said that he loved her. Yet, I ask: what is love?

And so, a product of rape grew into a beautiful woman who looked like her father. Oh how, that must have pained my mother to look at me; to look into the eyes of her cruel rapist. Perhaps that explains her psychological distance from me. I always felt it. It would also explain her intrinsic need to consume copious amounts of vodka to deaden her flurried emotions. But she could never wish me away.

Yet, I am so much like her, for we both murdered our rapists. We have a killer instinct. She shot her abuser in the head when he tracked her down. They said it was self-defence, and her slate was clean. I electrocuted mine while he worked on exposed wires. They said it was an accident.

I hoped George's death would quell my intense hatred. It was like an insipid cancer eating into my soul; like a rat gnawing a hardened piece of cheese.

But I was the bait.

And then I was incarcerated at Fairlea's Women's Prison. I became the rat; the rat living in a prison cell, gnawing at the hatred that George's death had not eradicated. My hatred was part of me. It was my shadow that stalked my quiet times. All the while vengeance nibbled my bruised soul to a flailed insanity. Yes, that's what the judge eventually said in the iconic Supreme Court of Melbourne. *I was insane.*

By contrast, the prisoners considered me as Zed, the quintessential murderess. I was their hero.

90

Older And Wiser

At forty seven years of age, I had a new wave of bitterness in my spirit. This was caused by being dumped by Trent. In moments of self-pity, I would sit at home with a bottle of wine, and recall his empty flattery.

"You are so beautiful, Kellie," he'd whispered, as we snuggled in the king size motel bed. "I could spend the rest of my life with you. Let's run away and get married. I never want to leave you. Please just hug me. That's right. Move closer. Closer. Yes. So perrrfect."

He brought down my defences. I fell from my mind wall like a broken Humpty Dumpty. And then he left without a word. My once pliable heart was ossified like a bone. For a season, I hated him. I hated men. I didn't want any more pain or rejection. I didn't need it.

At the end of the day, I consider Trent Oliver to be merely a painful social experiment in 'male peacockery.' That is where self-centred, over-confident men build a peacock mound comprised of the broken hearts of the women and children they leave behind. And then they stand on their mound with all their beautiful, iridescent feather displays. Ironically, other females choose their mates according to the size, colour and quality of these ostentatious feather displays. How outrageous.

Over all, I guess that I was just another bird chasing Trent's fine feather display of masculinity. Stupid me. I should have thought with my head, instead of my heart. He took advantage of me. He knew my history. And he used this against me.

I pledged my future to him. I just couldn't believe that he would dump me after all we'd been through. Especially after I paid for the penthouse, fine food and chilled champagne. This rejection rekindled bad memories about Craig and our one-night stand.

Again, I became the frightened school girl who felt the world was against her. I felt all the pain and rejection from my high school friends: all the gossiping, snickering and side-way glances. It hurt like crazy.

Before I met Trent, I had my entire life mapped out. And it didn't include being emotionally hijacked by another spurious male. After he left, I had to promptly pick up the pieces of myself. I had to become a total picture, instead of being fragmented. Ruby-Rose depended on me. My readers needed me. They eagerly awaited the next instalment of my books. I had to make a conscious decision to get over Trent's skulduggery. I had to survive.

No more saccharine words and bullshit emotions. No more smooth talkers luring me into their fly trap. Instead of chasing love, I would throw myself into my work, and write another fifty books. And they would each be a different shade of my grey world.

Yet, there is some merit in being rejected. The fling with Trent added a new dimension to my writing. I would write about the abandoned woman. I would take my readers on her solitaire journey as she lies in her empty bed at night, waiting for the straying man who never returns. I would introduce a softer side to my protagonists as they put on a brave face, despite their bleeding hearts.

In one of my telephone conversations with Ruby-Rose, she said that she heard through the grapevine that Trent returned to one of his ex-wives. *That wasn't so bad*, I thought. At least, the children now had their daddy. Maybe it all worked out for the best.

In many ways, I am grateful for knowing the pain of infatuation. Yes, that is the label I will attach to my sentiments surrounding Trent. I can chalk it up to experience. Still, I had other challenges; other hurdles to clear. He was just one of the many annoying obstacles that would stand in my way of success. Despite my raw emotions, I had to forget him. I knew that I had to leave Melbourne and my bad memories. Time to move on.

If I were to grow as a person, I must shut out the harrowing voices in my head that say that I am a failure. Instead of dwelling on my pain, I had to listen to the echoes of other troubled women. To authenticate my work, I must shift my focus from me to them. I must make the best of my sandpit experience. So I stepped into a brave new world. I would fake it till I could make it. I had to collect my thoughts, and consider my options. In short, I had to think rationally.

91

Goodbye, Mama

I knew it was going to happen sooner or later. I dreaded the day I'd get the phone call, pleading with me to return to Melbourne. A district nurse informed me that my mother was dying and was begging for me to come to her.

"Dying. My mother is dying." I said the words out loud, as I walked around my apartment in The Rocks.

I was in shock and disbelief. I started shaking. Trembling. I felt cold. And then I felt hot. A myriad of emotions raced through my mind. I hated my mother. I hated her for what she had done to me. And yet I loved her. I needed her.

I quickly flew to Melbourne and caught a taxi to the Alfred hospital. Ironically, it was directly opposite The Octagon Motel. Fate had decided to rub even more salt in my wounds. I soon found my mother in the ICU unit of the hospital. She was tightly tucked into her narrow hospital bed. She was propped up with two hospital pillows.

She had a drip attached to her hand. Morphine and antibiotics were pumped into her veins. Instead of wearing her usual finery, she wore a plain, white hospital gown. Her white hair was cut extremely short. She looked frail and very, very old. Her pallid skin was almost the same colour as her bleached pillow.

One side of her once beautiful face had collapsed. I thought she'd had a stroke. But the nurse told me that she had Bell's Palsy. It is a viral infection that causes a sudden weakness of one half of the face. There is no cure.

"Oh, Mama," I said, as I rushed to kiss her. "What has happened? You have to get better. I will take you home and look after you. You can't live alone anymore. That house is too big for you."

She nodded as I stroked her hair. And then she whispered something. I leaned closer.

"Mama. What are you saying?"

"Kellie, I love you." She barely got the words out.

"Yes. Yes, I know you do. Everything will be all right. We'll get you better."

I gently squeezed her hand. She faintly smiled.

"I am sorry," she said, softly. "So sorry. Please forgive me. Please…" Her soft voice trailed off.

"It's all right. You don't have to be sorry. I know you had a hard time." She closed her eyes. "It's all right. You don't have to be sorry for anything."

I sat with my mother for the rest of the day, hoping that she would open her eyes and talk again. Hoping that she would get out of the bed and go home with me. Hoping beyond hope that we could sit together and share our stories. The nurse said that my mother had been given a sedative and was extremely tired.

I fell asleep beside her bed. I kept her hand inside mine. She didn't open her eyes again.

***

Alone again, I wandered the dusty city streets of Melbourne, breathing in the congestion of city life; listening to the sounds of trams, cars and buses as they tooted and exhumed fumes. I knew my past was behind me. My mother's lawyer told me that I would get a lot of money from the sale of her Armadale house. But money meant nothing. I wanted my mother back.

I had an emptiness in the pit of my stomach. My life felt like an archaeological dig in ancient Egypt. I had ample money to pay the workers to dig into my soul. Psychiatrists and psychologists were always eager to work with me. But the real me was hidden in the Pharaoh's burial chamber. Mostly, the tomb was pillaged before the archaeologists arrived. The coffers were dusty.

These thoughts stirred me as I walked along Bourke Street, Melbourne. The city no longer felt like my home. But it could have been any busy city street, for I felt displaced. I needed to return to The Rocks.

I heard the pounding of trams and cars. I heard the words of passers-by drift into space. I saw flashing colours in shop windows. I felt the crowds pushing against me. I smelled their body odours; some stale and some sweet with fine perfume. A shoulder bumped against me. Then another. It was congested. Dusty. Dusty. Like an empty coffer.

Maybe the congestion was simply a fragment in my thwarted mind.

As requested, my mother's ashes were scattered across the bay. I couldn't imagine life without her. It felt as if I were in a dream; a character in someone else's story. I felt abandoned. Restless. It was time to return to New South Wales. Time to sell up and start again.

"Goodbye, Mama."

92

The Rocks, 1985

At fifty years of age, I am older and wiser. Dye colours my greying hair, and exercise tones my muscles. My mirror tells me that I am still easy on the eye. More importantly, an enormous weight has lifted off my shoulders. For the first time, I feel in control of my life. That is, my real life; not my life on top of the mountain. Now I can live in the present and not be harangued by flashbacks. I can safely conclude that the writing of this book has laid my ghosts to rest.

Nowadays, my first priority is to write books. And if any seeds of self-doubt stir, the author-in-me always rises to the occasion. Sometimes, I am so immersed in my stories that I forget to eat. I have to contain my enthusiasm. I have to bring myself down from the mountain top to dwell in the lush valley below.

But I haven't forgotten my prison friends. I am currently paying a lawyer to work on Ruby-Rose's case. He is positive about getting her out of jail, sooner rather than later. The lawyer says that Travis Oandia should go to jail for quite a while. Justice will be served, and we'll find a happy end to her story.

Ruby-Rose regularly writes and calls me. She tells me that she will dye her hair blonde when she gets out. In our last phone conversation, she said to me, "You're not the only bomb shell who gets out of here." She is such a wag, and makes me laugh.

Despite all that life has thrown at her, her attitude is positive. She says that she can't wait to come and stay with me in The Rocks. I promised to help her buy her own home nearby. She says that she no longer wants a prosthetic hand. One hand is good enough for her.

I value her friendship, and anticipate the hot chocolate beverages she will prepare for me in the evenings. Soon we will make a film about her life. Several prominent Australian actors will play the leading roles. And it's coming to a cinema near you. Now I feel really excited.

I have so many dreams and ambitions running through my mind when I nestle at home. However, at times it feels empty, even with all my memories. Notably, Billy's painting of 'the medieval knight fighting the dragon' proudly hangs in my lounge room. I always treasure that masterpiece. It has a hand-carved wooden frame; something a Viking would choose. I laugh when I think about its acquisition. I wonder about Sandra Rogers and all Billy's other girlfriends. He would have made a great husband and father, if only he had the chance.

His treasured art work proudly hangs in my home. It always goes wherever I go. But I have mixed emotions when I study the picture. Who was the real villain in this masterpiece? I am not sure who Billy wanted to win the fight. Was he on the side of the brave knight who was well-equipped with intricately-patterned, shiny-metal armour? Was the hero protecting his princess? Or was Billy on the side of the fiery dragon that had exquisite blood-red and gold scales? And not forgetting its bulbous emerald-green eyes that could almost eat you alive. I wish I could walk to Station Pier with him to discuss his artwork. I wish. I wish.

I know Billy had a fascination with dragons and beasts. They were always fighting some battle or other on his behalf. His themes were always about fighting a formidable enemy, be it beast or man. But I know who the real beast was in Billy's life.

93

Gregor Flynn

Last week, I ventured out of my apartment to do some social research. That's what I call my regular morning trips to the local shops. There I pick up snippets of gossip from other patrons. I call them my accidental friends; strangers who come and go; people whom I never become familiar with. I get inspired by their interactions. Some might call me a social voyeur.

On that occasion, it was a fine spring day as I casually strolled into a nearby café. That seems to be the place where I am most inspired to write; midst the scraping of chairs and the rattle of coffee cups. With a handy notebook and pen, I drew on my surroundings. I was fascinated by the assortment of shoppers and tourists who passed through the cafe. I listened to their chatter. For a split moment in time, I entered their world. Having a vivid imagination, I filled-in the gaps in their stories.

As I peered through the wide café window, I watched the outside humdrum of the locals as they prepared for the busy day ahead. They didn't seem to have a care in the world. The sun was pleasantly warm. It guaranteed a surge of tourists.

As I sipped my coffee, I was glad to be alive. I appreciated my move away from Melbourne's 'hit and miss' weather. I enjoyed my anonymity. I felt at home in The Rocks with its history of convicts, soldiers, sailors and street gangs. This creative and cultural arts hub fired my soul. I was always intrigued by its unfolding stories, and the stream of tourists who were attracted to this historic place.

Yes, I was content in my new home.

And on that lazy morning, as I sipped a cappuccino, I tried to shut off any discomforting thoughts. I wanted to be *in the moment*. And drinking coffee in a cafe was much kinder on my liver than consuming bottles of wine. I thought about Ruby-Rose sitting in jail, doing jigsaw puzzles. I was told that she was getting very creative with them. Perhaps she would sell them in my local markets when she lives here.

As I enjoyed my second cup of coffee, two strangers entered the café. One was a well-to-do middle-aged man. The other was an attractive woman in her thirties. They sat at a nearby table. I pushed my notebook aside, and feigned an interest in a newspaper that was on my table. I strained to hear their hushed conversation. Suddenly, he authoritatively blurted a stream of foreign words at her. He resembled a father scolding his wayward child. His frustration was apparent.

I stole a glance at them. Her frowning face streamed with tears. Did he give her good advice? Did she heed it? And then I watched them walk out of the café, chatting in a foreign dialect. Her heels clicked with her stiletto stride.

I peered through the crystal-clear café window. I watched the two strangers disappear out of site. I felt as if I'd missed a good story. Never mind. My imagination would fill in the gaps at a later date.

An air of silence filled the café as I pushed aside the newspaper. I wasn't feeling happy or sad; just resting in that place called logos. That place where you know you have done all that is possible, and you have to 'let it all go'.

The outside street was getting busy with tourists wearing cameras around their necks. The locals wore t-shirts and thongs, as they strolled along their familiar streets.

"Hello," a warm, male voice said, breaking my thoughts.

I looked up to see a handsome, suntanned stranger of about forty years of age, standing beside my table. He was wearing sharply-pressed, brown pants that accentuated his long limbs. His equally-impressive, blue-and-white checked sports shirt hugged his perfectly-toned torso. The top two buttons were open. To my surprise and delight, he positioned himself in the empty seat beside me.

"You're Kellie Earl," he said, as the overhead light caught his soft, blonde curls.

I half-smiled; not sure if I should welcome or rebuke him. How did he know my name? I thought I was incognito.

"I don't mean to be so forward," he half-apologised. "I'm Gregor Flynn."

He removed his designer sunglasses from his almost-pretty face, and offered me his soft hand. I felt compelled to shake it.

"Should I know you?" I asked. I left my hand in his for longer than was necessary.

"I worked at Fairlea for a while. I'm a lawyer."

I fidgeted with my dyed, blonde hair that hung loosely about my shoulders. I straightened my Moroccan caftan. I stared into his blue cesspool eyes. This handsome man caught me off-guard. But did I really want to talk to him? Did I want to revisit the past and open old wounds? My life was going so well, and I had too much to lose.

"It's ok, Miss Zed," he smiled. "I understand. And I've read all your books."

I was speechless; slightly flummoxed.

"May I buy you a drink?" he asked. "You look as if you need one."

I Am Kellie Earl

"I do now," I smiled, as I faced him.

"Two champers, please," he casually told the energetic, young waitress who hovered near our table.

"Champagne?" I quizzed. "So early in the day."

"Let's celebrate."

"Celebrate?"

"Celebrate our meeting," he continued, "and how I am going to help you solve a few mysteries. You know, write some chapters in your future books." He playfully touched my notebook. "You could put me in this story. I could be the handsome prince who rescues the damsel in distress. He slays the fiery dragon."

I smiled. "Now I am intrigued."

We thanked the waitress when our drinks arrived.

"Cheers," Gregor chirped, as his glass touched mine. "To love and happiness."

"You caught me unexpectedly," I self-justified, as I sipped my bubbly drink. "I am not sure what to say. I don't know you."

"You can get to know me. We have so much in common. For one, I love literature. And I especially enjoy your crime stories."

"And the romances?"

"Definitely, sweet lady. I get all horny just reading them."

His animal magnetism made me laugh like a skittish school girl.

"I am so pleased, Gregor. You have a way with words."

"I have so much that I want to tell you," he said as he gently stroked my hand. "And I believe in serendipity. This was not just a chance meeting. Our paths were meant to cross. And I will bring so much joy and love into your lonely life."

"Really?" I laughed. He'd just quoted from one of my novels.

I felt pleasantly nervous. He was handsome to a fault, and had a friendly spark in his soft-toned voice. Our age difference added excitement. He broke through my defences. Would he push me off my Humpty Dumpty wall, sooner rather than later?

For now he was the valiant Viking smashing, single-mindedly, through the wall of ice to rescue his eager princess; to embrace his destiny. He made me feel as if I were steering a run-away speedboat. My flighty emotions surged and dashed across foreign waters. I had no time to collect my thoughts or tell him to 'piss off'. No time to remind myself that I was damaged goods and wasn't capable of ever trusting a man again.

But my emotions were conflicted. Should I run or should I stay?

94

A New Beginning

"I studied your case in the newspapers," Gregor said, with a sweet-honey voice.

"And?"

"And realised there were heaps of discrepancies."

"That's what the judge said," I agreed. "And that's why I got out of prison early."

"It should never have happened," he continued. "I was disappointed with your murder trial. But I put all the clues together in your classical saga. And I reckon George Spiatis killed your brother, Billy, and got away with it. Car accident, my foot!" He leaned closer. "That's the real reason you killed him. Not that rape isn't good enough."

I took a long drink and reflected on his words. This man was a genius.

I sighed. "But George is dead. I think we have to pick our battles."

"We? I like the sound of that." He smiled. "You know, my office is in Sydney's CBD. It's not far away. And it is always open to you. And my services for you are free."

"Free?"

"I think we'll make a great team."

"Team?" I asked, as I trailed my fingers around my champagne glass. "Sounds like a sports match."

"Well, it is, kinda. It's us against them. Against the system that let George get away with it."

"I like that," I agreed. "I like that line of thinking."

"Of course, you do," he smiled.

"My friend, Ruby-Rose, weighs heavily on my heart," I said. "She was another misfit of justice. I pay exorbitant fees to a lawyer to get her out. It's all very intense at the moment. I'm going to make a film of her fascinating story."

"Interesting. I heard something vaguely about her, from Trent Oliver."

"Trent?" A lump hardened in my throat. I took a quick sip of my drink. "You know him?"

"We worked together in Fairlea."

"Oh, yes. Of course. How interesting."

"And you know him, how?"

"Did I say that?"

"It's pretty obvious to the trained eye."

I nervously fiddled with my hair. "It's a long story from Fairlea. Full of twists and turns. He rescued me once in a prison shower."

"How salacious," he stirred. "I heard rumours. Lucky man."

For the first time, I laughed about Trent. Gregor was the miracle I needed.

"Nothing salacious there," I said. "It was a prison fight. I got attacked."

"Ouch," he teased, and lightly rubbed my hand. "But I would like to help you with your story," he promised. "You know, find the perfect end for your readers."

"Story?"

"Yes, your tragedy about Billy, George and your confession. I want to get closure for you."

"Tragedy? Yes, it was. But closure? It's such an elusive word, Gregor."

"Ruby-Rose is getting closure. And you are making her story into a film. Now I want to help you to get closure."

"How would you get closure for me?"

"For one," he said, enthusiastically, "together we will prove that George killed Billy. We can do it. We will open a Cold Case."

I felt my heart beating for the first time since Billy's death. My life-blood flowed through my veins again. I welcomed the afternoon sun that broke across the city. It warmed me. Life was now good. Fantastic. All the butterflies were having a party. And all my jigsaw pieces were finally falling into place.

Over the next hour, we chatted about his Sydney practice. He told me that he planned to retire soon, and focus on writing books and movies with me. How presumptuous. I smiled at his audacity. I admired his driving ambition and sense of direction. He was a smart man who knew his mind. He would not be readily deterred. He trailed his soft fingers along mine. It excited me.

"Would you like another drink, Kellie?" he asked, as he kissed my hand.

"That would be nice," I purred, as one under a spell. He was driving me crazy.

He leant across the table. He endearingly kissed my lips. My body surged with an all-consuming, warm passion. I wanted this stranger, right then. Right now. I wanted his heart and soul. I was being swept away by 'love at first sight'. It was a beautiful dream that I didn't want to end.

I reached out to him, and held his sculptured hand. He smiled. I trusted him. I truly think I loved him; not just for his allure and honey words, but for the way he soothed my troubled soul. He had the key to my heart. He would pave the way for my return to normality. He would prove that George killed Billy. Then I would have the peace I craved. At last, the opposing forces in my life would balance. No more jails and self-flagellation. Just a layback logos life.

As I gazed into the alluring eyes of my Adonis, I felt incredibly peaceful. Lady Justice's scales were finally tipping in my favour.

95

The Poet's Pen

Last night, I kissed your dear face,
In my steamy dream.
Somewhere between here and there.
Caressing in between.
The waters wavered on the shore,
Where lovers' dreams set sail.
Open hearts yearn for more,
And friendships never fail.
That lush place inside my mind,
Quenches seething fires,
Of rampant passions cruel and blind,
Fanned by wild desire.
Sweet birds sing love's pure song.
Across sun-bleached sands.
Where fossil shells once belonged,
To the hungry seas of man.
Remorse plays no role or part,
In this tranquil scene,
To mar passion's graceful art,
Of vivid, fanciful dreams.

EPILOGUE

It's time for me to reflect again,
To remember when I lingered on my mountain-top,
Where the air is fresh and the flowers are sweet.
A sacred place where spirits meet.
There is a cross at its base,
A dark space where I buried George,

***

Blessed peace to my readers: to the followers and leaders; to the abandoned and broken with their words unspoken. May you find your mountain top and breathe fresh air, or fly like a butterfly without a care. The world is cruel. The world is kind. I pray that you have peace of mind.

Yours truly, B.M. Rising, aka Kellie Earl